ADVANCE PRAISE FOR
FIRST PERSON IMPERFECT

"Paul McComas has taken a group of young writers with big hearts and collected their stories in a big-hearted book. The poignancy, humor and craft contained in **First Person Imperfect** make this anthology much closer to perfect than the title suggests."

—Tim W. Brown, author of Deconstruction Acres and Left of the Loop

"A varied and wonderful collection of new voices."

—Kathryn Montgomery, author of Doctors' Stories

"This is a charming and diverse collection of original, emotional stories sung with passion; many pulse with angst and aspiration. The delightful 'I Was A Teenage Disco Prince' and 'My Mother Never Understood My Hair' are but two of the many gems found between these covers."

—William Hart, author of Never Fade Away

"There are fine moments within these pages. Very fine."

—Timothy Doyle, author of Going to Dolpo

"I was hooked from the very first story. And I stayed hooked as I met a variety of characters who were at once messy, violent, sad and again playful, loving, vulnerable. Stories where everyone wears their human-ness on their sleeve. Which is my favorite kind. On the page, and in real life."

—cin salach, poet, author of Looking for A Soft Place to Land

First Person Imperfect

Todd,

Thanks so much for checking out my first attempts — don't be too hard on me. Anyway, there are some great writers in here, so ENJOY! All the best,

[signature]

First Person Imperfect

Stories edited by Paul McComas

iUniverse, Inc.

New York Lincoln Shanghai

First Person Imperfect

iUniverse, Inc.

For information address:
iUniverse, Inc.
2021 Pine Lake Road, Suite 100
Lincoln, NE 68512
www.iuniverse.com

On the cover:

"Two Are Halves of One," sculpture installation by Chicago artist Darren Holliwell. Photo by Paul McComas.

Back cover photo: Jason Leo Grocholski.

ISBN: 0-595-30195-9

Printed in the United States of America

For Hazelyn McComas,
gifted educator of countless students,
among them
her loving son.

Contents

ACKNOWLEDGEMENTS

"Dig and Drive" appeared in *The Awakenings Review*, Vol. 1, No. 2 (Winter 2001). All other works are previously unpublished.

This project was funded by the Norris Minicourse Program of Northwestern University. The editor and contributing authors wish to thank Debra A. Blade, the Minicourse Program and Northwestern University for their encouragement and support.

❧   ❧   ❧

EDITOR'S INTRODUCTION

Perhaps this is how it feels to be a grandparent. While reading the work of my Advanced Fiction Writing (AFW) students—each of whom I've taught for one to five years—I catch glimpses here and there of my own approach to character and narrative. At the same time, each of the nine voices is unique, distinct—and distinctly *not* my own.

What's more, my students are also my colleagues; their influence is evident in my work, just as mine is in theirs. In my "…Disco Prince" story, for example, the paragraph describing the curbside area onto which Phil is ejected grew out of a suggestion from my longtime student Lisa Janis to "play up the contrast" between the glimmering interior of the Park Avenue dance club and the dark, dismal street outside. Every story here has benefitted from similar suggestions, for each has been "workshopped" by the group, in part or in whole, and is thus a team effort.

Each of the contributors to this collection began studying with me at Northwestern University in Evanston, Illinois, where I have taught the non-degreed, non-accredited Fiction Writing in Depth "minicourse" continuously since 1998. Each subsequently was invited into the AFW, which I founded in 2001 and teach out of my home. Of the nine, Betsy Doherty and Lisa have been with me the longest, while Carla Ng, having first taken my course a year ago, is the "new kid"—not that you'd know it from her work.

The 18 short stories and one borderline-novella in this anthology are, as the book's title suggests, all written in the first-person voice. In addition to this stylistic connection, each originated in and/or was further developed through our collaborative workshop/critique experience. But what about their content? Can a common thread be found there as well?

I believe it can. For as I dip into the minds, hearts and lives of these wonderfully varied lead characters—seven women, seven boys, three men and two girls—one theme continually presents itself: the quest for human connection. From Pete at the Lobster Shack and his dream of a life with Denny's waitress Sherry, "watching movies and having sex," to young Paula's need to make sure that her connection with her father is intact; from Karen Reyes' fiercely protective love for her older brother (and de facto father), the troubled Viet Nam vet Deeze, to the nameless protagonist of "Reflection" and her odd bond with a stranger glimpsed in a diner; from six-year-old Andy, who is offered a helping hand by the unlikeliest of neighbors, to Lenny, whose own neighbors spontaneously converge in the wake of tragedy to soften the blow; from the narrator of "Still Life," who longs for reunion with her loved ones just about as much as she fears it, to Marty, whose sister's suicide has left a void that no one can fill—though his "Gram" comes closest; from Phil, whose fake i.d. gets him into the disco, though not into the Disco Princess' bed (or her heart), to Alyssa, whose search for affordable housing in the Big Apple brings her life into quirky intersection—briefly—with so many others....

Our world gets bigger as its population continues to explode; our world gets smaller as information technology creates a global—albeit virtual—community. And so we navigate this bigger/smaller, fuller/emptier, ever-shaky terrain, stumbling along the way, each one of us very much a "person imperfect"—though united by a perhaps perfect goal: to reach and touch and know one another.

Which brings me to Boys Hope Girls Hope (BHGH), the independent, not-for-profit organization that my students and I have chosen to receive a portion of the proceeds from the sale of this book. BHGH came to our attention through longtime student Betsy Doherty, who worked for two years (initially through AmeriCorps) at the Girls Hope group home in Evanston, counseling "high-potential at-risk youth" from the Chicago area.

Explains Betsy, "Middle-and high-school-aged students who apply to BHGH are admitted on the basis of need, desire and performance." While continuing to be a part of their own families, each girl and boy in the program lives with as many as seven peers and three or four residential counselors for up to six years as she or he attends academically demanding secondary schools, prepares for college and learns to live and grow in a unique second-family environment. "The program," Betsy concludes, "runs on the belief that each scholar will develop the skills, confidence and compassion essential for leadership and service, both now and in the future."

The contributing authors of this book are honored to lend the voices of *First Person Imperfect*'s 19 protagonists to BHGH's resolute call. (For more information, call 847-256-5959 or go to **www.chicagobhgh.org**.)

In introducing this, a collection of my students' work, I would be remiss were I not to acknowledge both of my own faculty mentors (I'm lucky; some people don't even get *one*). In high school, Jan Martin taught Modern Lit in a way that revealed to me the "secret language" of fiction: symbolism and subtext, foreshadowing and framing devices. Her approach to literature made me want not only to read, but to write. Then, in college, Prof. Mark Dintenfass showed me *how* to write, constantly challenging me to stray outside my own comfort zone and dare to be true to my characters. I've modeled my own fiction-writing workshops largely on Mark's. Indeed, both he and Jan helped me become—for better or for worse!—both the writer and the educator that I am today.

The same goes for my students. Each of the contributors to this collection has proven instrumental to me in my growth as a writer, a teacher and—with this collection—an editor. I'd also like to thank the *newest* AFW student (too new to our group, unfortunately, to make it into this anthology), Kim McNabb, for bringing to the proofreading of this book both the expertise of a professional editor and the sensitivity of a writer.

In both of the classes that I currently teach, I share four key aspects of my own approach to fiction writing, the first being the **primacy of character**. Setting and theme are important too, but I challenge my students to all but *ignore* the plotline (I've been known to write the word "story" on a leaf and toss it out the window), instead allowing it to develop on its own. There's no need to outline, or to think too far ahead; if you create engaging characters and place them in a setting appropriate to exploring your theme, then the plot is, quite simply, whatever happens. Besides, how can you know the ending—or even the middle—of a story at the outset, when you barely know the characters? Character-driven fiction requires that the author exercise only *partial* control over the machinations of the plot—particularly, I think, when the story is in the first person. Ideally, you want to reach the point where you and the protagonist are writing the story together.

Secondly, I encourage my students to focus on **writing in the moment**. Many authors over-rely on back story and flashback, particularly in the opening pages. You've picked up a novel, and you're a paragraph or two in. The protagonist and the present moment have just been established, and then suddenly you're reading about the arrival of this fellow's grandparents at Ellis

Island 80 years before. Why should you care? You don't even *know* the guy. By and large, the reader should meet the characters the same way we meet people in real life: not by immediately hearing their life stories, but by watching and listening to them *in the moment*. How is his posture? Does she gesture when she talks? What makes him laugh? What pisses her off? Bring a moment to life in vivid detail, and then move *forward* from that moment—taking the now quite engaged reader along for the ride.

(Granted, writing in the first-person voice does give an author some leeway in this department; arguably, the reader is "in the moment" as long as he or she is paying attention to that which the protagonist feels compelled to say—whatever it may be.)

Thirdly, I extol the virtues of **the plausible surprise.** A plot development can be plausible but predictable (reader response: "I believe it, but I figured that would happen"), unpredictable but implausible ("I didn't see it coming, but I'm not sure I buy it"), predictable and implausible ("I had a feeling that would happen, but it doesn't ring true") or—the Holy Grail of story development—plausible and unpredictable ("I didn't expect *that*, but, wow—it makes perfect sense!"). How does a writer grab said Grail? Simply by composing non-outlined, character-driven, in-the-moment narrative that, by its very nature, ushers one's unconscious into the writing process. You can't *plan* a plausible surprise, but it's a natural byproduct of writing what I think of as "organic fiction."

Finally, I introduce a theoretical construct that I call the **Tightrope of Disclosure.** As author, you stand at one end of a tightrope: the beginning of a story. You must make your way to the other side—the end—disclosing information all the way. If you lean too far to one side, you'll fall off the rope and into Confusion: the reader will have no idea what's going on. Lean too far the other way, and you'll land in Obviousness: you're hitting the reader over the head. Throughout the narrative, you must strike the perfect balance. How? Here's my shortcut solution: while the reader should at no point wonder *what* is going on, it is acceptable—even advisable—for him or her to wonder *why*.

As you read the stories in this collection, I think you'll find that each AFW student has incorporated portions of this sensibility into her or his own writing. You'll also find places where they've gone their own way—and more power to them! In the words of the late Montana writer Richard Hugo—words (from his essay "Writing off the Subject") that I read aloud at the beginning of each term at Northwestern—"You'll never be [a writer] until you realize that everything I say today and this quarter is wrong. It may be right for me, but it is wrong for you. Every moment I am, without wanting or trying to, telling you to write like me. But I hope you'll learn to write like you."

Betsy, Carla, Drew, Elizabeth R., Elizabeth S., Emile, Laura, Lisa and Sarah: my congratulations. Each and every one of you has learned to write like you.

OUT OF THE LOBSTER TANK

Sarah Morrill Condry

I have this piss-ant little job down at the Lobster Shack. It's attached to Chicka-Dees, which does a hell of a lot more business than we do on account of people would just rather eat chicken or drive to Point Judith and get lobster fresh off the boats than eat the three-day-old crap we practically have to keep on life support around here. But that's all right with me because it keeps the place slow, and rather than actually work, I can mess around with the dismembered lobster claws or read the Sports page. One time I tried to bring in my friend Tom's portable TV that he let me borrow because he moved in with his girl-friend who had a 27-inch Sony. Wouldn't you know that the son-of-a-bitch owner, Bill, who comes in like once in a fucking never, stomps in that day when I'm right in the middle of a Sox game and gets pissed about the TV like nobody's business. When I told him that no one even comes into the place any-way, he really got bent out of shape. The only reason he didn't fire me right then and there is because all the summer help, the college brats, already left for their prissy little schools and shit. So, no more TV.

So, it's another lousy day at the Lobster Shack and I'm sitting there pretty bored out of my mind, so I decide to look at the Employee Handbook, which I realize I've probably never even seen except the day I got hired. Bill also gave me a Lobster Shack T-shirt that day, which I wound up using to wipe the grease off my hands when I was helping my buddy P.J. down at his garage. I'm pretty sure I pitched my handbook. That guy P.J. has it made. His father up and left with this broad from Westerly and just told him to run the garage and send some of the profits to Arizona where he and his babe are living. So P.J. sends a check once in a while with this note saying that things ain't looking so good, times are slow, business is tough and shit, but really he's rolling in the dough. He has this quickie oil-change deal going that the beach day trippers just can't get enough of because he throws in a free beach bottle or ball, your choice. P.J. is top notch. I mean he really has his life together. Hell, if I had a garage or something of my own, no telling.

Anyway, I'm reading the Employee Handbook I found under the register and it lists these nightly chores that I've never heard of before. All I do at night is turn out the lights and splash the water in the lobster tank, just to fuck with the lobsters. They probably think I'm dipping my hand in there to grab up one of them for some big fat man's dinner. The manual actually says that the tank needs to be cleaned out once a month. I pour fresh salt water in there once in awhile but I've never seen anyone clean that sucker out. It just has rocks at the bottom and some crab decals stuck to the side. There can't be much to it. I'm the one who's here the most so you would think that I would know. So that night I decide that I'm going to clean the tank out just for the hell of it. There's nothing else to do. Like I said, all the college kids have gone back to their little campuses, and that means all the beach tourists have headed home, too. I'm thinking I'm not going to be moving a ton of product today. So, hell, I'll clean out the tank.

It turns out to be a lot more work than I planned. I can't believe all the lobster shit and slime that is under the rocks. It's really sick. I think about leaving it for the sucker who has to work tomorrow cause it's my day off, but I already put all the lobsters in tubs out back. (I also took the rubber bands off their claws so they could go at it with each other.) So, I'm right in the middle of scraping some shit off the bottom of the tank when the faggy little bells on the door start to ding-a-ling. I wipe the crap on my jeans and look up to see who the hell would be coming into this dump, especially on such a shitty day. It's this chick that I think I should know but I have one of those brain-fart moments when you can't remember a person's name even though you *know* it and you look like a real asshole. This chick is pretty hot in my opinion and maybe that's what makes my brain shut down. Then it comes to me and I shout "Sherry!" like an idiot. She says in a quiet little voice, "Hi, Pete." And I'm relieved a little cause she knows me too and I'm not just being totally retarded about the whole thing.

For awhile Sherry stands there asking me how long I've been working there and stuff and I'm thinking all along it's really weird that she just happened to walk in the store. We hung out a few times. When she first moved here she would show up at the bar once in a while but then she faded out of the bar scene, I guess. She was cool and all but I got the feeling she liked P.J.'s friend, Teddy, by the way she looked at him, you know that hair-swing-and-sip-on-your-beer look. One night we were all hanging out at this bar down at the Misquamicut docks and I asked if she wanted to walk on the beach, just me and her, but she wanted to stay at the bar. The waitresses were passing around test tubes filled with shots and Teddy bought her one every time the waitress came around. Teddy was hitting on her something bad and I knew it too but he respected universal guy code (the "she's with that dipshit so I'll reel her in later when he's not around" code) that no one talks about, they just follow. He didn't cross any lines. Sherry and I got real shit-faced that night and wound up having sex in a car at P.J.'s garage. I felt like a loser for doing a girl in the back of a car that wasn't even mine, but like I said, we were shit-faced.

Sherry kind of blew me off after that. She probably didn't dig guys that would take a girl to a garage to screw them, but I live with my Ma so what was I supposed to do? My mother would lose it if I brought a girl back to the house and then just slipped her into my room. My mother doesn't pay attention too much but she has this radar for things like that. Anyway I figured that Sherry probably had eyes for Teddy anyway and it wouldn't be long before they would be doing it under the pier or something.

So now Sherry checks out the cuts of flounder and I ask her if she wants some, and I tell her that she can just have it cause we would probably throw it out the next day. The front row of fish in the case there is kind of like fish death row. She doesn't want flounder and it starts to bother me that I can't figure out what she wants. She's pretty hot, like I said, so I figure she probably isn't there for a pea-brain Lobster Shack worker like me. Plus which, I smell like fish shit. I start fiddling around with the rocks in the tank and then wonder if maybe she wants me to ask her out. I tell her that me and some buddies were going to have some beers across the street at Sandy's. I haven't officially made plans with the guys but it's kind of a given that we're all there every night.

"No. Maybe some other time," she says, and grabs for the knob on the door. I say that's cool maybe some other time and that I'm usually there after work or down at the docks in Misquamicut if she ever wants to just stop by. Then all of a sudden, out of nowhere, like a bad dream or a movie or something, she says, "You have a son."

And I say, "What are you talking about, Sherry?" I mean, it's so unreal that I feel like she's talking to some other guy behind the counter and not to me.

She stands there all still and just says it again. "You have a son," just like that with her hand still on the door like she's seconds from being on her way, just like any other customer.

It was like the first time I told my mother to fuck off and she hauled her hand back and slapped me like she was a freaking prize fighter, and then she said, "What did you say?" and I told her, "Fuck off," just like the first time, except this time I said it because she asked me, not because I was really saying it to her, and BAM, she slaps me again and melts the sting right into my cheekbone.

So now Sherry is looking at me with her pretty face. I'm thinking "no way" but I have nothing to say to her. She hands me this picture and tells me she'll call me later. And she leaves making those goddamn faggy bells go ding-a-ling.

I stand there for a long time until my back actually makes a creaking sound when I shift my weight. I watch her pull out of the parking lot like a stunt driver and I try to see if she has a real kid with her or if maybe one of my loser friends put her up to pulling a fast one on me. I think about the shit-faced night and try to remember if I used a condom but I don't have sex enough to say I really make a habit of using a condom. I can't remember, can't remember, can't remember.

I pick up a rock from the waterless lobster tank and chuck it right through the front window, and the whole thing shatters and falls. Bill is really going to be pissed but at the moment I don't care. I realize I've dropped the picture of the kid, so I pick it up and take a look. It's of this little boy sitting half-naked with a bandanna and cowboy boots on this plastic-looking motorcycle. He has these huge puppy-dog eyes that look just like Sherry but that's the only thing I could see that related him to anybody. He is cute as far as real little kids go but that's it.

I leave the Lobster Shack. For some reason I lock the front door like I always do, even though some thug could just step right through the front window that I busted wide open. I left the lobsters sitting in their metal tubs out back and I didn't really give a shit if they suffocated their brains out. In my opinion if I hadn't started cleaning their stinky-ass tank then I would have been out to lunch when Sherry came by to drop her little grenade and none of this mess would have happened.

I walk across the four lanes of traffic to Sandy's and sit by myself at the bar until P.J. shows up with one of the other mechanics. I tell them both the story about how I'm just doing something at my pissy little job and then Sherry walks in. They both are as blown away as I am except it's neither one of them who's being accused of being a father so their attitude is a little less concerned than I'd like them to be. I ask them if either one of them has some pot on them because this is turning out to be even too much for Budweiser to handle. The mechanic does. P.J. is always getting big fatties from the mechanics that fix boats for the New York drug runners. He has some more serious shit on him, too, but I tell him I just want the pot for now. I take the joint and smoke it in my car on the way home. Being at the bar with people is just too much.

When I walk in the door my mother, who is wearing the same housecoat I swear she was wearing in the hospital the day I was born, is watching "Wheel of Fortune" and screaming at Vanna White and Pat that their contestants suck. She sees me and says that Sherry called and her number is by the phone. My Ma acts more interested than she has in years because some chick has called the house for her son.

I shove the number in my pocket and go to my room. I lie in the dark on the twin bed that I've had since I was about two and just go to sleep.

Sherry calls again in the morning and I wake up to my mother shoving the phone in my face and saying that I was going to take this call because besides that girl from Providence who called to say she found my wallet, they don't come that often. Sherry talks a lot for a few minutes, saying that she hopes she didn't scare me and shit like that, and she didn't know how else to say it. And then I find myself getting a little pissed off and I let the throbbing from my headache kind of pound out the words. I yell at her, saying things like why is she telling me now, maybe it's not mine and stupid crap like that. All the while I'm saying this stupid stuff I know that Sherry is probably telling me the truth because she just doesn't seem like a chick that would pull some psycho-girl thing. She tells me to come over today and see the kid and gives me directions to her sister's house where she and the kid live. I don't even think much about if I should really show up or not, I just go.

Sherry answers the door with the kid on her hip. He's this big chunky boy, a lot bigger than the kid in the picture I left on the floor at the Lobster Shack. He turns his head into his shoulder which makes me feel like he knows I'm his Dad and he doesn't really like what he sees. Sherry says he's just shy and that all kids his age do that. Their house is pretty nice, a lot nicer than mine but still nothing special. Sherry and I sit on the couch while the kid kind of wiggles around on the floor like a lobster when you turn it on its back. I ask her if I am supposed to marry her or something like that. She says no a lot quicker than I would have liked her to, but I'm relieved she said it. She is totally a hot girl but I don't know shit about being married and Sherry can't tell people her husband is the guy at the Lobster Shack especially since I didn't even know if I still had a job because those lobsters were probably dead by then, or else stolen.

Sherry says she thinks I should know because it's my right. Bound by law to tell me, she says.

I say, "Oh, sure," like I knew that she was bound by law. We sit there for a while watching the kid wiggle some more and then Sherry says she has to change him. He smells worse than the shit on the bottom of the tank, and I tell her it's a good time for me to go. I quickly step over the boy and tell Sherry that I'll call her as she picks him up and swings him back onto her hip. Sherry breathes in with her lips pressed to his head like she's taking a drag off his hair and kisses the kid on the forehead as she exhales. Her lips look pretty touching his perfect skin.

"Oh, shit"—I forgot to ask what his name was! "Uh, sorry, Sher'—I shouldn't say words like 'shit' around him, huh?" I felt like this whole thing was a huge fuck-up. I shouldn't be standing here in her house. This was something that happens to older people. People who know how to handle the curve balls. "What's his name, anyway?"

"Robby," she says with this look like, *duh?* She can't believe I don't know something like that.

I feel dizzy.

I go back home because I have the day off from the Shack and I'm not sure if I have a job there anyway. My Ma is all over me when I get back, asking all sorts of stupid questions about Sherry. Like why was such a sweet-sounding girl calling me and how did I know her, anyway. I ignore her and walk down the hall to my room. I sit on my bed and look at my Metallica poster. If I were a girl I would cry or something.

❧   ❧   ❧

There is a plywood board over the front window of the Lobster Shack when I drive up the next morning. Someone painted the words "Lobster Shack" on the plywood in red letters and then this thing under it which I am sure was supposed to be a lobster but that looks more like a red jelly bean with arms. Bill the Bossman is behind the counter, putting rocks on the bottom of the large empty lobster tank. "Any idea why I have 25 dead fucking lobsters, asshole?" He takes a long drag off his Camel and with a flick of his head and through the corner of his mouth says, "Get out of here."

Usually I would have just left and not looked back at the burning bridge, but now I have child support, man. I've thought about it a lot over the last few days. Maybe I wouldn't fuck this thing up. Sherry and I could get married and

I could work in a restaurant or something and Sherry could be the waitress and we'd see each other all the time at work and then we'd go home and there would be little Junior tucked safe in his bed, dreaming about puppies and popsicles and shit. Sherry could cook us dinner and we could sack out all night in front of the TV and watch movies and have sex.

"What about my paycheck?"

My boss points to the plywood covering the window. Without another word between us I rip down the faggy bells and try to slam the door behind me, but the wind catches it and it just stays suspended halfway open.

I drive around for a while and smoke the butt of the fatty that's left in my ashtray. It doesn't do much for me, but it's enough to take the edge off as I round the corner onto Sherry's street. I sit in front of her and her sister's house for a bit before I get the energy to get out of the car and walk up to ring the bell. I am going to ask Sherry to marry me. I know she said that was not what she wanted the other day, but I'm sure Sherry is just a real traditional girl: she wouldn't ask me to ask her to get married. I'm sure she was just playing it cool.

Her sister answers the door with little Robby hanging like a bunch of seaweed off her arm. She's a fat chick with thick eyeliner. Nothing like Sherry.

"Sherry here?" I ask, trying not to stare at the food that's smeared all over the kid's face.

Fatty curls up her lip at me and snaps, "No, she's at work like the rest of the world."

I let the fake smile drop from my lips and snap back, "Jesus, what's with the attitude?"

"Just leave her alone, OK, Prince Charming? I have to get Robby down for his nap. So, if you don't mind…" She turns her back on me and starts to close the door with her heel, but I nudge it back open.

"Why don't I do that for you? Robby and I can read some books or something before he goes to sleep." I reach out and try to tickle him, but the kid goes wicked and flips out on me like some kind of wild animal. He buries his face somewhere in her mammoth T-shirt. He sounds like he's screaming the word "no" in between sobs.

"He doesn't like strangers to touch him." She uses her free arm this time to shut the door practically on my face. Robby is still screaming. He frees himself from the T-shirt to catch some air, and I swear I can see his tonsils as he points at me and screams even louder.

"Where does she work?" I yell through the screen door.

❧   ❧   ❧

I drive over to the only Denny's in Westerly because through all that noise the kid was making, I think that's what Sherry's sister yelled back at me. This is perfect, I think, because Sherry already works in a restaurant and she could probably help land me a job there too, seeing that my references might fall through.

I see her as soon as I walk in. You can't really miss her because she's the only one whose shirt is clinging to her chest, giving every guy in there a boner. Her hair is all tucked up in this visor thing. She sees me as she's putting down some plates and she looks surprised, but she points to this little table that must be in her section. It takes her a while but she finally gets over to me.

She asks me what I'm doing there and how she can't believe I found her at work. She doesn't seem pissed or anything but I don't tell that her sister told me how to find her because right now it seems like she thinks I'm sharp for finding her. She asks me if I want anything, and I almost say "hot chocolate" but I stop myself and say "coffee" cause that sounds smarter. She leaves and I rub my hands against my jeans to try to get all the fucking sweat off of them. I don't have a ring or anything. Sherry won't care; she's probably good like that. She comes back and says she sorry for the bomb she dropped on me, I must be freaking out. I lie and say "no problem." She sits down at my table with the pot of coffee between us. She has this look like she's about to tell me something I don't want to know, like we actually have more kids together or something. Like after she had Robby they just kept coming out of her, one little Robby after another.

She leans toward me. "I'm getting married." Then she leans back. This satisfied smile on her face that makes her look really sexy.

"Yeah?" For a second, it's like she's talking about me. Us working in the restaurant together, us with Robby, us watching movies and having sex.

Sherry pauses, a putting-all-the-pieces-together pause, and I suddenly realize she's not talking about me.

Sherry just keeps talking like, OK, that's normal if I already knew she was getting married because everyone in the whole freaking state of Rhode Island seems to know. Everyone but me. Everyone probably knew she had my kid, too, and felt sorry for Sherry that the dad was me.

She leans back in the booth and says that she wanted to tell me about Robby because her boyfriend wants to marry her and adopt the kid, but they need my permission or something. She wants me to write a note like the ones my Ma wrote me in high school saying let me out of class cause she says so. My hands are getting all clammy again and I feel like pitching something through another window. Sherry's getting all worked up as she's telling me their plans—my plans—to live like one happy little family. She takes her visor off and smooths her hair back. She's leaning forward over the table like what she's telling me can't come out fast enough. She goes on and on like I'm not even there, telling me that this guy has his own place and a yard for Robby to play in. He wears a company uniform, and Robby calls him Poppy. They were dating when Sherry and me got together, but he's cool with it all now. He loves Sherry. He loves Robby.

After a while she stops jabbing on about this stud, and I tell her how great that is and that it sounds like they have a good plan. Then I actually tell her, "Well, thank God," cause I was real nervous that she really did want me to marry her or something and she was just playing it cool hoping I'd come around to the idea. I explain that was why I was so pissed when she called the other morning cause I'm involved with this fire-hot babe from Providence who I met because she found my wallet, and she wants me to marry her too. I'm like the Bachelor of the Month or something, I tell her. I say to just give me a jingle when I have to sign the stuff, and then I say something annoyingly polite, like, "I'm so happy for you, Sherry."

I wave to her as I walk out of Denny's, and I smile this smile like "catch you later." I get in my car and start the engine. I try to put on my seat belt but the strap is stuck in the closed door. I don't stop the car to get it out of the door because Sherry may be watching from the window. I don't need a seat belt anyway. I drive slowly with my window down and my arm hanging outside the car door. That's cool. I'm cool. This is better.

I take a right on the highway, and I can see the intersection where the Lobster Shack is. I turn my car toward the pulloff for the Lobster Shack parking lot and flick on the radio. This cheesy love song is playing in this guy's voice and then this woman starts to sing with him. I search for any remainder of the pot in the ashtray and pretend I'm not leaking tears like a goddamn baby. I light up and take a hit from the tiny butt. All I can do is sit there with my engine off and the windows down and smoke this joint so small I can barely even hold it and stare up at the little jelly bean lobster painted on the plywood.

THE WAR OF NORTHERN AGGRESSION

Sarah Morrill Condry

My brother was running down the dirt driveway with his backpack swinging off his shoulder, the dust from his pounding feet swelling up toward the enormous umbrella of century-old oaks that lined the drive. I could hear Buddy's faint shouts between his steps. He tripped and almost wiped out, then he was up and running toward me like a boy on fire. I just sat on the front steps of our house as I did each day, waiting for him to come home from junior high.

I always sat on the third step. The two below were bowed in the middle, but Mama said that only added to "the authenticity of our home." The Pinkerton Plantation. It was never as historically well-known as Drayton Hall or Magnolia, but Mama assured us that at some point in time it had participated in the agricultural growth of South Carolina. "The Pinkerton," she said, "survived so the South could thrive." That was the little line she used whenever she believed the importance of the Pinkerton was being questioned.

The Pinkerton was a dump. It was on the outskirts of Georgetown, known more for its smelly paper mills than for our so-called plantation. Officially our home was a tourist attraction, but we didn't get many visitors. Most of the people who stopped by were beach trippers on their way to Pawley's Island who'd read the 20 or so signs Mama had made Buddy and me paint. Mama put them out about 50 miles away, where they invited the tourists to "Come sit for a spell at the Pinkerton Plantation" and "Step back in time."

Then, a mile from home: "Last chance."

Mama told the few tourists who visited that it was her great-great-grandfather's house, and that her grandfather was the distinguished George Lockwood Pinkerton of Charleston. She would lift up her chin like the queen of the realm, her eyes tilting down to look directly into those of her minimal audience, and say, "The Lockwood Avenue, in Charleston." If she sensed their unfamiliarity, she would add, "Down by the marina."

The person she was pretending to be was a second cousin by marriage. Thanks to a heart attack, cancer and some lousy estate planners, the house came to Mama by default. She never mentioned, or minded, that the trail that had led the house to her was a broken one, and that the property had arrived to her near ruins. It was hers. Hers and my stepfather's—Tony DiRussi.

"Tony's coming!" My brother unleashed the book bag from his shoulder as he reached the steps, completely out of breath.

The look in his eyes burned a fear into me that would never leave.

"He's mad, real mad at Mama. He's really gonna kill her this time."

My brother was two years older than me but invariably failed at the role of older brother. He stared at me, frozen with terror. We stood on the steps, face to face, the only sound his heavy breathing. Sweat rolled from his temple and balanced on the tip of his chin; with the back of his hand he rubbed his chin, and the sweat soaked back into his skin.

"Tony ain't gonna do nothing," I said calmly. "What makes you think the Italian Stallion is gonna hurt Mama?"

His breathing was still heavy from running and fear, but not labored from an asthma attack—not yet. Buddy had horrible attacks when he got too worked up. He constantly had his hand in his pocket, running his fingers over his inhaler like a revolver ready to draw.

I moved from the step to the rocker on the front porch, or "piazza," as Mama called it. She hated when we called it a porch. During her tour guide spiel, she would explain that the piazza was built to face the south, catching the breeze from the river. Then, acting like she hadn't told it a million times before, she'd lean in toward them and add, in a hushed and intimate voice: "You see, a Southerner would never be caught facing the North"—then follow up with her gentle laugh. She was right about the breeze, though, and today it held a particular chill that perhaps only Buddy and I could feel.

"It's real this time, Chip, I swear." He stood still on the step, his body sideways to the house, and the words spilled out of him like water from a broken dam: "I was with Hunter and we met up with his dad down on the creek. Hunter's dad's the one with the construction company, you know, he has that big blue truck and all those Mexicans. Hunter's dad told me the whole thing. Said I should go home and watch out for Mama. He said there might be a fight at home."

There was never a fight. It was always Tony, the Italian Stallion in one corner, weighing in at 195 pounds of flesh and five pounds of hair, vs. Millie, The Southern Belle—who usually got KO'd in the first round.

My brother stopped talking, his face pale and damp with the humidity that clung to everyone and everything down there like spider webs. He snapped his head toward the long drive, cocking an ear for any sound of Tony's pick-up.

"Turns out Mama's gone and hired Hunter's dad and all the Mexicans for a whole bunch of construction on the Pinkerton."

"So?" It didn't seem unusual to me. About once a year, Mama would do some planting or buy a new chair, usually after she got back from the Charleston Home and Garden show. She said these new touches would add to the authenticity of things.

"She went and cleaned out Tony's bank account and put it in her purse. It's the money Tony's been saving to start up that Yankee pizza chain."

"Who—how does anyone know that?"

"I'm telling you, Fartface, Hunter's dad saw the money! Mama told him she was going to fix the house up right, and she hired him for the job."

"Does Tony know?"

"Sure as spit. He's been down on the river for the past two days, drinking Jack Daniel's and Pabst Blue Ribbon." Buddy was quiet for a moment; then, in a low voice, he said, "I saw it for myself. I just came from spying on him. I got down low in the bushes like when we're pretending to hunt deer. I had him in rifle sight. He's all fired up. He's got his shirt off and howling and grumbling. It's bad, Chip, real bad."

Tony would often disappear for days between "business deals" with customers. Usually he would go fishing, or all the way to Columbia for the "gentlemen's clubs." We didn't care, and I don't think Mama did, either: the house was better when he was gone. Mama would rub our backs while we watched TV at night, me on one side of her and Buddy on the other, and the three of us would sit there on the couch until the news, when Mama would send us off to bed. If Tony was home, we tried to stay in our rooms. When we were forced out of hiding for dinner, I would see Tony try to pinch Mama on her butt or swipe a kiss. She would always wiggle away or get stiff as a board. I don't know why she married Tony.

The truck came bouncing down the driveway. You could hear beer cans hitting and rolling in the flatbed as it jerked to a stop, almost landing on the first step. Tony sloughed out of the truck. All he wore was an undershirt and soiled Duckhead khakis. The brown belt cut under his bellybutton, squeezing him

tight at the hips and making his body swell above. I could hear Buddy beginning to wheeze.

"Where's that mother of yours?"

I saw my brother as a shield. He was useless as a mentor, but he did have two
more years of growth than I did. If Tony had been drinking for two days, which
it smelled like he had, I didn't want to be in striking distance.

"It's shopping day," I told him, peering out from my brother's side. "She's
not here."

"What are you hiding from, ya little pussy?" His chin was buried in his chest
as if the weight of his hairy head was too much for his neck to support. He
seemed to choke on a burp before he continued. "You tell that whore-bitch-
thief of a wife that she has Tony DiRussi to answer to." Then he pounded on his
chest with one hand like he was Tarzan or something. He looked at us dead on,
something he never did. He stumbled up the first step, towering over us like
one of the oaks, his hair clumped down like dangling moss. His hot breath lin-
gered over our heads, and then he sneered, "I should burn this place down
with all of you in it."

He turned back to the truck and reached inside for something on the passenger-side floorboard. Buddy grabbed my wrist, ready to pull me along if we
needed to run. Most of Tony's body was strewn across the front seat.

It stayed that way.

My brother and I stood staring at the grill of the truck, waiting for move-
ment inside—held hostage on the steps, afraid even to take a breath. I knew
now that it was true. He was not just going to kill Mama; he was going to kill all
of us. I couldn't help wondering what Mama was doing, stealing money from
Tony. It was stupid; even I knew that. He smacked her around just for serving
him scrambled eggs instead of poached. For now, at least, she'd been saved by
Tony himself: he was passed out, stinking of alcohol and snoring away. We held
our stance, afraid that if we dared move, we might awaken the sleeping Stallion.

"Please don't come home, Mama," my brother whispered, tears cutting
through the sweat on his face.

"Shh," I said. "Shhhh."

❦   ❦   ❦

We waited at the end of the dirt drive that led to the Pinkerton Plantation.
We sat a few feet from a brick column that served as an entrance marker.

Mama had found an old sketch in the attic of the original gateway, built by the slaves of her not-so-related relatives. The columns were like monuments on either side of the drive: low to the ground on the outer part, then climbing three or four feet taller than the man in the sketch at the peak of the wall. In the drawing, each column was topped with a huge pineapple. Mama said the pineapples had been a sign of welcome for the master of the Pinkerton when he returned from his trading expeditions. Mama said, in her just-between-you-and-me voice, "It was well known that Master Pinkerton's wife liked to en-tuh-*tain* guests while her husband traveled. So you see, if the pineapples could be seen on top of the columns, her 'friends' would know to stay away because Mr. Pinkerton had returned. If no pineapples were on the columns, well..." A pretty little smile crept onto her lips.

I teased Mama because she never had any pineapples on those columns. With that, too, she smiled.

The wall and columns had no definite lines as they did in the picture. The lowest points had crumbled into the same hot earth we were sitting on now, facing the road. It was a long highway that looked the same in both directions. I saw it as a road that led to, but mostly away from, the Pinkerton. No cars passed. The only sound came from the insects in the nearby marsh: a chorus of humming and screeching.

Buddy sat with his knees tight to his chest. I took watch duty, resting my back against his. Neither one of us spoke, each too serious about our obligations.

My brother lifted his head. "Oh, no—look, Buddy." We both were as still as rocks so as not to be seen by the beast.

Tony fumbled out of the driver's side of the truck, holding onto the window frame of the door for support. He scratched himself, then stumbled to the back of the pickup. We watched with fear and intrigue.

"What do we do now?" Buddy asked, and looked at me with his tired face.

"I don't know, Retard, just shut up and stay still." We didn't move to swat at the bugs dancing by our ears or to wipe the sweat rolling out from our hair. We were stillness itself.

❧   ❧   ❧

Tony had hated Buddy and me from the moment he'd seen us. He growled at us as soon as Mama left the room, and when he was drinking he would lock us in the tiny bathroom until Mama came home from her shift at the truck stop. But he loved Mama's little figure and the fact she'd just inherited a big house. Neither Tony nor Mama had ever had a house of their own before; Buddy and I usually slept on one of her boyfriends' floors in front of TVs with bad reception. We dreamed amidst the cigarette smoke being exhaled over us, which tasted like being unwanted. Tony's trailer was the last of those places before we moved, like a family, into the Pinkerton.

He and Mama got married one night while we were asleep, right after she found out about the Pinkerton. They had gotten drunk and driven 40 miles to a seedy little wedding chapel. She said she was going to need a husband who would stick around to do the handy work on our new place. She didn't want to move into a new house all alone. Mama said that this was her one shot, and she was going to take it, and Tony was going to help her do it.

When we pulled up to the Pinkerton for the first time, us in the wagon and Tony in the pickup, I thought the last trailer park looked a lot better than this weedy brick building. Mama got out of the car and practically flew up to the front door. "Welcome home, boys," she hollered, as if she'd lived there all along. She toured the inside, seeing things that we didn't. She saw where the generals had eaten during the war and where the servants had brought the ladies their tea. It was a lonely, hollow place, but Mama walked in like she was hearing music, dancing from room to room. She named the rooms, using words like "*pah*-luh" and "*foy*-yeh." Buddy and I laughed at her enthusiasm. Tony even cracked a smile and slapped me on the back before heading out to the back porch.

❦   ❦   ❦

We watched Tony as he hung his head over the side wall of the flatbed for a long time. He jerked his body once in a while and rested his head on his forearm, then back over the wall. We couldn't hear anything from where we were. I knew he was throwing up, and I hoped it tasted as bitter as Tony himself.

"Choke on your own furry hairball, you freak," I spat out in nearly a speaking voice.

My brother shot me a glare that was an order to shut up. It reminded me for a moment that he was still the older of us two. His glare changed and reached past me; we both saw her. Without a word, we broke our stillness and ran as fast as we could toward the station wagon cruising up the road.

"Boys, boys, I am flattered you are so glad to see your Mama," she hollered, stretching to roll down the passenger-side window. The radio was playing a soft big-band tune on the AM station she loved so much. The car was loaded with brown paper grocery bags in the back seat. Today must have been her day at the beauty salon, too: her ashy blonde hair was pinned up and folded around itself in the back. It was the way she usually wore it, only neater. Sometimes I'd watch her fingers twist and turn her hair until, as if by magic, it stayed folded on her head. Her lips were shiny with a color that was not her own.

"Look at you boys, all sweaty and such. I declare, one day you'll want to be fine gentlemen, but all your clothes will be sweaty and soiled, and don't you think your Mama is still going to be doing your laundry." She began digging through the sweetgrass basket that she used as a purse—I strained to see its contents—then pulled out a handkerchief, all the while lecturing us for the thousandth time about the training of gentlemen. We stood there panting into the passenger-side window without a word to offer.

"Well," she said, "get in."

Buddy sat in the front, and I slid myself next to a grocery bag that felt cool. I thought that coolness might have been ice cream, and maybe we could all go back and sit on the front porch (piazza) and have huge bowls of butter pecan, and Tony would be gone. Mama would sit in the rocker as Buddy and I gulped down our dessert, and she would tell us her made-up history of the Pinkerton—one she somehow believed to be the honest-to-God truth.

"My, you two ran a long way to catch me out here. What's the occasion? What did you break?" She put the car into DRIVE. "Never mind. We will just go on back to the Pinkerton and fix it." Whenever she said the word *Pinkerton,* she assumed an aristocratic tone; even her posture tightened. "I've got something to tell you boys. Some very exciting news."

I thumped my brother on the head, urging him to speak.

"Ouch!" He cupped his hand over the spot where I'd hit him, right behind the ear. I knew he wouldn't be able to put together what to say until some time next week.

"Stop the car, Mama!" I knew my voice sounded panicky.

The car jumped back into PARK.

"What is it, Chippy?" She turned to the back seat, inspecting me for bodily harm. "Lord, I thought part of you was still hanging out of the car. Don't scare your Mama like that. I just paid for this blonde, and you are gonna turn it gray before next week."

She turned to Mister Macho, who had burst into tears in the front seat. He was sobbing. Sobbing with wails that roared out of the car and well into the next county.

"My goodness, Buddy, what is wrong with you?" She reached for the handkerchief on top of her purse. Pulling his head into her chest, she whispered to him, "Buddy, hush now, my sweet boy. What's wrong? What's wrong?"

The three of us sat in the station wagon, stopped right in the middle of the road, listening to my brother gasp and howl to the rhythm of the big-band tune still playing on the radio. Finally, my mother turned her head to me and, in a scolding tone, demanded to know what we had done.

"Mama," I said, "Tony is home."

She tried to turn up the corners of her mouth—"Well, that's fine"—but I could see the flash of fear in her eyes. "That's all?" she continued, letting out a nervous breath. She patted Buddy's head, which still rested on her chest. "When did I make y'all into such Mama's boys?" But I could tell she knew there was trouble on the plantation.

"Everything is fine." She pushed Buddy upright and repositioned herself behind the wheel. Mama was trying hard now to protect us by ignoring what was to come. "Just fine, just fine." She put the car back into DRIVE.

"Oh, Mama," I cried, "please don't go. He's been drinking again, and he is furious with you."

My brother sat comatose in the front seat. His long, lanky body didn't seem to match the whimpers escaping from his bubbly lips.

"Tony is all right, boys. You know he likes to overindulge now and again."

The only problem was, "now and again" always seemed to result in someone lying face down with blood on the floor.

"Mama'll be fine as wine."

"Did you steal his money?" I said it loud and clear.

She jerked her foot on the brake pedal, then let up as soon as she realized she'd done so. "Shit."

"Hunter's dad told Buddy. Tony said he's gonna kill you this time, kill all of us, Mama!"

"Boys, I want you to be good for me. Tony and I will work this out. Just a misunderstanding of sorts. When we get to the house, I want you two to go straight to the attic. That's been needing some rummaging through for some time. I bet there are a few artifacts to be found that we could clean up and put on display." She pulled onto our dirt drive. "I think there are some old dishes from way back. Find those for me, and we can put them on display in the kitchen; they'll look real nice hanging in the butler's pantry. You see, it is those touches that count."

Buddy stared out the window, and I stared at the back of his brown head, trying to ignore what Mama was saying and come up with a plan of my own. And drawing a blank.

"Why'd you go and steal his money, Mama? The Pinkerton ain't nothing but a shithole anyway." My swear hung in the air like a cloud. I had never sworn in front of Mama before. It felt like I had struck her with my own fist.

She stared at me, her mouth a little bit open—but no words came out. She turned her head toward the Pinkerton, which looked abandoned except for Tony's muddy pickup truck parked haphazardly close to the house. The only sound was the buzz from inside the truck, warning that the door was open. It sang back to all the creatures in the marsh behind the house.

"It's my house, boys," Mama finally said. "This is all I got to make something of myself." She slumped in her seat and continued staring at our brick house with its small white columns in desperate need of painting. "I'm like one of those slave girls, except I'm not running away to find freedom. I've done plenty of that. This is our house." Her words were very paced and sure. "Tony doesn't know anything about business. You've got to spend a penny to make a penny. You remember that."

Then she put the car into PARK and began collecting her things.

I remembered when she first told us we were moving to the Pinkerton. She was possessed, packing all of our belongings into the back of our wagon, moving as if she was in a race. Now she grabbed a bag from the back seat and clenched her purse like a shield as she walked up the steps, Buddy and me tagging along behind. The light weight of her body still made the last step squeak. The front porch clapped with the tap of her heels until she reached the front door.

Tony swung open the front door—"Welcome to the Pinkerton Plantation, y'all"—his boozy breath electrocuting the air in front of us. "Get yourselves off the piazza, and come on in."

He had a nine-iron golf club in one hand and a bottle of Mama's cooking sherry in the other. "Don't be shy now, this *is* the Pinkerton, full of historic value." He was imitating parts of his wife's tour around the house in an exaggerated southern drawl. He pointed to an oil painting on the wall: horses and hunting hounds. Mama had bought it at a starving artists' art show at the Charleston airport. It wasn't exactly historically accurate, but Mama hung it in the entry hall anyway and said it was very well done. Some tourists had even commented on the rich colors. Tony drove the club through the oiled canvas. None of us made a sound. Mama clutched the bags more tightly with her skinny arms, and my brother and I stood in the doorway, each of us holding the groceries we had mechanically taken from the car. Tony brought the club down and tapped the floor like he was about to putt.

"Go upstairs now, boys," Mama said in a low, hollow tone I had never heard.

"No yoozh don't," Tony slurred, pointing the half-empty bottle of cooking sherry at us.

"Let them be, Tony." She let her grocery sack slide from her breast, through her arm and past her hip. *Thud.*

"No, no, no, baby." His voice grew softer. "Can't just let 'em be; we got work to do." He slid his fat gut toward her and held her face between the bottle and the club handle. "We're doing some reconstruction here at the Pinkerton today." I could see Mama close her fists as Tony dragged his unshaven face across her cheek. "Everyone in town knows my little tramp has stolen my money to dump into this pit." Then he glanced around as if he were lost and was looking for the right way to turn and head off. Go, I thought, just go.

"Tony, sweetie, of course I was going to get your approval." I saw her switch her personality in an instant, becoming again the trashy blonde that Tony had fallen for. She maneuvered her body away from him. "I just wanted to surprise you, darlin'. Make you the fine home you deserve. You know, the king of your castle." She made her way to the kitchen without him stopping her; the club, the cooking sherry and the Stallion followed. She put her basket purse down on the kitchen table. "Now, let us talk about this, sweetie."

Tony stood there, looking dumbfounded at how Mama had diffused the situation.

Before I heard the sound of his grocery bag hitting the floor, I saw my brother running down the hallway toward the two of them in a full junior-high football tackle position. He was hollering louder than I had ever heard in practice. He slammed his head right into Tony's pelvis, knocking him off balance over a kitchen chair, and the two of them landed together on the kitchen floor. My brother's mind was still in the faraway place he had retreated to since the car, which was good because of the pain that followed.

Mama ran over to my brother, jerking him up off the ground before Tony got his bearings back.

"Little prick!" Tony grabbed Buddy's ankle and crashed him back onto the floor with one pull. Mama screamed words that I'd only heard Tony use as she tried to get him off Buddy. She was grabbing onto Tony's back like a cat climbing a tree. He backslapped Mama twice, but she didn't let up, pounding like a housefly banging into a window pane. Even with Mama on his back, Tony had Buddy by the neck and was bouncing his head on the floor like a rubber ball. Tony reached for the nine-iron under the kitchen table.

"Bastard fucks! All of you!" He kicked my brother one last time, and then a rage exploded from Tony's body that seemed impossible. He started swinging the club at every fixture and piece of furniture in Mama's house. Again and again, Mama lunged to stop the clubbing, and every time he came back with a crack at her delicate bones.

I stood there the whole time with my grocery bag, hugging my chest. My eyes were paralyzed by the sight of my brother's battered body. He looked like an infant, a bloody infant just born on the kitchen floor. Mama screamed in the next room between cries and blows to her body as the plaster walls of the Pinkerton gave way around her.

"It's a shithole, Millie!" Tony hollered and hit, hollered and hit. It was the very same word I had used; I could even hear my own voice echo in his. I watched the base of an old brass lamp roll to my feet: there was no shade, and just a shard of the bulb still connected to the base. That lamp was the first thing Mama had brought down from the attic when we'd moved in. It was the only light for weeks before Mama started dragging Buddy and me to garage sales to find more lights. Now it spun in a perfect circle by my feet before slowing to a stop. It seemed to take with it all of the noise, the screams, Tony's voice echoing mine. I wanted to move my legs; I just couldn't.

The Pinkerton smelled like plaster dust and blood. It swirled through my nostrils and into my head, making me dizzy. Everything in the house was moving, but without sound. Large, gigantic movements in silence. Tony was standing in front of me, speaking, but the words I could not hear. His sweat-drenched belly swept two inches from my face, speckled with our family blood. My muscles tensed and quivered from my legs up through my spine. I couldn't get my body to move. I was trying to awaken myself from a deep sleep, coming to slowly, so slowly.

And then, all at once, it came. I felt the heat in my shoulders burn down to my fists. I felt the bile race up from my stomach and into my throat. My pounding heart ordered me to move. With my fists, my head, my entire body, I hit Tony in the gut as hard as I could. It felt as if I had run head-on into his pickup. The thunder of his fists rained down on my back as I fell to the floor. I placed my palms on the hardwood and felt the Pinkerton beneath me. I didn't cry; I would not cry. He beat me and beat me until I could no longer feel the pain.

Mama sat balled up, rocking back and forth next to Buddy.

Tony, still now, heaved out a sigh and asked, "What have you gone and done this time, Millie? Why'd you make me do this?" He shook his head in disbelief, as if *we* had caused all the destruction. Tony let his forehead rest against the icebox door. He sighed and then yanked open the door. He stared inside while the coolness swept over us all. He reached inside and popped open a beer, as if he had just finished a hard day's work. Letting the brown bottle dangle between his fingertips, he stepped over Buddy, then shuffled through the front entryway, letting the screen door slam behind him.

Tony was gone, and the house was filled with a particular kind of quiet: the softness of three breathing together instead of four. He had fled our family as quickly as he had entered it. Like a storm crashing onto the beach, then racing out to sea—a powerful undertow taking with it all seaweed, all wood, every remnant of the watery underworld it had brought.

We stumbled through the house as through a cemetery. With a newfound strength, Mama scooped Buddy into her arms, and I followed behind. The sun was dancing through the limbs of the trees; it would have been a good day for crabbing down at the marsh. She could barely see out of her own eyes, yet she moved as surely as ever. She sat down on the first step of the porch.

Blonde shards stuck straight out behind her ears. I could still see the print of Tony's hand—the impression of his thick red fingers wrapped around her neck. She cried. And she breathed the same soft breaths I'd heard in her sleep, when she would crawl into one of our beds late at night, thinking we didn't know.

I sat down beside them. Buddy's towel-wrapped head rested next to my thigh. His chest rose and dipped as a blade of sun spread up his leg and over his hand. The blood oozing from his head soaked through my shorts, slow and warm.

I could smell the salty earth that had been exposed by the low tide. I could smell the mud, the fish swimming in little tidal pools; I could taste the motor oil from the boats that puttered up and down the waterway. I could see the rectangular slave cabins that still stood after all those years. I could feel the hot wood of the steps. But mostly I felt Mama and her swollen hand wrapped around my shoulder. She began to hum, and I could feel the vibration through my scalp as she pressed her head on top of mine. We sat on the steps of the

Pinkerton, just as I had each day, staring out at the enormous umbrella of century-old oaks that lined the drive.

MESH

Elizabeth C. Rossman

She sat on her suitcase, waiting for a taxi. Even from this distance I could make out the bag's faded floral brocade. When I was a child, those pinks and oranges and greens had provided endless fascination, and I had traced them over and over with one chubby finger and all the single-mindedness of a four-year-old. Looking over at her now I felt my throat close, and I swallowed with some difficulty. The chain links were digging into my hands, marking them.

How can she be doing this again?

The floppy straw hat—her beach hat, the one she had purchased so that the sun would not lend a brassy tint to her dyed-dark hair—curved out, hiding all of her face from me but the smooth plane of her right cheek. From here, the pale brown eyes and delicate crow's feet were not in view, nor the straight nose that ran down from her arching black brows. When she tilted her head, I caught a glimpse of her mouth, but the laugh lines that strained the edges were faded, smoothed away by distance.

And even though I stood there so close, I couldn't have called out if I'd wanted to. The words wouldn't form. The images that coalesced in my memory were muddled and imperfect, sensory data firing amongst tangled synapses: Gunther, our old cat, scurrying across the big four-poster bed; me struggling after him, learning to crawl as his tail enticed me. In the background she folded laundry. Her hair—natural then, and long—curled into fat, bouncing spirals as she called for my father to come and see. Her laughter made her voice husky.

I don't even know if that memory is my own or one that she supplied in response to my incessant requests for stories about when I was a baby.

Gunther had liked to nap inside that very suitcase, disgruntled and indignant as we packed around him in preparation for a holiday outing or a trip to the coast to visit relatives. Back then, she and my father had shared the giant bag, their clothes neatly lying side by side, the edges just touching. My things had gone in a matching carry-all, along with the toothbrushes and razors and shampoo. That smaller bag was still in the attic, fresher for its confinement, the colors less muted, less dulled by wear.

Mother! Diane!

Neither, or both—it didn't matter. My throat was too tight to make any sound beyond a whisper. A raspy sob lurked below the surface, and dammed behind it were waves of less coherent images, roiling and building.

This time was no different from any other.

The yellow taxi grew into view, then stopped at the curb beside her sandaled feet.

I forced myself away from the mesh gate and trudged up the sandy incline, not looking back, unable to see the path ahead.

REFLECTION

Elizabeth C. Rossman

Fall leaves skittered off the tall front windows, swirling into the foyer as the jangle of bells announced each customer's arrival at Sara's Café. Truth be told, it wasn't a café at all, but rather a restaurant that the owner had chosen to *describe* as a café in order to attract the type of clientele drawn to the quaint and the faintly romantic. Still, the place was cozy and the food, though predictable, rather good. Best of all was the convenience—a short walk down the street and I could be there without getting too chilled or too tired or too anything. I didn't even need to move my car.

And on that blustery Friday, I suppose I needed the convenience of the place—as well as a bit of its premeditated charm. Smiling at the thought, I returned the petite coffee cup to its glossy saucer, then glanced up as the bells sounded again. Near the entrance, newly arrived couples and families milled about, hair askew, noses running, cheeks ruddy from the stinging wind.

My own hair had been pulled back when I'd left my apartment, but—courtesy of the walk over—most of it now straggled about my face, entangled with small bits of leaf. Feeling like the ragamuffin I'd been dubbed as a child, I'd untied the rest of it and struggled to work my fingers through the unruly mass. Still, it wasn't as bad as it could have been; I tried not to stare as an older lady passed me on the way to her seat, hat askew and several frenetic white strands dangling from her coif.

I dropped my eyes back to my latest purchase from the campus book fair, trying to find the sentence on which I'd left off. Though it had proven difficult, I had managed to refrain from beginning the book until after I'd graded all the essay exams and turned everything back in to my professor. But now that the time had actually come, I couldn't seem to read more than a phrase or two before my eyes stopped registering what was written. A few minutes later I would find myself staring at the bottom of a page I hadn't read, wondering how far ahead I'd gone without learning a single thing pertaining to the ancient Egyptians' beliefs about death and the afterlife. A few times, I'd even caught myself staring sightlessly toward—well, through—other customers before realizing how rude I must have seemed. My embarrassment on each such occasion only served to heighten the vague churning of unease with which I had woken up that morning.

A plate full of Greek omelet and hash browns appeared on the glass tabletop in front of me, followed by syrup and a smaller plate full of pancakes and whipped butter. The waiter efficiently, and wordlessly, refilled my coffee—no decaf today—then strode off to check on the booths along the back wall. I watched him go, my pleasant-smile-of-sincere-appreciation still plastered onto my face. By now, I knew each server by name, and they knew me well enough to recognize that when I had a book I didn't need to be asked if everything was all right or whether there was anything I needed. Still, as I watched my waiter move amongst the tables, I wondered whether I should have said "thank you" or asked for more cream, or something. A little casual banter might have lifted my spirits.

When I had begun stealing off here to read, I'd found it a balancing act to juggle a hardcover book, multiple dishes, napkins and utensils and still manage to eat my food before it turned cold. But I found, in short order, that I genuinely liked to dine with just myself as company, and it wasn't long before I could bury my head in a book while my fork managed to find its mark—and my mouth—without much effort. Today, as the steaming eggs cooled, I nibbled on the pancakes—salty from the butter, and with very little syrup—and tried to pick up where I'd left off. In Chapter One. Still in Chapter One.

In only a matter of minutes, I found my attention drifting back up and around to the other diners. I sighed around a mouthful of hash browns, planting myself a little lower into the vinyl of the booth and flipping the book upside down on the glass surface. If someone had asked me what I was reading about, I doubt I'd have been able to say.

A couple of blocks away sat my car, packed up and ready to go. It was only now as I stared off into the distance, out through the restaurant's tall front windows, that I could admit to myself the reason why I'd walked right past my car and continued down the street more than an hour before:

Nathan.

My stop at Sara's was a delaying tactic. Despite my rationalizations that I needed coffee and breakfast before hitting the road, what I really wanted was an excuse to hang around town a little longer. Maybe just until noon, which was about the time he usually made it out of bed…

I had known, even planned on the fact, that he would still be asleep when I'd dropped off his gift. His roommate, Kevin, had been a bit bleary-eyed even as he'd assured me that I hadn't woken him up. He had invited me in, but I had declined, my stomach swirling now that I was there at the townhouse. Embarrassed that I had awoken him, embarrassed that I was there, I stood looking at the pavement, a gawky freshman all over again, hoping to catch a glimpse of the guy I had a crush on—and hoping with equal fervor that he wouldn't see me. Kevin had taken the package and shuffled back into the dim and drowsily quiet Unit 2-G. I had hurried down the walk, back toward the curb where my car was idling. My cheeks burned as I squinted into the biting wind.

…And now it was 11:30, more than an hour past the time I'd planned to leave, and I was halfway through a needless meal that—should I manage to consume it all—would fill me up for the next two days.

I felt my attention wandering again, my eyes sweeping the perimeter as I continued to ponder. I thus was startled when my gaze seemed to snap to the front of the restaurant. My heartbeat sped up and, for an instant, I thought that Nathan must be there. Then I registered the slender young woman in the camel-colored coat.

Her hair was as awry as that of every new arrival, but hers was a becoming dishevelment: dark, glossy-brown wisps escaping a small chignon to stray about a stark and somewhat angular face. The paleness of the woman's skin contrasted with the top of a deep red turtleneck that emerged from the collar of her coat, setting off the thick fringe of black lashes that I could clearly see, even from that distance. Of her eyes themselves, I could not tell.

I felt the small hairs at the nape of my neck quiver and rise.

The young woman stood before the front counter, stiff and still, her head cocked to one side and down as though she were listening to someone. Or for someone. She looped her fingers lightly over the back of an empty chair at a nearby table and continued to stand there, slight and strangely out of place amidst the bustle of the brunch crowd.

I swallowed a rather large quantity of coffee and continued to stare, this time fully aware of my rudeness. And baffled by the fact that I seemed so drawn to this still, small figure. With some effort, I looked away.

When I glanced back to the front, the woman had moved slightly and seemed almost perturbed, although she had yet to raise her eyes.

This was absurd. Annoyed with myself, I flipped my book back over, preparing to direct my attention elsewhere, or to at least give the appearance of doing so. It was at just that moment that the black-fringed eyes rose and bore straight into my own.

Uncanny. Uncanny because I could see that the slight woman with the porcelain complexion had eyes the precise same pale gray as my own...eyes that now stared into mine with the self-same intensity that I had been leveling upon this still stranger.

Goosebumps rose on my skin, and I felt my eyes widen.

The space of a breath passed.

Then the woman looked away and turned slightly toward the door.

I felt tired and fuzzy, as though I were just waking up. I took another bite of omelet, now tasteless, and stared sightlessly down at the pages of my book.

I decided to dismiss the moment. I decided to not look back up until I had finished the chapter. I decided I'd had too much coffee.

Then the overhead lights went out.

The background music cut off in mid-melody; the fans and motors no one ever noticed whirred to a stop; even the clanking of dishes ceased. There was an instant of complete silence. Diners—strangers—looked around to each other, seemingly seeking an explanation. Then, just as suddenly, people resumed their mutterings, at first hushed and strangely nervous, then strident, as if to lend the incident less credence.

I looked back up to where the woman had been standing, but she had moved again. Scanning the vicinity, I found her seated at a table by the window: coat still on, hair still unkempt, looking out the glass toward the street beyond. Servers crossed in front of her. Sitting lightly on the edge of her chair, she made no move to pick up the menu that rested by her place setting.

My coffee was tepid; as the server refilled my cup, I hoped the addition would be enough to warm it up. I added more cream, stirring slowly, deliberately, then laid the spoon off to the side before looking back to the front of the room, back to the narrow table where the woman sat.

Where the woman *had* sat. All I glimpsed was the back of the camel-colored coat as the stranger strode out the door and into the swirling leaves of late fall.

MARCH

Betsy Doherty

2/1—"False Start"

The school is putting out its first student-writing compilation this year, and I mean to be a part of it. (Hello, my 80-year-old self! Probably the only one who'll ever <u>read</u> this notebook...) I will glean from my meager adolescent existence something grand.

Michael, my best friend (and a mentor, though I won't tell him so), gave me this advice today after reading my first attempt: "If you don't know struggle, Marty, you can't know victory. Know what I mean?"

"You don't see the struggle? I mean, this guy lost a leg; what's not to...?"

"No—I know...the leg. Hmm," he considered, handing back the stapled pages. "Maybe I'm not picking up what you're laying down." He winked. "Could be me, man. Later."

Tonight, I broke in Dad's new paper shredder.

2/4—"Gram"

Gram smiles brightly, with relief, when I visit her nursing home after school. "Well hello there, Marty. I'd hoped you'd come today!"

"Hi, Gram. How are you?"

"Fine, fine," she replies predictably, releasing me from a hug. "How about a walk?"

A middle-aged assistant enters the room, her cart knocking into the foot of the bed and then the dresser. She ignores me. "Hi, Barbara." She tucks her gum between her lip and bottom teeth. "Lemme get your tray."

Gram looks around the room. "It's under the paper, Lilly." After Lilly leaves, Gram cups her hand to her mouth and confides, "I have a can of Lysol in the closet, Marty. I swear that woman smokes cigars."

We leave the room in a fine Mountain Fresh fog.

In the dim hall, I ask Gram to point the way. She holds her hands together, prayer-like, her elbows propped on the arms of her wheelchair. "I'd like to just go out back."

"OK."

"I wonder if Mr. Stevens will be there. He had surgery on that heart of his again last Thursday."

With a hospital bed in the way, I have to do a three-point turn. "Oh, really?"

"Yes."

I push Gram through the long corridor toward the back exit. As we reach certain doors, I slow so she can peek inside and say hello to the neighbors she knows.

Almost at the end of the hall, we feel a breeze through a room whose door is propped fully open. Mrs. Campbell's shadow brushes across the floor tiles where a "Welcome" mat used to be, a strange, bristly thing with purple-paint flowers. The administration made her move it because it was hazardous to the ambulatory residents.

Mrs. Campbell is the liveliest person in the home, and it always surprises me that someone so intent and vigorous lives here. She has what must be her whole wardrobe spread across the bed. She speaks with Gram as she paces, a strange sadness swallowing her cheer after each comment.

"I can't hardly fit any of these any more, Barb! Would you believe it? Not even my blue dress."

"Oh, I know—it's the food they serve here," Gram offers.

"Huh?"

"The food. The breads and sweets…"

"This lovely blue dress." Mrs. Campbell clicks her tongue. "I just got it last December."

There's a long pause.

I pick at the rubber handle of Gram's chair. "Uh, maybe you could get a green one this year."

Mrs. Campbell looks vacant.

"Or red," I try.

She lifts the dress by its shoulders, shaking it gently. Slowly, she looks down at the piles of garments on her bed.

"Ann," says Gram, "I'll save you a seat at dinner tonight." And we move on.

Gram pushes open the glass door to the back walk. She has to lean forward, as if to touch her toes.

"Got it?"—her veiny, splayed fingers hold the edge of the door.

"Got it"—I catch the bottom with my foot and force the door open a little wider to get the back wheels through.

The narrow cement path winds around a cluster of tall evergreen bushes. There are just a few splotches of rusty needles in the full branches. Gram tugs at the thin, ropy limbs that crowd the path. She manages to snap off a few and tosses them into the underbrush. From this vantage point, you would almost think you'd stepped into a lovely, wheelchair-accessible wilderness. But around the corner, the path's laid out in such a tightly snaking way that you feel like you're standing in line for a big roller coaster: shuffle, shuffle, practically double back on the turn; shuffle, shuffle again.

Gram looks around for Mr. Stevens. "Wish I had my sunglasses."

"We could go back."

"No, no. That's all right. Maybe that's him in the shade."

I'm sweating. Wafts of Gram's lemon verbena cologne come strong and steady—so steady that in time I lose the scent. I wonder if I should give Gram my baseball cap—her scalp looks so vulnerable.

The man in the shade is not Mr. Stevens.

Gram finally grows uncomfortable in the sun. Her voice is tired: "I'll look for Mr. Stevens later. Just take me back to my room now."

"OK."

"Thank you for the walk, Marty. You're a good boy."

We return in silence.

Lilly is coming out of the next room as we reach Gram's. "Barbara! Hon', it says here you're gonna need some imipramine after dinner—a little accident last night, huh?" She opens the closet door, looks inside, shuts it. "I'll get a set of fresh sheets just in case and put 'em in here. Remind the night nurse about that so she'll check in on you every couple of hours…OK?"

Gram twists her ring, clamping its stone in her palm for a second, then turning it back. "Yes, Lilly."

Lilly leaves a blue-flowered Dixie cup on the dresser and walks out, flipping through her chart.

Gram speaks into her lap. "Say hello to your father, and to Jake."

I bend to kiss her, and she pats my cheek.

"Goodbye, dear."

"Love you, Gram. I'll be back soon."

And now, as I lie in bed, I picture Lilly roaming the halls, ducking in and out of rooms, trailing cigar smoke everywhere. Her shift ends, and she pushes that stupid cart all the way home. In my mind, she breaks her fucking back when she slips in the puddle her fucking dog left on the floor.

2/6—"Wad"

After school, I head for the book store downtown. It's full of college students and quiet perusers. For a while I weave through the stacks, reading jackets here and there. I walk under a couple of sliding ladders, touching their yellow-wood steps as I go.

Eventually I sit down with a steaming mug of something I don't really like and start to write:

> Opening the door to Dr. Elliott's clinic, I almost hit a wheelchair. The woman sitting in it is facing the door and swinging one foot off its hold like an old bull pawing the ground.
>
> I start, and smile. "Were you on your way out?"
>
> A man sitting to my left looks up from his magazine to observe the scene. No one in the waiting room claims the woman with eyes or action. Most of them shift in their seats to show that she is now mine to worry about or dismiss as I see fit. The man lazily shifts his gaze to the reception desk. He is still watching.
>
> The pain in my chest has grown from a distant pulse to a full throb since I woke up this morning. I muster another smile for the woman—she is blocking my entrance. "Excuse me, then."
>
> She puts the foot in reverse, but it just rubs against the floor. After a moment, I bend down and push her backwards. Her eyes widen, and she stares at my hands on her armrests.
>
> "Sorry, ma'am. I hope that's all right. Here's a good spot, huh?" A shooting pain pulls my arm to my chest.
>
> She speaks. I can't understand the words, but on the last one she straightens her torso and raises her voice. Nothing hostile, just emphatic.
>
> "I'm sorry. I—um—I have to check in."
>
> The receptionist is looking at me expectantly, sympathetically. She moves her something-a-day calendar and name plate aside and pulls the patient register closer. "Hi. Do you have an appointment?"
>
> "No, but I called this morning. Dr. Elliott said he might have time for me after two. I'm Daniel Neuman."
>
> "Oh, OK." She looks at the handwritten notes at the bottom of the page. "There you are. Dr. Elliott should have a good half hour open soon. Most of them are just waiting for blood work."

"Thanks."

"Mrs. Steinmetz?"

The woman in the wheelchair turns her head. "Ya?" comes out, deep and shaky.

I slide past Mrs. Steinmetz gracelessly to a blue armless chair by the end table.

"Would you like me to call the ride service again? It's been an hour."

Mrs. Steinmetz nods. Still talking over her shoulder, she says something about her dinner. Then, almost indecipherably: "It's been an hour."

"Yes, it has, hon'. I'll call again."

For some reason, I can't finish this story. I hate Daniel Neuman. I hate all of them, just sitting there watching the control and happiness leak out of this old woman. Pretending not to stare at the trickle of piss and vinegar.

The streetlights have flickered on—I'm not sure when—so I gather my things and go out to the curb, just as the bus pulls over. The bus door shakes open. The driver cocks an eyebrow and lifts his chin. I realize that I'm sneering, but I'm not sure if this guy is curious or just impatient.

"Hi," I mutter. In a fit of impetuosity, I meet his look with my own jaded gaze. I look away quickly and survey the seating: no open rows. I head for the back, picking my way past shopping bags and shoes. I pass up a seat next to a woman holding a baby who mouths her shoulder. I pass a drowsy businessman who blocks another seat. Then, like a puppet, I turn on my heel and plant myself next to a man with torn-up corduroys and glasses taped at the bridge. I soon notice a wet-dog smell.

Two stops into my ride, the man rumbles and hacks up a substantial wad.

"'Scuse me," he manages through his mouthful.

"Sure." I turn away.

"'Scuse me." He's staring at me with anxious eyes.

"Oh, sorry." I swing my legs into the aisle.

His stench, as he maneuvers by me, meets no barrier in his clothes. But I—catching sight of the driver eyeing us in his rearview mirror—inhale sharply, purposefully. Wrinkles appear in the skin around the driver's eyes as he silently snickers.

I reply with a look that's bolder than the one I gave him before. I <u>like</u> being immersed in life's untidiness. I like being challenged, damn it. I like the stench of humanity, and I'm not afraid of my fellow man, whatever his circumstance. I will <u>not</u> respond with mere amusement or disdain. I am a writer.

2/20—"Leah"

I found this in Leah's diary. (I need some new ideas for my story since my English teacher's suggestions haven't panned out.) I think Leah was talking about her college advisor or someone like that. The entry is from two weeks before her suicide:

> We engage in two types of communication. The first, an earnest intellectual dialogue. The second, a receding but still apparent visual acknowledgment of our youth and inexperience, an admission that her expertise is yet to be established and that my honesty hesitates. I am not used to sharing so much…
>
> I guess it is inevitable that the rich and boiling chaos in the mind can be only partially conveyed in logical narrative. So do people essentially understand each other, since all of us face this same dilemma? Or is it foolish to think that anyone can truly understand another, since each of us sifts through such varied chaos to present a public face?
> I don't know what to have faith in…
> Whether I desire faith in anything…
> What faith is.

I wonder if Leah ever thought about getting old—about what she could have figured out with time…

Unlikely. She was pretty stuck in this existential crap. She probably believed that gray hair and dentures would never be her lot. She never did say much about what made her so unhappy.

I can't write about Leah now.

2/29—"Welcome"

Michael looks exasperated. He isn't talking fast like he usually does. It's dark outside, and we're walking across the playground at the top of my block. "What happens next, Marty?"

I'm watching my feet take me forward, in stride with Michael. I don't know how to meet his look, but I know this is a question that he would like answered. By me. "Well," I shrug, "I'm working on it."

He doesn't talk for a while. "Of course you are." His tone is flat. I think he might be high.

"Fuck you, man. What makes you God almighty? Why does <u>your</u> opinion of art and humanity count for so much?"

I don't think Michael cares about helping me get ideas for a story any more. From the back, he looks almost tragic.

I scan the ground, looking for wrappers or rocks to somehow anchor this blur of green. I want to leave. "I'm going home. My dad needs me for something."

Michael stands quietly for a second, then walks away.

I become aware that no audience witnessed this strange scene.

A tide of indifferent discovery washes over my brain, across my eyes.

I blink. Michael means so little in this world. I mean so little. And we are desperate to grasp a meaning we could glorify, capture, debate. We are small and selfish and stupid.

I think he knows it.

Back home, I walk into Leah's old room with my notebook and sit down on the floor.

Fuck Michael, anyway. I won't believe that Leah might as well have thrown her life away. Or that Gram is just marking time.

I lean back against the bed and close my eyes.

I picture Gram wheeling herself through the nursing home halls, peering through each door frame. "Leah?" she calls out. "Leah, dear?"

My sister sits in the far corner of one of the rooms, hunched over a desk. Her pen is dry and she is crying.

Gram can't get there: an enormous "Welcome" mat barricades the doorway.

And I am out back on the narrow path, where a woman in blue is blocking my way. Each time I get past her, I am somehow turned around, and there she is again. She grabs lightly at her blouse, and she looks right through me.

3/1—"Early Morning, March"

Dad wakes me in the morning. "Hey," he coughs, "you sleep OK?"

My neck hurts, but, "Yeah."

He looks around the room, then at me. "Can't have been too comfortable." He is looking down from a great height.

"What time is it?"

"Seven-thirty." He seems to feel the need to say more about the fact that I spent the night on Leah's rug. But he doesn't—just takes a couple of breaths and closes his eyes. "Hurry up, now. I need to leave for work in ten minutes."

"OK." Suddenly, I want Gram there.

I go to my own room and open the closet door.

One day, none of these clothes will fit me.

DOOR MEETING FRAME

Betsy Doherty

After eighth period, I shove my Social Studies book into my locker and pull a bag of Combos from the top shelf.

"Hey, Niel." Megan's voice is so darned soft.

I scan the hall to my right, then turn to her. "'Sup, Meg." I slam my locker and flash my cheesy smile before jogging over to the fountain by the gym. Megan is giggling behind me.

The shoulder strap of my duffel bag is digging in, so I flex, and my flesh turns to metal; the strap pulls smooth against my mighty arm-pole.

There's Drew. "Drew, man, you comin' tonight?"

Drew sticks his tongue out and makes these crazy eyes. "Yeah, man!" He drops his shoulder into my chest and pins me—cuz I let him—to the wall for a second. "Better be sharp today!" He turns down the music hall to drop off his trumpet.

I shake the bag of Combos into my mouth, half chew the crunchy rolls and pull cold water through my lips.

Football season's over, but the coaches are rounding us up for a scrimmage. I've got another year at Gompers Junior High, but most of the team will be freshmen at LaFollette in the fall. Coach Simon won't say it, but he wants me starting at wide receiver next season, and we both know we're losing the best QB ever. Coach is giving me some glory with the old crew cuz next year's gonna suck. Oh, well. Today'll be fun. Once I get to the park.

Jason and What's-his-face are crouched between the glass doors. I stick my hand in my bag and look the other way when I pass them. Disinterested—that's how Mr. Tse put it. "Just try not to engage, Niel." I feel Jason's eyes on me, and I flex my arms again. He smacks his lips, kind of the way Mom does when she disapproves—but Jason's noise is hostile. I swallow and unleash the loudest burp my churning gut can muster, followed by, "Dude, get some Maalox, man."

"Bitch," he answers, and that breaks my stride. But I'm not about to get into it with this punk. I just walk to the bus.

My day gets a little worse: it's the puny, squirmy driver again. Man, I hate being the biggest person on the bus. Too much responsibility.

"'Sup, man," I offer to the mini-driver. ("Minnie Driver"—ha. That's good. Gotta tell Drew.)

The little rat barely looks at me. He keeps checking the pre-teen wasp nest in his rear-view and rubbing his palms over the giant wheel. "Um, yeah, 'what's up,' kid."

Whoa, man—don't dis your reinforcements. I push past the nerdy kids and spread myself across two seats toward the back. Somebody took a knife or maybe just a pen to the plastic. It peels away like a good scab.

I guess my courage hasn't caught up with my body, cuz I still won't park it in the way-back. Gotta have a clear shot at the door. Jason and his sidekick aren't far behind, but I'm not worried. Not yet. They lunge at a couple of the dorky ones up front. Tracy is too ballsy for her own good, and she shoves Jason back—I mean, her palm on his chest and just shoves! Damn—I don't think *I'd* even do that. Jason's in the seat with Tracy in a second. He's got her smashed against the window, and his face is right up in hers. What did she expect?

Maybe a minute passes, and the bus is getting quiet. When this girl from geometry looks at me funny from across the aisle, I notice that I've pulled off like half of the seat back where there used to be just that rip. She raises her eyebrows, and I scoop up the peelings. "For you," I offer.

She laughs. "Niel, you are so weird sometimes."

Yeah, she likes me.

Man, why hasn't Ratty pulled Jason off Tracy yet? I pocket the plastic shreds and kind of start up the aisle. "Pete, you goin' to the game, or what?"

Pete's crouched over his Nintendo. He's got his gray hood pulled low, and I grab at the strings to pucker it up, but he slaps my hand away. "Knock it off, man. And, no—you know I've gotta clean the garage tonight. Dumbass—thanks for rubbing it in." Pete can play it cooler than I can, but I know he's kind of watching Jason, too. He's only a couple of seats back from where that asshole is now squeezing Tracy's leg, hard, just above the knee. Jason's holding his backpack across both their laps so the driver can't see, and he's blowing a steady air stream at her eyes as she clenches her jaw. Her chest moves like she's got the hiccups.

The bus starts to shake, and we jerk away from the curb. Perfect.

"Whoa-ho!" I shove my handful of plastic scraps down Jason's shirt back. "Shit, man, sorry—bus caught me off guard, y'know?"

The insult snaps him to his feet, and he pivots in a flash. You'd think I'd dropped ice down there. He glares at me.

I could throw up, I'm so tense.

I can tell Sidekick doesn't want to get into this, but he's watching from the front of the bus. He's got one heel on the sneaker-toe of a kid who's sitting next to him, a sixth grader.

Jason reaches back, grabs his collar, and shakes out the scraps. They fall slowly behind him. The kids up front are watching. Ratty rolls through an intersection and hits the gas. Jason and I each grab a pole for support.

"Oh, look at that"—I draw out the next word—"bi-i-it-*ch*: you're shedding."

Enunciate. That's another thing Mr. Tse is always telling me.

I'm ready to duck a swing. Jason is smaller than me, but meaner. I wouldn't be surprised if he had a knife on him somewhere.

"Sit down, you two!" Ratty's eyes jump from the road to the mirror and back at least a dozen times.

Jason leans toward me, slowly.

To my left, Tracy is almost frozen. Just her right hand is moving, tapping gently on her leg.

"Sit down!"

Jason's face is getting close to my chest as he keeps leaning forward without moving his feet. What the hell is this kid doing? He hasn't taken his eyes off me.

Now in one motion he turns his neck to the window and spits. Hard. He barely had to let me out of his sight to hit the side of Tracy's face, dead-on.

The kid at Sidekick's mercy gasps, then yells a little as Sidekick grinds a heel into his foot.

Jason pushes past me. I hear him stumble; Pete must have stuck out a leg.

I can't look at Tracy. I grab two fistfuls of Sidekick's jacket—he's even scrawnier than Jason—and basically throw him toward the back of the bus.

Now Ratty's itching to pull over—too much action, I guess—but his timing sure sucks.

"Hey, man," I say, "it's cool. We're cool."

"Just find a seat, young man!"

My Dad told me not to talk back to adults. I return to my seat slowly, and no one looks up. Jason and the kid I threw flip me off, one after the other.

Geometry girl—Sarah, I think—watches a thermos in another seat.

I sit and watch it, too. It jumps when the bus tires hit potholes. Head turned toward the one-level houses and dogs and fences that we're passing, the owner makes a claw with his hand and steadies the thermos so it won't fall.

The driver is pulling over: first stop. There's a PDQ across the street and a trailer park down the hill. Usually only the new boys—two brothers—get off here, but Tracy is walking to the front door as they go out the back.

I can't really tell from here, but the driver looks angry; he doesn't wait any longer than he has to. He pushes a lever forward, and there's a rubber-metal flapping noise of door meeting frame.

Tracy and the brothers are kind of coming together as they walk toward the store. One of the boys cuts toward her even more—Jesus, now what? The bus is moving again, and I stand to see what's happening outside. I'm ready to push through the back doors since the little green light's always on—they'd give way. Dude—where's a Superman T-shirt when you need it?

But now it looks like Tracy's got her hand out and the kid's just dropping something in—Skittles or something. My legs and stomach relax. If I were Clark Kent, I'd be rebuttoning that top button and straightening my tie.

In the back seat, Jason and Kick sit as far apart as possible, staring out opposite windows. They look bored, but when Jason catches me watching him, the finger is back up like he never moved.

"*That's* original."

"I'm just trying to get a point across, Niel." Jason uses the same tone as Mr. Tse.

I snort.

Sarah looks at me, and then at Jason. Incredulous, I believe, is the word for her expression.

When Jason gets off two stops later, Kick leads the way. Jason turns to me on the last step, tips his middle finger in a kind of salute and jumps to the curb, shoving Kick into the gravel as he lands. The door closes and the bus pulls away.

I don't stand up this time. My palm traces the jagged edge of the plastic that remains on my seat back, and I try to think about the game ahead.

DIG AND DRIVE

Paul McComas

South Side of Milwaukee, July 1981

It's Tuesday morning, quarter to 11, and we been called out to lay some replacement pipe at this house on Pulaski. The folks who live there are moving out, and I guess their realtor said to get the gas line fixed because otherwise she can't sell the place. Anyway, our Machine Op's on another job, so we get out the shovels and dig the holes by hand: one by the sidewalk, one right up by the house, each about four feet deep. While we're digging, the owners keep carrying boxes and furniture out the front door and loading them into a rental van, a yellow Ryder parked right behind our truck. It's awful hot out, and I guess the owners have some idea what it's like for us, digging away under that blazing sun. One of them does, anyhow, because pretty soon this guy's coming towards us down the walk with three cold Schlitzes.

"Thanks," J.G. tells him, "but no thanks. We can't drink on the job."

I laugh. "Like that's ever stopped you."

"Boss is comin' to inspect the site. Remember?"

Old Merkel has his sunglasses on, but I can tell his eyes are getting all narrow and mean behind them from the way his wrinkles kind of rearrange. "He is, is he?" Merkel spits at the ground. "Little piss-ant. When I crewed with him, before he got his goddamn promotion..."

"He used to get soused. He used to drink his lunch. We know." J.G. shakes his head. "You're repeatin' yourself, old man. I swear you get more senile every day."

Merkel gives him a little shove. "Senile my ass."

The guy's still standing there with the beers, so I say, "I guess we better not, but thanks for the offer."

"Well," he says, "the hose is right over there if you fellas want to cool off." And he takes the beers back to the house. Pops a can himself as he goes.

Well, we go ahead and drink from the hose like he suggested; the water ain't beer, but it's cold, anyway. Then we get the gopher out of the truck and hook it up to *its* hose—the one attached to the truck's compressor. See, the gopher's this heavy, missile-shaped tool about three feet long. The compressor pumps air through the hose and into the back of the gopher, making it jerk forward and burrow its pointy tip right through the ground. It makes its own tunnel—just like a real gopher—pulling its hose along behind.

So we stick the gopher inside the hole by the sidewalk and aim it at the hole by the house, then we start up the compressor. Like always, the gopher makes a lot of clangy, rattling noise—it's a real powerful tool. But then, as it starts disappearing into the earth, the noise gets softer, not so much a clanging as a muffled *thunk-thunk-thunk*.

The gopher, like I said, has a lot of power; what it *ain't* got a lot of is speed, so J.G. and I go and sit under a big tree on the front lawn. J.G. lays down on his back with his hands under his head and shuts his eyes. I've got a root beer I bought on our 10 a.m. break, so I pop the tab and take a sip. Then I scoot back a little and lean up against the tree to watch old Merkel.

He's standing there just past the hole by the sidewalk, trying to figure out where the gopher is at that exact moment entirely by feel. The earth is trembling under his feet, and that makes Merkel tremble, too: the backs of his pants legs are shaking, and so's his collar, and even his head; his sunglasses are bouncing on top of his nose. He reminds me of some two-legged animal character out of a TV cartoon.

Merkel starts walking towards us.

"Come on out of the sun," I say.

"Yeah, yeah." With a grunt, he squats down and sits next to J.G. who, being J.G., is already sound asleep. "Ding dong, ding dong."

Never understood why Merkel always says that. He makes those bell noises just about every day, sometimes more than once, without any explanation. I never asked him about it. "It's all dig and drive, boys"—that's another one of his big expressions, though that one's pretty clear-cut.

I hold my root beer out to him, but he shakes his head, so I take another drink myself. "Gonna be a while," he says. "Ground's kinda hard here."

"Hey—what'd you guys use before the gopher was invented?" I been wondering for a while but never bothered to ask.

"Now what makes you think I been around that long? I look *that* old to you?"

I don't say a word.

"Yeah; I guess I do. All right." Then he starts in with that voice he always uses in situations like this—that kind of teacherish tone. "Well, Rick, the gopher has been around for many years, though it wasn't very, y'know, sophisticated at first. Took a lot longer to do its job, and hard ground like this here woulda…"

"Merk," I cut in, raising my hand, "I said, *before* the gopher."

"I know," he says, a little bit pissed. "I'm gettin' there. That was just what you call your background information. Usually we'd have to dig a trench that went the entire length of the pipe we was gonna lay. If there was a sidewalk, well, we'd just have to take our shovels and tunnel down under it. Nowadays"—he gestures over to hole number one—"you boys got it easy." As we can hear, the gopher's still hard at work. Next to me, J.G. kind of chews in his sleep.

"Easy?" I ask. "Who do you think dug those holes?"

"We did. But now we're sittin' on our asses in the nice, cool shade, you drinkin' pop and him in fairyland, while *that* poor bugger chugs away, pumpin' its little heart out."

Across the street, this pretty young blonde is coming around the corner. "Nothing wrong with doin' that," I say. "Check it out."

On second look, she's even younger than I thought: maybe 14, with long white legs and short white shorts, carrying a grocery bag. She hasn't developed all the way, but she's getting there, all right. An early bloomer. I shake J.G. till he wakes up.

"Wha' th' hell…?" he mumbles, wiping a hand across his mustache.

"Look."

He looks.

She crosses the street and heads straight towards the very house we're working at. As she makes her way up the walk to the front door, paying us no mind, Merkel's eyes don't leave her for one second. He even tips down his sunglasses for a brighter view.

"Christ," J.G. says. "In a coupla years…"

Merkel folds his arms. "Looks plenty ripe to me."

The girl opens the door, and in she goes.

"Merk," J.G. says, "she can't be more than 14—15, tops."

He shrugs. "'Old enough to bleed, old enough to seed,'" he proclaims, and J.G. laughs. Then Merkel starts in on him. "Now don't be tellin' me you wouldn't love to—to Mount her Saint Helen." *I* laugh at that; it's a new one, at least to me. "I remember it well, John-Boy; I know what it's like. Your wife is, what—eight months along now?"

"Nearly," J.G. says.

"Been a while, ain't it? Or do you got a pinch-hitter stashed away somewhere?"

J.G. laughs, but he doesn't answer. He turns to me. "Nothin' you didn't go through 'in country,' I expect."

"Damn straight. We went weeks, even months without a piece."

"Well," Merkel says to me, "that ain't a problem for ya now, is it? How 'bout yerself, Rick—makin' any babies yet?"

"Gettin' plenty of practice," I say.

"Shootin' blanks, huh?" Merkel laughs at his own joke.

"Sure as hell hope so. Christ, Merk, we only been married a year! We can't afford a kid—not yet, anyway."

"Who can?" J.G. says. He rolls onto his stomach, sticks his hands under his chin and gazes off at the ditch next to the house. Nobody says anything for a while. Then the front door opens, and two guys—the beer guy and another one—come out carrying a big desk. They have to twist it sideways just to get it partway through the door…and then it gets stuck.

"Hey," Merkel says, "maybe we oughta give 'em a hand."

J.G. shakes his head. "Bad back. Can't lift nothin' heavy." He grins. "Wife's gotta help me take a piss."

I've heard that one before, but I laugh anyway.

"Well," Merkel says, "looks like they got it now." We all watch them carry the desk over to the Ryder, load it into the back and then return to the house. All the while, 30 feet north and four feet underground, the gopher keeps on *thunk-thunk-thunk*ing away.

I nod towards it. "Sound a little slow, guys?"

"Yeah," Merkel says. "It's hit some clay."

"Or a rock," J.G. suggests. He flicks his finger at a blade of grass, sends a bug sailing.

"Nope. No rocks here. Nothin' big, anyway—nothin' it couldn't shove aside or go right around."

J.G. raises himself up on his elbows. "Merkel, how the hell…?"

"I been on plenty of jobs in this neighborhood. This ain't rocky ground. Just a little clay. Maybe a pebble here and there."

"Guess you oughta know," I say.

J.G. rolls back onto his side. "How long you been with the Company, Merk?"

"Thirty-eight years."

"And you never got further than Mechanic-One?"

Christ, J.G., I'm thinking, but as it turns out, Merkel doesn't seem to mind. Just shrugs and says, "Never tried. Never applied."

"How come? I mean, you at least could've made Machine Op."

"Why the hell I oughta do that? Don't need the money. My wife, she works at IBM. Makes a lot more'n I do." He's glad about this, I know, but he sounds a little ashamed, too. "Two years and I'll be out—full pension, full benefits. Less time than that: 20 months. Then I'm home free. Little scrap of family land out in Wyomin' me and the Mrs. gonna go call our own. Beautiful land. Fascinatin', too—like my buddy Pike out there always says, you never know what you're gonna see next." Did I mention old Merkel has a tendency to ramble? "That's where we're headed, all right. Hell, I got life by the short 'n' curlies! No point workin' any harder than…"

"But *before*, I mean." When J.G.'s wife filled up his lunch box this morning, she must've forgot to pack a clue. "Back when you were young—you coulda been a supervisor, like Cramer. You been here longer."

"That's true," Merkel says, his voice getting kind of hard. "And I ain't makin' the kinda scratch he is. But on the other hand, *I* ain't a *son* of a bitch. And Cramer is."

We both have to agree, because Cramer really is a son of a bitch.

"Boys," Merkel says, "I remember it like it was yesterday," and we both know what's coming. His eyebrows press down around the top of his sunglasses, and he picks at the dirt on his palms as he talks. "We were partners back then, me and Cramer. And every so often he'd have a couple too many at lunch and, well, that was all she wrote. It's in his blood, I guess. So I'd get him into the truck and drive him home, 'cause when he'd been drinkin', he wasn't in *no* shape to work.

"When we got there, he'd drag me down to the rec room in his basement and show me the 'authentic wood paneling' he'd put up. And the 'western-style mahogany bar.' And the stuffed largemouth bass he'd caught up north. I heard that same tall tale about that same goddamn fish 100 times if I heard it once! I could prob'ly tell you boys the whole bullshit story from memory, word for word, to this day."

"Don't," J.G. says. He looks over at me, and I know we're both thinking the same thing: that we must've heard him *complain* about that bullshit fish story 100 times.

"So I'd leave him there and cover for him back at the station. I'd tell the supervisor—the very fella Cramer later *replaced!*—I'd tell him Cramer had come down with something, fever or stomach flu or whatnot, or that he'd hit his head on a pipe. And I'd do *both* our work for the rest of the day.

"Then," Merkel says, his voice getting even harder, "he up and gets promoted, and he starts gettin' this idea he's better'n me. Starts orderin' me around, tellin' me how to do my work. Last week—no, week before, it was—he says he's noticed I'm takin' nearly 45 minutes for lunch, and that this'll have to stop. Jesus H. Christ! 'Nearly 45 minutes.' So I says, 'Look, Cramer. I seem to recall a time when your lunches took the whole afternoon, mainly because they came from a *bottle.*'"

"What'd he say?" I ask.

"He just stands there, wanting to hit me but too chickenshit to try. Then he sends me out on the shittiest job he can find. Little ass-wipe. If I was him, I swear I'd have to stop shavin', 'cause I couldn't stand to look in the mirror. Goddamn traitor's what he is. And all it took was a little power…"

"That's all it *ever* takes," I say. "My C.O. in the Nam? Same damn thing. And look at the other supervisors here: Rutley, McCutcheon…"

"Y'see?" He takes off his sunglasses and wipes them on his Company shirt. "Just as well I *wasn't* promoted."

I notice something funny going on inside the house, up on the second floor. They've opened a big double-window and laid the edge of a sofa up on the sill; it almost seems like they're gonna just push it straight through. "Look at that," I say, pointing.

"Huh," Merkel says. "Guess it wouldn't fit through the door."

"So how'd they ever manage to get it *in* the house?" J.G. asks.

Merkel takes the words out of my mouth: "Doorway mighta narrowed since then, from the humidity. Prob'ly swelled up a little."

J.G. grins. "Mine's more swollen when I put it *in* than when I take it out."

Merkel doesn't bite on that one; he's still looking up at the window. "They're gonna have to lower it somehow." He's quiet for a while, thinking. Finally, he turns back to us. "Gopher's back on track. Hear that?"

He's right: it's returned to its normal, steady clip. I get up and walk over between the two holes, feeling with my feet to see where the vibrations are the strongest. The place I locate the gopher at's a little more than halfway to its goal. I stand there, look up at the guys and nod; they nod back. I return to the tree and sit back down.

"Won't be long now," Merkel says. "It won't be hittin' any more clay."

J.G., of course, takes the bait. "Now how the hell do you know that?"

Merkel shrugs. "Just do. There's *some* clay in these parts, but not much."

J.G. shakes his head. "You're crazy, old man. In-freakin'-sane."

"Insane?" Merkel asks. "Thought I was senile."

"That's right," I say. "*I'm* the crazy one. Must be: Vietnam veteran. Hell, don't you watch TV?"

"Tell ya this," Merkel says. "I ain't so crazy I don't know a good bet when I hear one."

"What," J.G. asks, "on whether the gopher hits any more clay?"

Merkel nods.

"Now, wait." J.G. points over towards the place where I stood and nodded. "Thing's more'n halfway home. Just by sheer, y'know, *probability*, it prob'ly won't hit no more clay. What kinda odds you gonna give me?"

"Even odds, John-Boy: a six-pack either way. I say it's out in 15. Prob'ly less."

J.G. hesitates. He looks like he's deep in thought—which makes this a special occasion. "OK, you're on! What time ya got, Rick?"

I check my watch. "Eleven-twenty."

"Eleven-twenty," J.G. repeats.

Merkel smiles. "We'll see who's crazy."

"I'll tell ya who's nuts for real," I say, "is that nasty old bag on Teutonia. The place we serviced last Friday—the kitchen leak…"

"Oh, Christ!" J.G. says. "'Catwoman!' That house—I never smelled nothin' so awful in my life."

Merkel laughs. "She must've had 50 of the buggers in there if she had one. And I didn't see no litter boxes in that basement, nor anywhere else." His nose wrinkles at the memory; he pinches it shut. "JAY-zus!"

J.G. picks up a twig, tosses it across the lawn. "Maybe we shoulda reported her to the Health Department."

"Maybe we ought to yet," Merkel says. "I didn't know if we was gonna make it, workin' down there."

"Well," I say, "it was about the quickest repair job *I* ever seen!"

We all begin to laugh, but then Merkel stops; he nods over towards the house and talks under his breath. "Speakin' of filth…"

We look: someone new's just come out the door. This time it's a woman, about 35, long-legged and blonde. Looks like what that younger girl we saw might turn into when she grows up—almost like we been stuck on this job for 20 years!—except that if it *was* the same gal, then at some point, her life took a turn. This one's got shiny black boots with stilleto heels, a solid inch of makeup on her face and the kind of trampy, tight black mini-dress most women wouldn't wear in public, let alone daylight. Quite a sight; all that's missing's the whip.

We don't say anything as she struts past us and heads for this hot pink Pinto, shaking her not-bad butt for all to see. She gets in, revs it and pulls away.

Of course, J.G.'s gone and gotten himself all worked up. "Oh, she'd be a kicker, I bet. Give ya a sore back in the mornin'."

"Sore throat's more like it." We both laugh at Merkel's joke. But then his voice gets all serious and wise in that same old way—like when he told about the time before gophers. "Boys," he says, "a whiskey glass and a woman's ass made a horse's ass o' many a man." He nods at his own motto, which I've heard him deliver many times before.

"You speakin' from experience, Merk?" J.G. asks.

"Only way to learn." Merkel stands, stretches out his arms. "Gopher oughta be out any minute."

"Dream on," J.G. says, then looks over at the house. "Now they got it tied up."

He's right. The men upstairs have attached a couple of ropes to the sofa, one on each end, and they're pushing it a little further out the window. Once they've got it halfway through, they stop and talk. Then one of them walks away from the window and out of view.

"Yup," I say, "they're gonna try and lower it, all right. Must have it anchored to *something* up there, though God knows what. Lucky they had those ropes."

J.G. laughs. "Prob'ly got 'em from Madame Pinto!" He's looking at me out of the corner of his eye, waiting, so I go ahead and grin at his dumb joke. Might as well, it makes him so happy.

The guy who disappeared upstairs walks out the front door and goes to stand under the window. He raises his arms. We can hear the two of them talking back and forth: "Careful." "Easy, now."

Merkel stands up and starts walking towards them. "Hey, fella! Why don'tcha go back upstairs and help yer friend? I'll handle it down here."

"Yeah? Are you sure?"

"Looks like a three-man job to me. Go on."

"Thanks a lot."

The guy walks back inside the house; he reappears upstairs. Then him and his friend edge the sofa the rest of the way out. Slowly, they start lowering it down towards Merkel. It's swaying a bit from side to side, and for a second it looks like it might swing right into the top of the big first-floor picture window, but pretty soon it's just outside Merkel's grasp; reaching high, he steadies it with his fingertips, then takes hold.

I hear someone pulling over, and I turn to see that it's a white Company car. Cramer. He parks in front of the house, gets out and starts waddling toward us. Cramer's maybe a dozen years younger than Merkel, but on account of his desk job, he's gotten pretty out of shape. He comes up and stands right next to where we're sitting. From the look in his little pig eyes, I know there's gonna be trouble—though not for me or J.G. "Hey, Ned," I say.

He nods. "Rick."

"Gopher's just about through." I'm trying to sound casual. "We should be out of here inside 45."

"Uh-huh." He starts walking again, this time over to Merkel and the couch, which by now has landed safely. Those two men come walking out the front door to thank Merk. But before they even have a chance, Cramer starts in. "Merkel, what the fuck do you think you're doing?"

Merkel stands there kind of stunned. I guess even he hadn't expected such a sudden attack, and in front of strangers. Who seem, by the way, pretty uncomfortable. One of them—the guy who offered us the beers—says, "He was just giving us a…"

Cramer grabs Merkel's sleeve and leads him away; the two guys just look at each other, pick up the couch and haul it back to their van. The boss drags Merkel over towards the gopher—close enough to me and J.G. for us to hear them, but not close enough for us to really get involved.

Merkel's come around by now; he pulls his arm away and puts his hands on his hips. "Those boys was tryin' to lower that couch, and I figured they could use another pair of hands. One of 'em coulda got hurt…"

"What about you? What if *you*'d been injured, Merkel? I'd be out a worker, and the Company would have to foot the bill. You'd be sitting pretty on workman's comp because, strictly speaking, you'd have been injured on the job—even though you weren't *doing* your job!"

Merkel shakes his head. "I don't see the harm…"

"If you're so goddamn eager to help people, do it on your own time. Volunteer at a hospital. Put on a skirt and be a goddamn *candy* striper for all I care.

But on Company time, you do our work—*Company* work—and that's *it*. Is that clear?"

Merkel speaks really soft at first—almost too soft for us to hear. "What about drinking, Cramer? Drinkin' on Company time? You oughta know *all* about *that* policy." Then he shouts—and I mean, *screams*—right into the boss' face: "C'mon, Cramer! What's the rule on *that* one?"

J.G. and I look at each other, and then at Cramer, whose stubby little fingers are twisting at his sides: every word is hitting home. "Merkel, this isn't the first time I've had to warn you about 'helping' on Company time, and..."

"God forbid I should *help* anyone!" By now Merkel's over the edge—all sing-songy and out of control. "Used to help *you*, Ned. Used to lie to the boss, time and again—for *you*."

"What if that couch had slipped? You think you'd have gotten out of the way in time—old man?" Cramer laughs, once. "You can barely tie your *shoe*."

Merkel's body tenses up, and I just know he's gonna deck that prick. And he starts to...but he stops. It's almost like some kind of comedy routine: he actually grabs his own fist and just stands there, frozen, fighting with...himself, I guess. Then he spins away and walks back towards me and J.G. His steps are shaky, and his face is red. I want to say something...but what? He moves right past us and goes to stand by the back of the truck.

Suddenly, the *thunk*ing of the gopher gets a lot louder, like it's about to come out. "Got it!" I say, jumping up, and I run over to the hole by the house. At the same time, J.G. heads off to man the compressor switch in the cab of the truck. He stands there looking at me, waiting.

I get to the hole in plenty of time. Little wisps of dirt come tumbling down the inside walls, then whole clumps start to drop, and then finally, out comes the tip, streaked with clay from earlier in its trip. I grab the short-handled shovel we'd left next to the hole and dig out some of the dirt, helping the gopher through. When it's nearly all the way in and clanging like crazy, I wave my arm. J.G. flips the switch, and in a few seconds the tool rattles to a halt.

As I walk back towards the truck, I notice that both Cramer and his car are gone. J.G. hops out and meets me halfway. "Where's the boss?" I ask.

J.G. keeps his voice down: "Guess he figured he'd done his job."

I run a hand through my hair, which is damp from the digging, and I lower my voice, too. "I could've sworn Merk was gonna belt him. Hell—*I* sure would've! Wonder what stopped him?"

"He'd have been fired before Cramer's fat ass hit the ground."

"But with the union at bat for him, and you and me..."

"No way. Cramer never touched him. Merk wouldn'ta had any kinda case, no matter what you, me *or* the union had to say."

I look over at Merkel. He's standing with his back to us, hanging onto the side of the truck with one hand. "So what if he *had* been fired? He's about to retire anyway. I mean, there's only so much shit a guy can take."

"Well, he's gonna have to take a little more, and he knows it. You heard him: he wants his pension and benefits. That means waitin' it out another 20 months. And you'd better believe Cramer's gonna make every day of every *one* of those months an absolute livin' hell."

Merkel turns around to face us. He stares at us from behind those sunglasses of his and rubs his palms against his Company shirt.

"Hey, Merk," I call out. "You were right. No more clay; gopher made it straight through." I check my watch. "Twelve minutes flat."

J.G. folds his arms. "Guess I owe you a sixer."

Merkel nods. "Guess ya do."

"I shoulda known better, Merk."

"Yup," Merkel says, his face a blank. "Well, it's all dig and drive, boys. All dig and drive." And then the man who has life by the short 'n' curlies climbs kind of stiffly into the back of the truck and grabs a length of orange pipe.

After a second, J.G. and I walk over to give him a hand.

"Ding dong, ding dong."

I WAS A TEENAGE DISCO PRINCE

Paul McComas

.

…but please don't judge me till you've walked a mile in my platforms.

You see, while the mid-to late-'70s disco craze was widely viewed as the last word in mindless conformity, for me it signified the opposite. In our lily-white, upper-middle-class suburb, and particularly at Hyper-Homogeneous High, disco—with its roots and popularity in both urban black and blue-collar-white culture—was scorned for reasons more ethnic than aesthetic. Within our student body of 1,200, most of whom favored the arena-friendly cock-rock of REO Speedwagon, Journey and Styx, there were perhaps two dozen rebels who dared crank their Chic and do "Le Freak" for all to hear and see. This gutsy crew included most of the black kids bused in daily from the city, several members of the Modern Dance Club…and me.

Even among the misfits, though, *I* mis-fit a bit. Musical tastes were the chief means by which we teens bonded and, for that matter, self-segregated—a tribal dynamic, in essence—yet my own taste was wildly eclectic. I was as enthused about pop-rockers Boz Scaggs, Rita Coolidge and E.L.O. as I was about disco; like my stoner friend, Cheryl, I dug the harsh, guitar-driven sounds of Cheap Trick, Blondie and the Knack; and I found myself increasingly drawn to the offbeat lyrics and strange syncopations of new-wave pioneers Devo, the B-52s and Talking Heads. Call me broad-minded, but there wasn't much contemporary music I *didn't* like.

Except, of course, for the irredeemable pap churned out by REO, Journey and Styx.

By the summer of 1980, disco was on the wane…yet I, being just shy of 17, still had never "stepped out" at an honest-to-God discotheque. There was something else that I had yet to do, too, something even more ambitious—something that would require the full cooperation of a willing young woman. And so, one humid summer Saturday night, I repaired to my bedroom to blow-dry my hair, don silver shirt and white polyester pants, slip into midnight-blue dancin' shoes, sling a faux-gold medallion around my neck and slap on some Brut. My mission was clear: to strut into the city with my fake i.d. and cruise for chicks at the area's preeminent discotheque-cum-pickup joint, Milwaukee's answer to Studio 54—the Park Avenue.

As I drove my Mom's AMC Pacer downtown at 9:30 (under the auspices of meeting friends for mini-golf), my heart raced in anticipation. Was I ready for this? I'd seen *Saturday Night Fever* three times: the R-rated original once, the PG reissue twice. I'd taken two disco dancing courses at the YMCA (yes, the Village People *were* on the play list) and practiced my moves religiously at home. Then there was that night the previous March when my friend Danielle Payton and I had driven out to working-class West Allis to shake our respective groove thangs at an alcohol-free nightclub called DiscoTeen…

As it turned out, we didn't linger long. For when Danielle and I walked in the door, a black girl with a white boy, you'd have thought we were *Close Encounters* aliens straight off the mothership. Kids pointed and whispered and stared; dancing to black music was one thing, but apparently having an actual black person amongst them—on the arm of a fellow Caucasian, no less—was quite another. Many a hostile glance was aimed our way; as we hit the floor (to the strains of Foxy's all-too-apt "Get Off") I leaned in close and joked, "Did we take a wrong turn and cross the Mason-Dixon?"

But Danielle didn't laugh—just looked up at me with anxious eyes and said, "We crossed a line, all right. I'm thinkin' we'd better go."

…Now, while pulling into a just-vacated street space a block past my destination, I found myself wondering whether I should have invited Danielle along tonight. I'd considered it—the downtown crowd was bound to be more open-minded—but Danielle had never seemed inclined toward anything but friendship. My best shot at adult-type intimacy lay within the venue's indigenous population, and I certainly didn't want any potential Park Avenue paramours to see Danielle and me together and presume I was taken.

Of course, in striving to accommodate a hypothetical interest in me on the part of these as-yet-unmet older women, I myself was presuming up a storm.

I got out of the car and, with the chicken-scratch-guitar intro to "Stayin' Alive" playing in my head, strode up the street, jaw set, arms swinging—not quite Tony Manero, but a passable Tony-in-training, *sans* paint can. I paused in front of the Park Avenue's black-tinted front window to check my hair and admire my shirt: shimmering silver with a thick, red lightning bolt zigzagging across the front from shoulder to hip. I adjusted my fashionably wide collar, took a deep breath and stepped inside.

"I.d." I heard the man before I saw him; I couldn't have been carded sooner. With a practiced casualness—literally; I'd rehearsed at my bedroom mirror—I removed my wallet and smoothly produced the goods. The mustachioed door-man peered at my card, then at me, then at the card again before handing it back. "Five-dollar cover."

I handed him six singles—"A little somethin' extra for ya there"—and waited for a word of gratitude that never came. Rather, if his narrowing eyes were any indication, I seemed only to have aroused the man's suspicions. "Thanks"—the word was mine, not his, and after speaking it I hurried past him into the vast, pulsating space beyond.

The Park Avenue was everything I'd hoped for: swanky and sumptuous, a grand, glimmering, bi-level disco palace. The dance floor was laid out in a multi-colored grid and illuminated from below by hundreds, perhaps thousands, of bulbs that flashed, rapid-fire, to the rhythm. Suspended above, a rotating mirror ball the size of a satellite sent a spectral web of light cascading across everything in sight. On the upper level couples stood, drinks in hand, elbows on the rail, gazing down at the dancers—who unquestionably merited the attention: dodging and swirling, twisting and twirling, hard-eyed young men and haughty young women, black and brown and white together, united by the beat, by the heat, by their predilection for garish inorganic fabrics and, at this moment, by the powerhouse falsetto of Sylvester:

> You make me feel…mi-ighty real.
> Ooo! You make me feel…mi-ighty real.

Of course, the Park Avenue may have been many things, but "real" wasn't one of them. Then again, people didn't go there seeking reality; they went to escape it. And as for me, standing open-mouthed and agog in the midst of it all, my own desire was to find, within and through that utmost *un*reality, one absolutely authentic woman…someone who, if I played my cards right, just might make *me* feel real. Mighty real.

Seated together at a table near the dance floor were three dazzling prospects: a blonde and two brunettes in their early 20s, stunningly attired in sparkling satin dresses, each of a different shade. Nursing her drink, the highly animated short-haired brunette did nearly all of the talking while the others, flanking her, guzzled and grinned and hung on their friend's every word. The trio displayed true esprit de corps—Charlie's Angels, I thought, in between assignments. They seemed to be enjoying themselves, the one recounting some comically convoluted story and the others prodding her on. Still, every so often, one or another of the three would glance over toward the dancers as if yearning to join them.

Had no one yet asked these lovely ladies onto the floor? It seemed unlikely, given their looks. Or was that the problem: were the women prohibitively beautiful? Did no one here dare tender an invitation? Was there not a man in the house brave enough—or, as in my case, desperate enough—to risk rejection and shoot for the stars?

Apparently there was not. But, I told myself while in motion, if the men were afraid to act, then perhaps a brazen boy was what the job required.

"Hi," I said, making fleeting eye contact with each woman in turn, then followed up my snappy opening line with the equally droll "How ya doin'?" I winced and thought, *At least my voice didn't crack!*

The storyteller glanced at her cohorts, then back at me. "We're doin' good," this apparent group leader said, sizing me up with lively green eyes. "How 'bout you?"

"Me too." I nodded, hands in my pockets. "Real good."

Straight-faced, she nodded back. "*Good* to hear."

The blonde stifled a laugh; the longer-haired brunette shushed her.

"I'm Cassie," the talkative one said. "This"—indicating the shusher—"is Tricia, and that's *Ahn*drea."

"Nice to meet you...all. I'm Phil."

The brunettes, together: "Hi, Phil!"

*Ahn*drea, drinking, gave me a wave.

Cassie indicated an empty stool. "Care to join us?"

"Thanks," I said, and sat down.

"Don't think I've seen ya here before, Phil." Cassie turned to her friends. "Does Phil look familiar to you?"

Tricia shook her head. "'Fraid not."

*Ahn*drea tried to answer, but her words degenerated into another squelched titter.

"It's my first time," I said.

"His first time!" Cassie placed an arm around each of her companions. "Didja hear that, girls?"

Finally, the blonde spoke—"That's…hot"—then lapsed back into laughter. "Now, *Ahn*drea," Cassie chided, "be gentle with our new friend. After all…" The three spoke in unison: "It's his first time!"

"My first time here, at this club," I hastily explained, face flushing. "I've been to *others*," I added—then wished I hadn't, as the only club name currently coming to mind was DiscoTeen. Tricia took out a compact, checked her make-up; I fiddled with the medallion around my neck and studied my shoes. I was in over my head. I felt like a double-agent whose cover had been blown by a troika of *femmes fatales*. No: more like live prey being batted back and forth amongst a pack of feral cats. I was about ready to locate a mouse hole—or a mercifully quick trap.

Maybe Cassie picked up on my distress; maybe not. Either way, she proceeded to switch gears. "So tell us, Phil. What do you do? You in school, or…?"

"I work," I said evenly. "Building services and property management"—a reference to my summer job as night janitor at the office building that housed my father's cardiology practice.

My answer took the women aback; like everyone at whom I had flung my departmental title, they didn't know what to make of it, though Cassie for one seemed mildly impressed. "Is that in, like, administration?"

I deliberated: that would be a *good* thing, right? "More or less."

*Ahn*drea, bored, played with her swizzle stick. "Well, how about that."

Cassie raised her own drink, took a sip. "Where?"

"Meigs-Childress. It's this big professional building on—"

"I know," she said. "I'm a teller at First Wis. You're just down the street."

"Yeah!" I heard my own ebullience, brought it down a notch. "My savings account's at First Wis." Encouraged by even so distant an affiliation—and by the apparent cessation of Phil-teasing—I steeled myself and went for broke. "Uh…Cassie, was it?"

"Yeah?"

"Wouldja like to dance?"

Her friends, amused, exchanged another look, but this time Cassie's eyes stayed on me. "Y'know what, Phil? I would." And with that, she stood.

Out on the floor, a couple of feet apart, we slipped into the rhythm with ease. Cassie's steps were flawless and her movements fluid and, oh, my God, what a *form*! Sleek and slender, she was nearly my height with a tall, tapering neck, ivory skin and perfectly-shaped breasts that bobbed a bit as she danced. Long, sloping calves; thighs till Thursday. As for her ass, I can only say that, my Methodist upbringing notwithstanding, I began to contemplate founding a new religion. For each time she spun, her dress—a short spaghetti-strap number the same gumdrop green as her eyes—whipped up and to one side, exposing the perimeter of a rounded realm that well may have been Nirvana.

My gaze, as you may have gathered, had barely left her since we'd started dancing, but not until midway through the second song—"You and I" by Rick James—did it hit me that Cassie's eyes had yet to fall on me. A shame: bolstered by the bass line and swept up by the sax, I was *on*, adeptly executing the steps I'd learned at the "Y" and tossing some slick improvs into the mix for good measure. Still, what was the point of setting the dance floor aflame when the one you aimed to wow wasn't watching?

I reached out and took Cassie's hand and then, at last, she looked at me. Her face, framed by chestnut hair in a stylish pageboy, would have been striking even without its current cast: assured, collected, self-possessed. Swallowing, I stepped forward and eased my arm around her waist; she placed her free hand lightly on my shoulder. Just then a new song began: the celestial, synth-driven title track from the recently-released film *Xanadu*—an abysmal "modern musical" that I, upon viewing, had confidently crowned "Worst Film of the '80s," regardless of whatever else the next nine and a half years might have in store.

"Hey," Cassie shouted over the intro, "you seen the movie?"

"Yeah," I answered, "last week."

She smiled at me. "I loved it!"

I smiled back. "Me too!"

Though we'd done well apart, we moved even better together. Gamboling with abandon, Cassie was more relaxed in my grasp than expected; I'd danced with a few girls in my day, but not a one endowed with such freewheeling looseness. I guided her one way and spun her back the other, Cassie responding so readily that it seemed neither of us was leading and neither following. A liquid energy coursed down her slender arms, into her palms and out her fingers; a rippling warmth enveloped me each time I pulled her close. And wafting around us all the while was the seraphim soprano of Olivia Newton-John:

> A million lights are dancing and there you are,
> A shooting star
> An everlasting world and you're here with me,
> Eternally…

My heart seemed to be swelling within my rib cage, pressing out toward my partner, aching for contact—but I caught myself, held my passion in check. I hadn't come this far to squander everything on an ill-timed kiss.

As "Xanadu" reached its big finish I double-spun Cassie into a dramatic dip. We held the position, catching our breath, my dream-come-true partner flung over my forearm with her head thrown back, lips parted, her gaze joined to mine. "Oh," Cassie sighed, "I hate this."

I almost dropped her. "Uh…"

She straightened. "This song—I hate it. Don't you?"

The deejay had selected a medley of Beatles hits performed by sound-alike singers to a thumping disco beat. Cassie, being several years older than I, was probably a Fab Four fan back when they were still an active band; thus, to her, "Stars on 45" no doubt qualified as sacrilege. "I…uh, you're a great dancer, Cassie."

"Not so bad yourself." She raised a hand, flipped her bangs out of her eyes: an innocuous gesture rendered with heartbreaking grace. "Let's sit this one out."

"Deal. Can I buy you a drink?"

"Rum 'n' Coke. Thanks." She turned and headed back to her table—*our* table—in the process presenting me with a most agreeable view. I'd developed quite a fondness for watching women walk away…appropriate, as my love life's rocky start had afforded several such opportunities. Heading for the bar, I recalled the most recent occasion on which I'd been jilted—then tossed the memory away. For somehow, with Cassie seated across that magical dance floor awaiting my return, that other night had lost its bite.

Trying to catch the bartender's eye, I found myself wondering if perhaps I was *supposed* to have missed that prior connection in order to meet Cassie. Then I found myself imagining a proper date on some future night, with Tricia and *Ahn*drea nowhere in sight. Then I found myself wondering how Cassie's tongue would feel against mine. Then I found myself being grabbed by one arm and emphatically yanked away from the bar.

"Your driver's license," the massive, bald-headed bouncer said from his vantage point a good foot overhead. "Please," he added, smirking—a little joke to himself.

I handed him my fake i.d.: a UWM student card with my own name and photo.

"This is not a driver's license." He didn't hand it back.

"I…I know," I said, voice shaky.

The bouncer folded his arms. "You have one?"

"I do." I cleared my throat, fixed my lips into a sheepish grin. "But y'see, the problem is, *on* my driver's license, if I *were* to show it to you…I'm only 16."

"Time to go"—he checked the card—"…Phil."

"I'm not even *drinking*," I basically whined. "I'm just here to dance."

"Song's over."

I gazed off toward Cassie and company. Perhaps they'd witnessed my initial "capture," perhaps not—but they certainly were watching now. "Can I go say goodbye to my friends?"

He shook his head.

"It'll only take a…"

"Do it from here." His tone invited neither bargaining nor begging.

I bit my lip. This time, apparently, it was the woman's turn to watch *me* walk away. *Do it from here*—that wasn't possible! Still, I couldn't just turn and go. I had to tell Cassie something.

Catching her eye, I pointed at my watch, then mimed holding a telephone receiver to my ear, then shrugged, then waved good-bye.

Her face registered confusion—and who can blame her? I mean, what the fuck had I just said? Even *I* didn't know! As she raised her right hand, fingers delicately opening and closing, a strobe light above started to flash, plunging Cassie's own farewell gesture into somber slow-mo.

I headed back to the entrance, my unwelcome escort at my heels all the way.

❧   ❧   ❧

Cursing under my breath, kicking at cigarette butts, I skulked about just outside the building on the off chance that she might come looking for me. This stark stretch of street was the disco's depressing antithesis. There were no strobes or lasers out here, just a slowly flashing DON'T WALK on the corner; there were no crowds—just me and, half a block down, a bum dozing by a dumpster. And the music, from this vantage point, had been reduced to a muffled, bass-heavy blur.

After a minute or two the door swung open, and my head shot up; a black couple tumbled onto the sidewalk, arm in arm, laughing. They were fashion-model-attractive and dressed to the nines. "Oh, you think so, do you?" the woman purred.

"I do," her man replied, deep-voiced. "You have somethin' better in mind?"

"Not tonight, I don't." She sighed—"Not…tomorrow night"—then snuggled up close. "Shit, Trey—not ever."

He rumbled out a low chuckle, his palm sliding briefly over her behind as they stepped past me and crossed the street.

I couldn't help it: I despised them.

I sat down on the curb and, staring at the pavement, put myself in Cassie's shoes. What did she think I was trying to say? "Oh, look at the time! I have a phone call to make. Places to go, things to do. Sorry, babe. Have a nice life." Would any woman in her right mind pursue a man—let alone an almost-man—who had danced with her and held her close, then stiffed her on a drink and told her *that*? Head in my hands, I found myself near tears.

Again, the door swung open.

"Phil."

The bouncer. Standing alone. The neon "Park Avenue" logo reflected on his shiny, bullet-shaped pate. My fake i.d. was clenched in his hand; he flicked it toward me, but as I reached out the card detached in mid-air: he'd cut it up. It landed in four pieces, two of them in the gutter.

"Now get the fuck outta here."

I scrambled to my feet, glaring, and mumbled something under my breath.

He took a step toward me. "*What* was that?"

"DISCO SU-U-UCKS!!!" I screamed, voice fraying, then tore off my medallion, cast it into the storm drain and ran back down the block to my mother's car as fast as my blue platforms would take me.

Heading for work on Monday afternoon, I got off the bus one hour and one stop early, at the base of the First Wisconsin. I swiftly ascended the granite steps, lunchbox in one hand, a lone red rose clutched in the other. Sweating profusely—from the heat, the humidity and the attire (I'd put on a sportcoat and tie, like the junior administrator Cassie assumed me to be)—I hurried toward the revolving door, eagerly anticipating the near-frigid conditions that surely awaited within.

As luck would have it, the building's overtaxed air conditioning system had blown out, and several maintenance workers—the First Wis version of *me*, I realized with a start—were in the process of erecting a series of ancient, wrought-iron electrical fans throughout the stale and stagnant lobby. As the crew activated each clamorous contraption in turn, the cumulative noise level quickly approached airport-runway dimensions. Wiping my brow, I got in line and began scanning the long row of teller stations…and there she was, in a crisp white blouse, off to the right in the second-to-last spot. As I waited, I silently rehearsed the short speech I'd scrawled back home and committed to memory on the ride down.

Soon after I reached the head of the line, a teller beckoned; I stepped aside, ushered forward the customer behind me. A minute later, Cassie's station opened up and I, with jittery steps, made my way toward her. Stepping up in front of her, I noticed a triangular blotch of perspiration on her blouse, right at the collarbone, and smaller stains under each of her arms. If you for one moment imagine that any of this turned me off in the least, then you have never been a 16-year-old boy.

Cassie, straightening a stack of currency, had yet to look up. "Good afternoon. How may I help you?"

For lack of a check or a deposit slip, I placed my rose on the counter and slid *it* forward—only then noticing how much it had wilted during the commute.

She looked up, and as she recognized me her mouth dropped halfway open. Glancing about, she grabbed the flower and tucked it out of sight. "Well," she said softly. "This is a surprise." She fiddled again with her stack of bills, eyes alternating between it and me.

"Cassie," I began…then paused, paralyzed by the smell of her: a perfume of some citrus scent—tangerine?—comingled with the frank fragrance of the woman's own sweat. The bulky stationery fan just behind her amplified the aroma, aiming it straight into my face. I nearly swooned, and though I vaguely recalled having readied a recitation of some kind, not a word of it came to mind. "Cassie…"

"I'm working," she murmured, again looking about. "I can only talk for a minute; they watch me like a hawk."

"I don't wanna get you in any trouble…"

"It'd help if you had a transaction."

"Oh. Right." I removed my wallet, pulled out a twenty. "Tens, please."

Eyeing me, she took the bill.

The opening line of my speech came back. "You're probably wondering what happened at Park Avenue the other night…"

"I assume you got carded; I saw Floyd take ya out." She slid me two tens.

I slid one back to her. "Fives, please. So you *knew* I was under-age?"

She took the bill. "Um, *yea-a-ah!* We all did, soon as we saw you." She slid me two fives. "Why'dja think we kept teasing you?"

I slid one back. "Singles, please. Then why did you dance with me?"

She took the bill. "Because you were kinda cute, and I wanted to dance, and, well, you asked. But, c'mon, Phil. What're you—sixteen?" She counted off five singles in front of me.

I slid one back. "Quarters, please. Yeah, I'm sixteen, but only for the next month. Besides, I thought that…I mean, the way we were dancing together and all…"

"I'm eight years older than you. That's half your life! You must know girls your own age who like to dance and…and who like you." She slid me four quarters.

I slid one back, and as I did, an image of Danielle came to mind. "There's one, but I don't think she'd want to be my girlfriend or anything."

"Ever asked her?" She slid me two dimes and a nickel.

I slid the nickel back. "Well…" I cut myself short; we'd gotten off track. "Cassie, are you positive that nothing could, uh, develop between you and me?"

Wide-eyed, Cassie looked right at me. "Sure—if I wanna get *arrested*!"

As if on cue, a short, pin-striped fellow wearing wire rims and a bad perm appeared by her side. I scanned his i.d. badge: Dale Seastrom, Accounts Manager. "How's it *going*, Cassandra?"—his tone accusatory.

"Fine, Mr. Seastrom." She flipped her bangs out of her eyes. "Just giving this gentleman his pennies"—which she proceeded to do. She also gave me a look: *Please leave before I get canned.*

The man folded his arms. "Quite the little tête-à-tête you're having, eh?"

Quite the little prick you're being, eh?—that's what I wanted to say. Instead, hands in my pockets, I somehow came up with this: "I was asking her about the different kinds of savings accounts the bank offers. I've…come into some money—inherited it, actually. I'm saving up for college, and I was, uh, interested in finding out what my options are."

Mr. Seastrom appeared to buy my story. "In that case, you should really speak with an accounts manager. *I'm* free, if you'd please come with me…"

As I followed him away from the teller station, that glorious scent receding with each step, I turned my head and glanced back.

Smiling faintly, Cassie mouthed her thanks. Then, just as two nights before, she raised her hand and waved.

❧   ❧   ❧

Half an hour later—armed with a brochure about money-market accounts, a First Wisconsin keychain and a receipt for my newly-purchased $1,000 certificate of deposit (I'd shifted it over from savings; Dale Seastrom may have been a little prick, but he was a *persuasive* one)—I made my way back through the loudly ventilated lobby toward the revolving door. I tried to sneak a peak at Cassie along the way, but some male teller stood at her station now. She must have finished her shift, or maybe she was on break. And though I don't put much stock in omens, at that moment I knew with utmost certainty that I would never see her again.

Leaving the bank with half an hour to kill before my own shift, I wandered along the steaming sidewalk, head bowed, dress shoes dragging. Halfway down that first block, my eyes fell on something carved into the pavement below: two sets of initials, nestled inside a heart. I made a point of stepping on the accursed hieroglyph as I passed it.

A dull clanging noise brought my head up, and I squinted out through the hundred-degree haze. Some big, brown dog—a thick-coated, overheated stray—had managed to capsize a curbside garbage can and was dazedly sniffing at its sweltering contents.

Never had downtown been more depressing.

In search of air conditioning, I trudged across the street to Radio Doctors, Milwaukee's best-stocked record store, and opened the door. Was it, in fact, cooler inside? I honestly don't recall. What I *do* remember is how the petite girl behind the counter—clad all in black, with short, spiky hair to match—looked up from the latest issue of *Record Mirror* ("Exclusive Elvis Costello Interview!") as I approached. "Hey."

"Hi," I answered, eyeing the Buzzcocks button pinned just above the nipple of her smallish yet lovely left breast.

"Lookin' for anything in pah*ti*culah?" An English accent, sexy as sin.

"Um…yeah." My hand shot to my collar; loosening the knot, I suddenly wished I'd worn a skinnier tie. And a hipper sportcoat: my jet-black one with the sharp-cut shoulders and narrow lapels. *Next time,* I thought. *Come back tomorrow and do it up right. But for now…*

I slid my hands into my pockets and shot the clerk a conspiratorial grin. "Where would your punk-rock section be?"

BALANCING THE LOVE SEAT

Laura Allen-Simpson

I dig my fingers into the dense wool pile of the living room carpet and wiggle the tips to leave ten holes. Then I turn one hole into a "hi" dot and two others into eyes. "Don't draw on the carpet!" calls Mom, rapping the wooden spoon twice on the edge of the pot.

We are having goulash for dinner as soon as Dad gets home. It has sauerkraut in it, and, at the last minute, Mom adds sour cream. She calls it "*Say-Kay* Goulash," which is Hungarian. With a half-smile, she claims that she can't translate it any more. She looks very beautiful with that half-smile—like a European princess: snow-white skin, red lips, black hair, light blue eyes, and a dimple in her chin. She dabs Chanel No. 5 behind her ears and on her wrists even when she isn't going out. It mingles with the goulash in the steamy yellow kitchen.

I stay in the living room and draw another face in the carpet. Then I go to the love seat to sit *inverted* (my new word). My knees are hooked over the top of the back of the couch, my shoulders where my knees should be, while my hair pools on the floor and my head begins to feel magnetized toward the ground. I grow dizzy as I mentally walk the new rooms above me. The world upside down is incredibly bare, but it has light fixture fountains and unexpected steps and stairs.

"What are you doing in there?" Mom is in the living room checking before I can right myself. "Oh, Paula! You're going to get sick if you hang like that! And your hair's going to be a mess—all staticky and snarled. You won't like that when it comes time to brush it out." I swivel my head to look in her direction and feel my scalp beginning to prickle. "Get up!" she says then, more insistent. "Come on! The dust down there must be terrible! I haven't vacuumed in weeks!"

I pretend I'm getting up but don't rush it, and as soon as she's gone I drop again for one last look at the other world that lies above us all. Then, feeling *queasy* as Mom calls it, I finally sit up, and while I let my mind settle like Etch-a-Sketch particles I wonder how much taller I've just gotten.

What to do now? I know: balance the love seat. When I kneel on the love seat facing the back, it's just light enough for me to tip toward the windows. All I have to do is jerk my hips out and lean into the fall. Then I have to push off the window frame with enough oomph so that the couch balances on its two back legs but not so much that it falls back down in front. I love that with just a slight push of one finger I can make the whole big love seat move and then, for whole seconds, float.

But I can't hold us at that balanced place very long. The love seat lands with a *thud*.

"Paula! How many times have I told you not to tip the love seat? You're going to crash through those windows one day!"

I know. I know it all.

The picture windows in houses like ours have rubber parts that are painted but when you pull the rubber back the paint crackles off. I discovered that just recently and have made this paint removal my newest project. Wondering how I could have forgotten, I return to it now. Making progress feels extremely good—like when you're peeling up the edges of dead, sunburned skin and suddenly get a whole big sheet of it off at once.

"Leave that alone!"

I jump.

"Why don't you play with your dolls?"

I run to get my black patent leather Barbie case with the satisfying metal clasp and am soon back in the living room, pulling Barbie from her pink plastic compartment. I have no Ken, but that's OK. He's just there to watch Barbie anyway.

Barbie decides to go for a swim. She always goes for a swim. "I think I'll go for a swim," she says. Then, la-dee-dah, she does a perfect swan dive into the glass-topped table. And just as her nose bumps the glass—*whoosh*—she's under the water, swimming. This pool is like the one at the Howard Johnson's where we once stayed when it was too hot to sleep at home, even with the big hallway fan on high.

Now Barbie comes up for air. Ken is watching even though I have to imagine him. "Oh!" she says, "I didn't know anyone was here!" This is a key moment in the drama because she is actually very excited by his having seen her. Just the thought of him having seen her in her suit makes her cheeks burn. But now she claims that she does not want him to see her in her suit. So she asks him to pass her towel over and look away as she dries off. But as she concentrates on drying off, he looks, and she knows—she can feel it—but says nothing. Then he asks her for a date, and she agrees. Since it is evening already, she goes off to change into her special evening dress. Soon I will need my little sister, Jenny, to play the bridesmaid, and then to play Madge, the nurse—when Barbie has her baby. That is where the game always goes and always ends—although sometimes there is no wedding. And sometimes they swim together—late.

But I don't want to play with Jenny now.

I'd rather go behind the love seat to watch the world underneath the evergreen bushes. Once I saw a bunny in there. But mostly nothing comes. Now as I watch and wait, I notice a lot of pine cones and consider telling Granny about them because she'd be so pleased. But no. She'd probably want us to pick them all up and make a big art project of painting their tips with red nail polish or something, which would give me an instant headache. And she's very fussy about how we do things like that, so I'm sure I'd get something wrong. I'm definitely not telling.

There are a lot of paint chips on the carpet back here. I wonder if Mom knows. I pick up the big pieces and poke them down the vent, but as the warm, cushiony air pushes up, some fly. One nearly gets in my eye. That's when I stop and begin to wonder if anyone will know where I've gone. I am very quiet. Mom is humming, and the goulash is bubbling. I hear her rap the spoon again and click down the flame. I scooch in further so that I'm totally hidden, scrunch up my knees and rest my cheekbones on them, and then wonder what I'll overhear if people think the room is empty.

I've been breathing the air near my knees for a while and listening to cooking sounds when at last I hear Dad's car roll over the lip of the curb. He turns off the engine. The door shuts. He strides to the door. Now his key is in and Mom is going to meet him. She and Dad kiss and mmmm. There is a lot of rustling. Dad sighs. I giggle into my hands, but a squeak gives me away.

"Where is Paula?" Daddy asks in that fake way so I'll know he's coming to look.

"I don't know, Daniel," says Mom. "She was in here a minute ago...I guess she's gone!"

I am a bird in the bushes who can't stop her cheeps! I cover my mouth, but it's too late. Dad has found me and his hands are scooping me up for a great big hug. I am snug as a bug in a rug, and the air is delicious with Say-Kay Gou-lash.

❋   ❋   ❋

The next morning, as I'm using the bathroom, I suddenly remember that Granny is coming over. I check for Dad and discover that he's already left to get her, so I have to hurry to make my cleaning bubbles. I've been letting the scum in the upstairs bathroom sink get super bad so that the sink will look really sparkly when I'm done, and Mom won't feel so bad about her housekeeping this time. But you never know. Sometimes Granny refuses even to come upstairs, saying that the downstairs bathroom her son has to use is good enough for her.

I pull up the thing to close the drain, let a little water in the sink, and start rubbing the soap over the bottom really fast. Back and forth, back and forth, backandforth. I've gotten about half a sinkful of bubbles up when I hear the front door squeak open and Dad call, "Granny's here!"

Knowing I will have to stop any second, I rub harder and faster, meanwhile listening to what's going on downstairs to figure how much time I have left. Granny is making fussy noises as if she doesn't want Dad to bother over her things. He's raising his voice, though, and putting spaces between his words—"It's...no...trouble"—probably so that she'll finally listen to him. But she just keeps fussing with her bags. She always has bags with her—bags for projects and snacks and lanyard and yarn and stones she's picked up and her nail polish and her nightgown. And by the time Dad gets home with her and her bags, he's always a little irritated.

Uh-oh. He's already climbing the stairs to find us.

"Paula? Jenny?" He raps on the door.

"Yeah?"

"Don't you want to go down and say hello to Granny?"

"Sure," I say. "Be there in a minute. I'm just finishing cleaning the sink."

"It would make Granny feel better if you came down *soon*."

I push the thing down, hear the dark, Lurch-like swallow of the drain, and splash water over the last of the bubbles. Then, as I'm drying the chrome edge around the sink so it won't spot, I hear Jenny thumping down the stairs on her butt and Granny's growly attempt at sweetness: "Ohhhh, there's my little angel!"

When I appear at the bottom of the stairs a few minutes later, Granny is clawing past a pink nightgown in one of her clear vinyl shopping bags. I don't know whether I should go kiss her hello to prove that I am an affectionate grandchild, or wait politely to be respectful. As I try to decide which she will prefer this time, I get hypnotized watching her ridged, pink-frosted nails gouging through the soft stuff in her bag. "Well?" She looks up, startling me. "What are you standing there for? Don't you want to kiss your Granny 'hello'?"

"Yes, of course," I say, stepping forward.

"No," she says, smiling tightly. "Let's say our 'hello' *properly*." Her eyes look past me, and obediently I step backward, up two stairs, stopping where I know we will be the same height. I wait there for her. Then, careful not to muss her stiff poof of hair or its tight little bun, I lean out, put my arms around her neck and kiss the cheek turned toward me. Her too-sweet perfume, cheek powder and hair spray make me feel kind of sick, but I say nothing.

❦   ❦   ❦

By early evening I am in the upstairs bathroom watching Mom in the mirror, putting on her makeup, while I use my index finger to dig chunks of homemade sugar candy out of my molars. Granny and Jenny are out back, catching fireflies. Dad is downstairs, buffing his shoes on the edge of the utility sink. I am waiting until Mom finishes her left eyebrow to tell her what I figured out about Granny.

Granny showed Jenny and me how to make sugar glass candy by melting sugar in a pan until it's brown liquid and then pouring it out onto a plate. Mom came rushing in at the end and wasn't too happy with it because Granny used Mom's new frying pan. But Granny didn't seem to notice how angry Mom was. In fact, while Mom was running water over the pan, making it hiss and steam, Granny just raised her voice and went on explaining how after the candy cooled we could break it into pieces, just like glass.

"Scorched," Mom muttered, her face flushing.

Anyway, when we sampled the cooled candy, it occurred to me that it was sort of like Granny: it started out all sweet and sugary but wound up tasting burnt and bitter—*scorched*, like Mom said—and being really brittle, with thin, sharp edges that could cut your tongue. I am just on the verge of telling Mom how Granny's candy is like Granny when Mom starts to talk. "Dad and I are going out tonight," she says.

"I know," I say, swinging my legs so that my heels thump the sliding vanity door. Did I mention I'm sitting on the vanity? I'm up on the vanity.

"Stop that kicking! You're going to scuff up the doors with your sneakers," says Mom. Then, after a pause, she adds, "Granny is staying with you."

I crash my heels against the door with a *thud*.

"Paula!"

"What about Grandma Hannah? Why can't *she* come like she always does?"

Mom answers me like a ventriloquist as she paints on her red lipstick with a brush liner. "Grandma's not feeling well." Our eyes lock in the mirror. Mine fill up as I imagine the long night ahead. Mom shuts the cap to the liner with a click and turns to me as if it's all decided. "You'll be fine." Then she takes two squares of toilet paper and closes her lips over them, pressing off the excess red.

"I won't be fine. I hate Granny, and she hates me. I don't want to stay home alone with her."

"You won't be alone. Jenny will be here."

"Oh, great. Jenny. She's some help."

"Now, Paula," says Mom, dabbing the glass stopper of Chanel No. 5 behind her ears, "I know that Granny's not the nicest person, but she won't let anything bad happen to you. It'll be fun—like a sleep-over! You can make popcorn and watch TV and sing songs. You like to sing camp songs with Granny, don't you?"

I look down into the toilet bowl and see Mom's kiss floating there. My throat is aching, and I can't look up or I'll burst out crying, I just know it. But if they leave me alone with Granny, I am going to die. Why can't they see that?

Mom presses her powdered cheek against mine and makes soothing sounds, but when I look up at her and my first tear spills out, she's already looking back in the mirror, fussing with her hair. "Come on," she says, now studying my face as if to see what it'll take to get me out of this mood. "How about I put a little Chanel behind your ears so that you can still have me around while I'm away? Would you like that?"

"I'd rather have *you*."

She kisses away my stupid tear and rubs my cheek lightly to wipe off the lipstick she left behind. Then she touches the cool glass stopper behind each of my ears. It tickles, making me squirm and smile against my will. So now she thinks everything is fine. But it isn't. "*Please* don't go!" I beg, throwing my arms around her neck and letting her drag me off the vanity as she backs away.

"Paula, you're too heavy!" she cries. "C'mon!" She eases me to the ground and pries off my arms, as if I've been choking her. She looks into my eyes for so long that I think she might just stay. But no. "C'mon," she says. "Let's go show Daddy how good you smell."

❦   ❦   ❦

All too soon, it's just Granny, Jenny and me. We're down in the basement, and Granny is telling Jenny what polite people do when they have company over. I know from her sweet but schooly way of talking that her lecture is really meant for me. It's her way of telling me that I am not being friendly enough. I am supposed to offer her snacks and a cool drink or a cup of hot tea so that she can say, all fakily flustered like some southern belle in the movies, "Oh, don't bother on my account." Then I'm supposed to insist that it's no trouble, and that even if it were, of *course* I'd want to bother. That way, she can finally agree to let me wait on her and not feel bad about it—feel, actually, quite special.

But instead I am sitting on the rec room floor, totally focused on my game of jacks—that is, until Granny suggests that Jenny encourage me to join them and "be sociable."

"No, thanks," I say, planning my strategy for swiping up the jacks this turn. "I'm having a really good game, and I'd like to finish it."

"OK," says Jen.

Granny makes a sound like Saran Wrap squeaking and finally speaks directly to me. "Is that any way to treat your little sister—especially when she's just trying to remind you to do the polite thing?"

"Jen's fine with it. She just said it's OK."

"Sweetheart," says Granny, as if she's coiling the word. "Come here." It is a direct order. Granny is looking straight at me, patting the floor beside her.

I heave a sigh, carefully mound up my jacks in a clump so that the ball will stay put on top, and crawl over to her.

"That's better. You know, we don't get to see each other very much. So I can't fault you for not knowing how to behave." Then, as if it's some sort of truth that she's just realized, she adds, "Your mother probably doesn't teach you manners, and your other Grandma probably doesn't even expect them. But, you see, a proper lady always wants to make her elders feel loved and respected. A proper lady focuses only on her guests, even when she wants to be alone or playing 'a really good game of jacks.' Now, let's be good to each other, shall we?" But as she gives me an awkward sideways hug, she wrinkles up her nose, inhaling sharply. "What's that smell?"

"What smell?" I ask, trying to sniff out something bad. I detect a trace of the burny sugar glass still lingering, but she can't mean that.

She stares at me long and hard, as if I know the answer and she can get it from me through my forehead.

"What?"

"Perfume!" she announces. "What are you doing wearing perfume—especially something like *that*?"

"Like what?"

"It's much too adult for a little girl like you."

I still don't understand what's wrong. "It's *Mom's!*" I say, thinking this will prove it's all right.

She shudders and yanks me up, her bracelets rattling.

I go limp, dropping back to the floor, and turn instantly into a blob of cement.

"Stand up," she says, five ridged, pink-frosted fingernails spread wide to grasp my hand.

I'm frozen. I can't help it. Her meanness does that to me sometimes.

"Stand up, *now!*" she says, her ripply nails closing around my arm.

"*Ow!*" I cry, scared.

"I didn't hurt you!" she says, yanking me back up to a standing position. She's right, but feeling scared is just like feeling hurt; it makes my voice jump out of me. Granny lowers her face to about an inch from mine. "We're going to wash that off." She starts pulling me toward the bathroom, and all I can do to resist is let my knees buckle. "You're not getting out of this that easily," she says, grabbing me by the arms with two hands and lifting me back to my feet. She's got me just above the elbows and has started shaking me. Even Jenny gets wide-eyed at that.

Jenny's terror magnifies my own. "I know you hate me! I know you want to kill me!" I cry, hysterical now. "But if you do, Daddy will never talk to you again. He'll hate you. He'll never want to see you!" It's all I can think of to save myself, but it seems to work.

"What are you screaming about?" she asks, startled. "Nobody's going to kill you." Saliva is foaming in the corners of her mouth, like she's been bitten by a rabid dog. I worry briefly that she has been and is going mad right now, turning rabid before my eyes. To calm myself I stop looking at the foam and concentrate instead on how one yellowish front tooth folds over the other—like warped planks on a picnic table. "Who put such crazy notions into your strange little brain? Did your mother tell you that? *Did* she?" Shake. "Or did you make it up all by yourself?" Long stare.

"Ow!" She's giving my arm an Indian burn. "If you don't let me go right now, I'm going to tell that you scared me and hurt me, and I'll have the bruises to prove it!"

"Brat!" she spits, tossing me away. I stumble backward and hit the cold basement floor, hard. "You tell them whatever you want. They won't believe you. They'll believe me—won't they, Jenny?"

She's not asking. She is telling. And Jenny, pale as milk, is nodding her head.

Granny turns back to me. "Now go get yourself washed up clean! And scrub behind those ears. I don't want to be able to smell a whiff of that perfume."

I run straight to the bathroom and immediately lock the door. I'm not coming out until they get home. I'm not washing anything off, either. But just in case she's listening, I run the water, wet my dad's wash cloth and ring it out. Then I sit down on the floor by the vent, where the air puffs up my top, and I try to swallow past the sharp rock that's stuck in my throat. I think I'm getting a stomach ache. I want my parents to be home.

While biting and sucking on the washcloth, I try to picture where they are. I imagine them at dinner: blue window, white linen table cloth, Mom looking glamorous. I see them dancing. Dancing, dancing. I jump the evening forward and picture Dad smoking as he waits for the valet to bring him their car. I imagine them on the dark road coming home. I *will* the tires to roll up over the curb into our driveway; I strain to hear the engine singing like crickets. But all I hear is the roll of the dice and the *click, click, click* of a game piece going around a board. Granny and Jenny must be playing some dumb, easy board game, like Life.

"One, two, three, four, five, six, seven!" counts Jenny.

"You can count up to seven!" exclaims Granny, clapping her hands like it's some big deal. I could count up to 100 when I was Jenny's age. And now I can count up to infinity, but Granny has never made a fuss over that.

After a while, I wet the washcloth again, ring it out, and lay it over my face like Mom does when I have a fever. It feels cool. I've tucked my knees up so that I can rest my chin on top of them. Every so often a trickle runs down my neck or into my ear, tickling me, but after a while I don't even notice because I am calmer and have convinced myself that I'm in a dark, damp cave, trapped by a landslide on one side and a rattlesnake, or maybe a grizzly bear, on the other. I try to decide what time it was when I came in here so that I can figure out how much longer it will be until they're home—correction: how much air

I have left in the cave. I figure it was about 8:30, which means I have about an hour's worth, maybe. I start counting the seconds, then the minutes…

When I finally hear the creak of the front door opening, Dad's "Hellooooo!" and Mom shushing him as she swishes past, I realize I must have drifted. Stiff, I try to stand; one leg buckles, asleep. Still, I pull open the door and limp-run up the stairs.

But I'm too late. Granny is already there—telling them *her* version.

❦   ❦   ❦

Sunday morning is bright and clear, as if the world has been scrubbed clean and is fresh and fine again. And it really sort of is, because even though Granny is still over, I'm out with Dad on morning errands.

I got to go by myself, too, because Jenny was still in her pajamas, sitting by Granny's sleeping bag when Dad and I were ready to go. Granny was telling her that sometimes you just have to say "I love you" even if you don't mean it. "People expect it," she was explaining. "I don't really know what love is, but I knew my husband needed to hear me say I loved him, so I said it. People like it when you say 'I love you.' It makes them feel good. I like hearing you say it to me. Will you say it to me?" Poor Jenny had looked up like she really wanted to go with us, but it was too late. We had to leave.

Now Dad and I are holding hands on the curb at Devon and Campbell, waiting for the red light to change. I am thinking about how to find out whether Dad believed whatever it was Granny said when I notice the blonde woman on my right looking at me. I say "hello," and so does she, and soon the two of us are talking about where my Dad and I are going (the camera store and then the deli), how old I am (eight and a half), where she is going (Shaw's Department Store), and how old *she* is ("Very old," she says. "Three of your lifetimes!"). Then the light turns green, we all start walking again, and it's like we're all back in separate cars, even though we're on foot. I turn and wave goodbye; she smiles and waves back. I wish she were my big sister. I wonder what it'd be like to have a big sister to watch out for me.

"You can make friends anywhere," says Dad. "That's a great gift. That means you're never going to want for friends." He also praises me for having a long stride, an adult stride. I match his stride, even though I have to sort of lunge to do it, and I feel very proud. I feel superior to all girls and children.

Maybe he didn't believe Granny's story. Still, I want to know what she said, just in case she told any really bad lies I have to correct.

The camera store is filled with glass cases and men and cameras and film. The movie cameras in the cases look like oddly shaped submarines, stranded on the bottoms of waterless aquariums. I squat to study them, pressing my forehead against the cool, thick glass, and I hear Dad tapping out the rhythm to a song. As I roll my head over to look up at him, sideways, he smiles down at me and begins using both hands, for variety: his wedding ring hand and the one with his father's ring. I listen to make out the tune and then, sure I'm right, I guess, "'Hogan's Heroes'!" He beams at me. It's my turn next, and I plan to do "F-Troop," but then the man comes to take care of us.

Soon we're out on the sunny street again, and Dad is saying, "On to the deli. Last stop!"

There isn't much time left to find out. "Dad?" I begin, but he's already opening the door into chilly darkness and commotion.

Hairy arms, patterned sports shirts, belt buckles and khaki slacks surround me. Dad takes a pink slip of paper from a red machine and shows me that we are number 56. They are on 48…49…50. As we wait, I notice some of the hairy arms reach and sway above the crowd to pass the little pink slips forward and wrapped white packages back. The old men yelling to each other behind the counter sound all gravelly and sing-songy, like the Rabbi. And the air smells of smoked fish and cigarettes, which is like being at the lake front—except it's dark in here, with red leather chairs and polished wood walls and floors, and occasionally big whiffs of aftershave, too. I worm my way to the glass case to see the silvery smoked fish with their pink jelly eyes staring up; the red, oily smoked sable; the coral-orange pile of lox. They're all lying on a beach of white crushed ice. When I try to see up over the silver rim of the counter, I spy big baskets of gold bagels along the back wall, with salamis of all sizes hanging down in front of them like a sausage curtain. The baskets are tipped so that the bagels half-spill out.

"Fifty-six! Fifty-six!" the old man is calling.

"Here!" says Dad, suddenly beside me. I feel his warm, reassuring hand on my shoulder as he passes in our ticket. I think he smells the best of any man in here: just like Safeguard soap. I lean against his hip and watch the old man through the glass to make sure he doesn't lick his fingers or anything before touching our food.

Then I remember my part of our job, take out our list from Mom and hand it up to Dad, who clears his throat importantly. "A dozen bagels (no egg)," Dad reads.

"A dozen bagels," the old man repeats. "You want a variety?"

"That'd be great, but no egg. How about some plain, some onion, and some sesame?"

"You got it," says the man, winking at me.

"Two small smoked fish," adds my Dad when the bagel bag is full.

"Two chubs," says the man, handing over the bagels. When he rips the paper to roll up the chubs, it makes the same sound old men make before they spit, so I watch him extra carefully then, but he still doesn't spit.

"Some smoked sable, if it doesn't cost too much—how much is it today?" Dad leans back to look at the raised red numbers on the white sign stuck in the fish. "Make it half a pound."

"Half pound."

"Let's see…nova lox."

I watch the man spear up a small mountain of orange strips and look to my Dad for approval. Dad nods his OK. Then, as if he's startled by the next item, Dad says, "Cream cheese! Paula, could you get us a large cream cheese from the refrigerator over there?"

"Got it!" I say, eager to fulfill my mission, and start winding my way through slight gaps in the forest of men.

I return in record time—just as Dad is getting a small tub of creamed herring, which I happen to know is just for him. Nobody else in our house can stand that sour, pickeldy fish with the little bones in it that feel like a mouthful of hairs.

The old man is staring down at me, and when I look up, he winks at me again. I remember what my Dad said about my being able to make friends anywhere, and I break into a grin.

"You want maybe some rugelach?" the old man asks. But then he answers himself: "I'll put in a dozen, how's about? The wife and kids'll like 'em. On the house." He makes a funny face at me, and now I don't know what to do, so I look away. Then I reach for Dad's hand and twist his ring—the one from *his* Dad, who died before my parents even met. Suddenly, I don't think I could bear it if Dad believed Granny.

"Dad?"

He doesn't hear me. He's taking the last of our packages from the man, thanking him.

"Dad?" I say, tugging on his shirt until he bends down so I can talk into his ear.

"What's up, sweetie pie?"

"Daddy, you didn't believe Granny, did you?"

It takes him a minute to figure out what I'm talking about. Then he exhales like he does when he's just finished a cigarette, and he gives me a big hug, but the packages are between us and slipping around. So he takes my hand and walks me over to the red leather chairs at the side, puts the packages on an empty one, sits down, and pulls me over between his knees to face him. "Paula," he says, looking at me very seriously, "I will never believe anything bad about you—no matter *who* says it. You're my sweetheart, and Granny…" He gets a sour look on his face. "Granny is a very controlling person who has very definite ideas about how children should behave. But they are *her* ideas—not Mom's, and not mine. Do you understand?"

I am so relieved that I start to cry.

Dad takes his white hankie out of his top pocket and hands it to me. "Come on," he says, "give it a good one."

His hankie smells a little like Mom's perfume, which gives me a great idea: as soon as we get back, I'm going to put a couple dabs of her Chanel on again.

Then I blow really hard and accidentally make an elephant sound that startles us both.

"*Good* one!" says Dad, adding a few other zoo noises until we're both giggling hard.

Then we go pay for our lox and bagels and cream cheese and smoked fish and sable and creamed herring—but not the rugelach—and I feel like I could eat it all, I am so hungry and happy.

But when we burst out the deli door into the white sunlight, white pavement, white glare bouncing off the cars, I can't keep my eyes open until Dad slides his sunglasses onto my nose. "What will *you* do?" I ask. I can't help it; I worry about him.

"I'll be fine," he says. "I can handle it. I'm the adult—remember?"

And for a while again, I do.

HOW TO WORRY ABOUT YOUR FATHER

Laura Allen-Simpson

I take a brisk lunch-time walk to feel hungry and fresh—and to forget that my Dad is having night sweats again, my mother may be having an affair, and all I have in my life is work, late-night cab rides home from the office and aimless walks when I can find the time for them.

Today I stride down Randolph, blowing my nose into the white carnation of a dried tissue I've just torn open again. When I get to Wells, I take a left and head into Greens 'n' Things. While I'm scanning the place and trying to decide whether I really want to wait in the growing line to pay for an overpriced salad, I see a man who's about 60, unpacking oranges, being ordered to "get to the lemons" by a fuzzy-lipped, fat-fingered boss.

"Yessir. Right away, sir!" says the older guy, eager to please—not even a trace of sarcasm. Then he rushes to the lemons as the young bully looks on, arms crossed, legs planted.

I leave, but the interaction plays over in my mind. At the end of a day, does the older guy make excuses for his young punk of a boss, or does he sigh away scenes like this and comfort himself by wrapping his arms around his wife as she does the dinner dishes? Does his wife suspect the indignities he suffers? In the morning, does she say anything to bolster him as she presses his kelly green apron, or does she hold her tongue so that he won't know that she knows and have to suffer the humiliation of that, too?

I wonder if *my* mother holds her tongue or offers my dad sympathy that would only cost him more of his dignity. If she does, I wonder if my dad scowls and snaps at her then, the way he did whenever she fussed with his pajama collar or pillows during his last round of chemo.

Before I get too anguished thinking about all this, I notice my chilly cheeks, my runny nose, and a few papery shells of leaves clinging to gray branches. As I turn a corner and sniffle back the mucus, I suddenly fight gusts of cold wind, too. I picture people in hurricanes clinging to light posts and signs. I imagine the wind as a malicious force that delights in tearing each leaf from its source of nourishment, its home. Then I consider this: the leaves are only being torn and bashed about because they're still attached to their branches. I wonder how long it will take for the leaves to let go—or if they've been trying to let go but can't because the tree is still holding on.

Back at the office, a co-worker accosts me with a question just as I step off the elevator. I listen to her as she trails me to my desk. I listen as I lay my coat on the radiator, exchange my boots for shoes and grab a fresh tissue. I'm still listening and wondering what her point is going to be as my phone rings and I reach to pick it up.

She doesn't even pause—in fact, I think she talks even faster—until I say, "Hello?"

"Hey there!" says Dad while my co-worker hovers, silent but tick-tocking with her head and eyes as if to ask, "How long is this gonna take?"

"Hi."

"Is this a bad time?" he asks.

I think "Yes," but I want to talk with him, so I ask, "Can I call you back?"

"*Nooo,* noo, noo, that's OK! No problem. Go back to what you were doing."

"*Please* let me call you back."

"Nope, nope. You can't reach me anyway; I'm at a pay phone. And I really don't have anything to say. Just wanted to tell you I love you and that you're a neat person. Gotta go."

"*Wait!*"

My co-worker is still near the edge of my cubby hole. I stare at her and then let my eyes slide to the books and papers on my desk and the items thumb-tacked to the wall beyond, but then I stop seeing these things and see my father instead. I see him at that pay phone in a chamber between the inner and outer doors of a diner that smells of beef vegetable soup and ammonia. When the outer door opens, traffic noises drown out what I'm saying, and the wind flaps his navy blue raincoat. A few ragged yellow pages flutter in the battered phone book at his feet. When the outer door thumps closed, the inner door bumps open on the cushion of air. I hear this *thump-bump* and think that the doors are like the two valves of a heart, with my Dad trapped between.

I say, "I love you too, Dadsy," just as the next person coming in from the cold makes it past him and opens the inner door. I briefly hear the clacking of plates from inside the warm diner and a male voice calling, "Order up!" and I hope my message has reached him the way I meant it to—like a lifeline, a hug. Then, my choice to listen made, I ask, "So, what's up?"

"Had a little extra time"—must have had another no-show—"and thought I'd call. I needed the break, though. Mom's right: I really should take more breaks during the day." Another plug for Mom. "Hey, do you ever do the acrostics? I find them really relaxing. I've gotten pretty good at 'em, too." So he's had a *lot* of no-shows lately, and today he's been at this diner long enough to finish another word puzzle—and, likely, a piece of apple pie, half a pack of Winstons, and a pot of licorice-black coffee off the thick, rough rim of some worn-down cup. He's probably gotten his waitress to laugh at least once and tell him a little about herself. And he can't even smell the beef vegetable soup or the ammonia any more—although the scent of both cling to his skin, along with stale cigarette smoke. Soon he'll pop a stick of Trident into his mouth and get back into his car. But right now he just needs to hear a friendly voice, to make a connection, to reassure himself that he's valued and loved. Maybe the waitress didn't laugh at his jokes. Maybe he saw the listless way she sloshed the coffee into his cup and saucer, thought *to hell with trying to bring the light back into her eyes,* felt the corners of his mouth twitching down, and realized he needed me...Mom...*someone.*

"So, have you heard the latest about our crazy neighbors? This is a classic..." As Dad launches into this story, a pink Post-It with a question scrawled on it appears before me. Unthinking, I stare at the scrawl until it phases into words and the words develop meaning. I look up and lock eyes with my coworker, who is silently pleading for some sort of an answer to her question. Then, with a sudden horror, I realize that my ears have pinched shut. My Dad is still talking, but his words are sliding over me like coils of movie film spilling out of a projector. They're spilling, spilling everywhere, but I can't hear what he's saying, can't take in the words, can't even see him. Panicking, I dive, dive, dive into the darkness, into the projector to reel in the slack, to rethink the sounds in my head and make them into words again.

I *see* the diner. I *see* the darkening afternoon sky and traffic: wet pavement, yellow headlights, red brake lights. I see white paper place mats, gold vinyl booths, an old woman with feverish eyes and bright red spots of rouge on her powdered cheeks. And I see my Dad seeing all this as he drags on his cigarette. I see the gray ash dissolving the paper. I hear the splash and sizzle of tires on wet pavement, horns honking, someone whistling for a cab. And, with all the strength I've got, I pull the outer door open. Pull the outer door open. Pull the outer door open and feel the rush of warm air, smell the beef vegetable soup and ammonia, throw my arms around him and hang on.

I hang on tight, so tight that I'm smelling the cigarettes on his skin and feeling the smooth, polished cotton of his navy blue raincoat. I hang on—even when the inner door bumps—and this time, I don't let go.

NAME CALLING

Carla Ng

Monday

"Hi, Amanda. Hope I'm not late."

The deep, friendly male voice belonged to an equally appealing male body. I peered through the open door at the tall, dark-eyed guy standing there. Italian, or maybe Cuban, dressed in jeans and a nice linen shirt. Yum.

He raised his eyebrows, smile dimming a little. "I'm Mitch?"

I didn't answer right away, preoccupied as I was by the view, then slowly extended a hand. "Hi, Mitch. What can I do for you?"

My smile was guileless, but my brain was engaged in some naughty thoughts. What was it he wanted to be on time for? For his part, Mitch seemed a bit perturbed. It looked good on him.

"You don't remember me? We talked a couple of times on the phone, before your trip. I was hoping I could do a column on you? I work for the *Voice*."

OK, Katie-girl. Time to think fast. I continued to stare and smile—blankly, I'm sure—while my brain was busy working. *Obviously, GQ here has never met Amanda, so he can't be blamed for coming to the wrong conclusion when you show up at the door of her apartment in a robe. Now, the rational thing to do is explain the situation to him, and…*

"Oh, Mitch, yes, of course. Sorry." I never did pay much attention to my brain. "I've been, um, sick. You know—Dengue? It's been going around down there. In Brazil. Where I was, for my trip? I've been suffering some memory loss. They tell me. The doctors, I mean." *Shut up, shut up, shut up, you idiot! Stop talking.* I blew out a breath, sending my bangs dancing, and smiled big at him. What the hell did I think I was doing?

Mitch eased from perplexed to sympathetic with hunky grace. "I did hear something about that." He laughed softly. "Actually, I heard you were dead."

My heart stopped for a moment, causing me to clutch the door frame as I smiled ever wider at him.

"But then, we've heard all that before, haven't we?" He winked.

Ha! So maybe I wasn't screwed.

"I hope you're fully recovered now?" God, the man even looked gorgeous when expressing concern. I could have watched him all night.

"Peachy." *Pay attention, moron.* "But, um, I'm not quite up to an interview tonight. Could we maybe postpone it until tomorrow? It would give me time to gather my thoughts." *Or get out of town.*

"No problem. This time work for you?"

"Yup, that'd be fine." I wondered what time it was. I was beginning to feel a little panicky, the slightest inkling of what I'd just done beginning to trickle down from my consciousness. I'm afraid I may have closed the door a tad quickly on poor Mitch.

His voice was muffled through the thick wood: "Nice meeting you!"

Crap. Now what? I leaned against the closed door for a minute, waiting for my knees to stop shaking. Here I was, standing in my jammies in a dead woman's apartment, and for some unknown reason I'd suddenly decided that impersonating her might be a good idea. I looked down at said dead woman's black silk robe and then yanked it off, feeling my skin crawl. It had been handy as something to throw on when the doorbell rang, but right now I'd rather be chilly. And, yes, the empty apartment did suddenly seem decidedly cold. I went in search of my own clothes, to see if I'd packed something more substantial than the nightie I was wearing. As I passed the big grandfather clock in the hallway it donged hollowly: quarter past 11. Seemed kind of late for an interview, but then I wouldn't really be surprised if the folks at the *Village Voice* kept strange hours.

The shrill ringing of the phone exploded into the now silent room, and I must admit that the tiniest "eek" may have escaped me. Abandoning my duffel bag, I hurried back to the living room and snatched up the receiver. "What?"

"My, aren't we genteel. You done yet?"

I was surprised the word "genteel" was even in his vocabulary. "No, I'm not done. I just got here this morning; what do you expect?"

"Well, how much crap could she have? I need to get this house back on the rental market."

"Donald, your sensitivity is absolutely touching. Never mind that your girl-friend's been dead for all of three days." My cousin always had been a sterling individual.

"*Ex*-girlfriend. And anyway, she's dead, ain't she? It's not like she's gonna need the place."

What had Amanda ever *seen* in him? "Listen, Donald, you said I could stay here until I had all her stuff packed up, and that's gonna take some time. There's lots to go through, and I'm sure you wouldn't want any of your things given away by mistake."

The silence on the other end told me Donald was cogitating. It seems I had struck the right note. "I guess that's reasonable. Say, you didn't happen to come across a nice silver ladies' watch, did you?"

What, was he crossdressing now? "No, I've barely gotten through the living room." I'd spent most of the day trying to sort the stuff in the living room into separate boxes for donation, sale and storage. It had turned out to be a harder job than I'd expected; too many of Amanda's possessions seemed to defy cate-gorization. I picked up a heavy piece of iron from the coffee table. It looked like nothing so much as pile of keys that had melted and fused together. Was this art, or a locksmithing accident? I answered Donald distractedly as I turned the object over in my hands. "I'm starting on the bedroom tomorrow. Do you need the watch for the funeral or something?" Big fancy artist that Amanda was, she'd probably want to be sent off in all her finery.

"Nah. Amanda was cremated on Sunday. She had a thing against being under the ground. Fast work, though, eh? Guess they need to move quickly when people die in the Third World. No facilities to preserve the bodies with all that heat."

"You mean they're not even sending her back here for burial?"

"Turns out she'd been traveling with instructions in case the worst hap-pened. Weird, huh? So the Brazilian officials or whatever went according to her wishes. Apparently, she wanted her ashes scattered in the rain forest."

Now, that *did* sound like Amanda. "Say, Donald, have you told anybody about her dying?"

His laugh over the phone line was grating. "Yeah, right, like anybody would believe me. Y'know, she never even let me tell anybody that we were going out. I called the *Times* yesterday to see if they wanted to do an obit, and the guy actually *laughed* at me. 'Like I never heard that one before,' he said."

I smiled, relaxing a little. Perfect. Amanda seemd to have a reputation for dying, though none of the previously-rumored causes of death had been as ignoble as the case of Dengue fever that had done her in for real. It looked like I was in the clear, at least for a couple of days. "So, what do you need the watch for, anyway?"

"I'm givin' it to Sandie. Tomorrow's our one-month anniversary."

"God, Donald! You are repulsive on so many levels." I hung up on him, then switched off the ringer for emphasis.

❧   ❧   ❧

The living room was a bit of an obstacle course, what with all the boxes I'd been dumping Amanda's belongings into. I paused in front of one of the larger ones, idly flipping through the canvases stacked upright inside it. Somehow I couldn't focus on the slashes of bright color, nor could I resolve into any logical shape the twisted sheets of foil decorating some of the canvases. Was I really going to go through with this interview? I looked up and, glancing at the gilt-framed mirror on the opposite wall, met my own eyes. Was I so desperate for a date that I'd pretend to be someone else, just for the chance to spend time with a handsome reporter?

I shook my head and looked away—not really up for a bout of soul-searching that time of night. I navigated my way out of the living room and went in search of the liquor cabinet. Tomorrow might be fun. And anyway, what did I have to lose?

❧   ❧   ❧

Tuesday

Brooklyn was the new Village. Or the new Chelsea—I forget which. According to Amanda—a supposed authority on the New York art scene—Brooklyn was *the* place for edgy new art. I had wanted to point out to her that most up-and-coming artists probably couldn't afford the rent on a beautifully restored brownstone in Brooklyn Heights, but as it turned out, I never got the chance.

And I certainly wasn't about to complain now.

Requisite cup of bracing Starbucks in hand, I strolled the promenade, admiring the Manhattan skyline and contemplating my interview with the lovely *Village Voice* reporter. Now that I'd decided to go through with this, I would have to figure out how to pull it off.

The interview would doubtless be a probing piece on the impetus behind Amanda's provocative artwork, or some such swill. Unfortunately, I knew next to nothing about art, or even how much of the stuff in Amanda's apartment *was* art. Like the box of videotapes I'd found tucked in a cupboard, each one marked simply with a man's name on the spine. Sure, they might all be pieces for one of her famous video installations. But what if they were something a little more private—and a lot more gross? I had put the box right back where I'd found it but hadn't been able to keep it off my mind. I might have to watch at least one, in the interest of familial duty. Donald had asked me to sort Amanda's belongings, and I should do the best job of it that I could.

The good thing about Amanda's weird kind of art—good, at least, for the purposes of my interview—was that there was really no telling what her work was supposed to be about. If I made something up, it's not like anyone could prove me wrong. Me, I like my art simple. Give me a nice matador painting or velvet Elvis any day. But there were some benefits to abstract art that I'd never thought about. Like being able to pass off your homemade pornography as a legitimate performance piece.

I tossed my empty coffee cup into a nearby trash bin, grazing the arm of an old man who was fishing for soda cans. I gave myself three points and winked at the guy, then hurried away before he could retaliate. Time to go home and get into character—not to mention clean up the living room. Marvelous Mitch might get suspicious if he saw all those boxes scattered around.

❧   ❧   ❧

It took me a couple of hours to clear out all the boxes. I shoved everything into the spare room, hoping Mitch wouldn't ask for a tour of the place. Then I went around, strategically replacing knick-knacks so the place would look lived-in again. Ha-ha. No pun intended.

It struck me, as I was arranging a collection of first-edition books on the fireplace mantel, that I really didn't know anything about Amanda. She'd been slotted, in my mind, under the heading "Donald's current girlfriend," which made her easily dismissible. True, she was probably the most interesting girlfriend he'd ever had, but she'd also been kind of a recluse. I'd only met her once, for an evening of stilted conversation and uncomfortable silences here at the brownstone. She'd just moved in; Donald, being a realtor, had found the place for her, and she'd wanted to give him a thank-you dinner. I suspect that wasn't all she thanked him with, since they became an "unofficial item" soon after. I'm not really sure why I was invited, except that I'd been in town at the time, and maybe she'd thought it would have been rude not to ask. Certainly, Donald wouldn't have given leaving me out a second thought.

They had kind of a weird relationship. They were never seen in public together—mostly because Amanda never went out in public. I don't think she'd ever allowed a picture of herself to be published, though her art was quite well known. It must have galled Donald no end. I couldn't see what the two of them had in common, and I couldn't help but think Donald was just a little star-struck. Or at least he thought he could milk the going-out-with-a-famous-person angle to help boost his business. I grew up with Donald—my Mom raised him as her own—so I had no problem seeing right through him. But for other women, he really knew how to turn on the charm. And when he really wanted something, he usually got it.

Still, I reasoned, *the fact that Amanda had been private to the point of phobia should work in my favor in the interview tonight.* I just needed to get in touch with her personality, make some sort of connection. I finished fiddling with the book ends, then used a fireplace match to light some candles on the coffee table. I grinned to myself as I shook out the match. *Maybe I should hold a séance.* I moved on to the bedroom.

I guess I'd been avoiding this room since the day before. I'd come in only to grab a blanket and pillow, and then had spent the night on the red velvet couch in the den. For the most part I'd made myself comfortable in the house, getting as much as I could out of this great space while I had it, but I couldn't quite get myself to sleep in a dead woman's bed. The room was still so full of her presence—her smells, her makeup, clothes she'd worn tossed carelessly over chairs and on the bed. True, I didn't know Amanda, her death was no great loss to me—except in a general, mortality-acknowledging sort of way—but the bedroom creeped me out.

It was done up in a mixture of velvet and sheers, with fabric draped everywhere. If it weren't for the color scheme—greens, oranges, blues and reds; I guess she was going for a tropical look—it would almost make you think of a harem. I ran my hands over the shimmery Bordeaux fabric that hung all around the bed, then sat down at her dressing table. Her makeup and jewelry were scattered all over its surface, and chains dangled from hooks on either side of the mirror. I spotted the silver watch that Donald had mentioned; it was sitting atop a carved wooden box. It was a nice watch. I picked it up and snapped it over my right wrist. *Huh—perfect fit.*

I grabbed a colorful silk scarf that was draped over the chair and wrapped it around my shoulders, then pulled my dark hair back into a tight bun—the way Amanda's hair had been done that time at dinner. I struck a dramatic pose in the mirror: shoulders flung back, chin raised, looking out through half-lidded eyes. Not bad. I grinned at myself—then whirled around as something dashed behind me in the mirror.

I let out my breath, hands clutching my chest: just a curtain, fluttering in the breeze from the open window.

Had that window been open before?

Maybe it's better I don't hang out in here. I went to the guest room, where my duffel bag sat among the boxes, to select an outfit. It wasn't weird to avoid the bedroom. No weirder than pretending to be its previous occupant. Still, I made no move to return the scarf, and I admired the way the watch flashed on my wrist as I walked.

❀   ❀   ❀

Mitch arrived right on time at 11. I appreciate a man who's punctual. *He* seemed to appreciate the black, short-sleeved cat suit and strappy heels I'd paired with Amanda's watercolor scarf. I offered him a drink, which he politely declined, and then we settled into the den for the interview.

Mitch proved to be a bit of a disappointment. He read his utterly predictable questions straight off a legal pad, like a bad actor with a new script, and dutifully recorded my responses with his hand-held tape recorder. He seemed uninterested in any diversions. The interview, however, was a blast.

"So, what would you say is your biggest source of inspiration?"

I arranged the scarf on my shoulders as I pretended to ponder my response. (Actually, I'd been thinking up answers to questions like this one all night.) "Well, Mitch, as you may know, my mother was Brazilian. Although I've never lived there, I've always felt a special connection to that beautiful country. This was part of the reason behind my recent trip there." This bit was true, as far as I knew. "The vibrant colors of the jungle, the unique rhythms of the culture, all inform my art." God, was I good, or what?

Mitch nodded sagely, as if he had any clue what I was talking about, and ticked the question off with a red pencil. Really, despite his looks, the guy was kind of a dweeb. "And which artists would you say have been your biggest influences?"

This one was a little tougher, since I knew so little about art. But I had been ready for this question, too. I clasped my hands, a bit primly, and tried to look earnest. "I really don't like to think along the lines of direct influence. I feel it's very important to practice one's art freely and individually; it must have one's own voice. This is why I have never been constrained by a particular school of expression, or even by a particular medium. I like to think that it all springs from my own unique consciousness, through my own experiences. So I couldn't point to any particular painter as having directed the way I paint, to any particular sculptor as having guided that aspect of my work, or to any director as having influenced the way I make film."

I settled back on the couch, recrossed my legs and smiled aloofly. Really, this was too easy…

❦   ❦   ❦

Wednesday

The next day dragged like it would never end. I was itching to see the article in Thursday's *Voice* and gauge how it was received, but the clock wouldn't cooperate.

I spent the morning puttering around the brownstone, going through boxes I'd packed Monday and taking out whatever caught my eye. I picked out canvases to hang but decided after a few tries that they looked better in their original positions, leaning against the hallway walls. This way, they looked like works in progress.

It wasn't that I was settling into the place; not exactly. I just needed something to keep me busy, and since I would be staying at least a week, I reasoned, I might as well be comfortable. My original strategy of clearing the apartment starting with the living room was probably impractical, anyway. Instead, I'd start with the least-used rooms, like the guest bedroom and the basement, and slowly work my way back.

By the time noon finally rolled around I was starving, not to mention sick of artfully arranging candles. I figured I might as well get out of the apartment, just in case Donald was feeling antsy enough to stop by. I had a quick pizza lunch—one of the best things about New York, as far as I was concerned—and headed over to the Brooklyn Public Library. It was a leisurely 20-minute walk from the apartment, and the calm library setting seemed likely to soothe my restless nerves.

I asked the librarian in the main lobby where I might find the Art History section, then sat myself down with a stack of books on female artists of the 20th Century. So maybe Amanda Brown wasn't exactly Georgia O'Keeffe. Art was art, and inspiration was inspiration. Who knew when I might have to do another interview?

❦   ❦   ❦

Thursday

It had been ages since I'd read the *Voice,* but Thursday morning, bright and early, I was in Starbucks, settling down with a large black coffee and the new issue. I normally drank my coffee with cream and tons of sugar, but it seemed more Amanda-ish to drink it black. And really, the bitterness was kind of good.

I sat at a table right by the window, partly for the light and partly to justify the sunglasses I was wearing indoors. As I flipped the pages to find the interview in the Arts section, I enjoyed the way the sunlight reflected off the silver watch and danced against the facing wall. I imagined the other coffee drinkers around me could tell that I was someone.

And it's not like I *wasn't* someone. I mean, I didn't need to be Amanda in order to be someone important; I had my own life waiting for me back in Buffalo. Well, except that I'd been put on "involuntary permanent leave" from the public library, and now that Mom had decided to sell the house I didn't really have a place to live. Not yet, anyway—not until I found another apartment…

But, regardless, this was just a lark. Something to do to entertain myself while I was here in New York—whatever it was I was *doing* here in New York. Regrouping, I guess. Or maybe finding myself.

As I read over my responses from last night with relish, I decided that the latter was the more likely. And when I went looking, who knew what I might find?

❦   ❦   ❦

I spent the day touring the city, walking through the museums and art galleries, riding the subways and generally enjoying the feeling of being a real New Yorker. I'd always loved the city, even though I'd never gotten to spend much time there. But now that I didn't have to worry about missing work, and with this great apartment to stay in…

It would be easy. I could just, I don't know—slip in and pick up where Amanda had left off. She'd left plenty of canvases behind, and at the end of next month, when rent was due, I could just sell a couple. Heck, I could even put together a gallery showing if I wanted to. I had certainly pulled off the interview, hadn't I?

I stopped at a trendy little trattoria to pick up some take-out, then made my way home in a happy fog. Home. I was already starting to think of it that way. *And what a nice home this is,* I thought, looking out over the tree-lined streets, lit a cozy orange by the streetlamps. Couples walked arm in arm, enjoying the crisp October night, and here and there a dog barked; strains of music floated out of open windows, and the cool blue light of television shows flickered against closed drapes. I'd never seen anything so inviting. Certainly not back in Buffalo, where the streets were deserted and no one stayed up past 10.

When I got into the apartment, though, none of the lights seemed to work. That bastard! Donald must have had the electricity turned off. He was trying to smoke me out so he could put the place back on the market with a new, jacked-up sticker price—a portion of which he, as the leasing agent, would receive. Well, he was out of luck.

I walked carefully through the dark living room and over to the fireplace, where Amanda had kept the long matches she used to light the gas fire. Lucky for me, Donald didn't seem to have gotten around to the gas yet. *Ha! You won't get rid of me that easily.*

Between the fireplace and the numerous candles Amanda had scattered around the house, the place was downright cozy. I settled in at the coffee table to enjoy my Penne alla Vodka. The only thing missing was a little mood music. In the quiet, I could hear cars swish by outside, the occasional creaks and groans from the house settling around me. It would have been spooky if I hadn't been in such a good mood.

A bellyful of pasta and a few glasses of wine later, I rose to take my dirty dishes to the sink. As I rounded the sofa, my stockinged foot tripped on something sticking out from underneath the velvet slip cover. Penne nearly went flying, but I managed—barely—to keep my balance, with the aid of some well-placed swear words. I put the plate and glass down on an end table and bent to pick up the offending item: a photo album, black and leatherbound. Intrigued, I brought it over to the fireplace, where the light was strongest. This was the first evidence of any photos I'd seen in the entire house.

I opened the heavy cover and felt an immediate chill. There, staring up at me, was Amanda. A crisply printed 5x7 photograph, in black and white, showed her from the shoulders up, black hair drawn into that tight bun she favored, lips firmly compressed. She looked pale and grim.

I turned the page—and nearly dropped the book. Flickering candlelight played across three photos: 4x6s, arranged in a column. In the first two her eyes were closed, in the third open, as if she'd suddenly woken up. Except that in the first two she didn't look like she was sleeping. God, this was creepy. These looked like morgue photos, or like she'd been to a shoot for *Night of the Living Dead*.

I flipped quickly through the rest of the pages, and they were all the same. Row after row of stark black-and-whites in different sequences, eyes closed to open. I set the book on the mantel and stepped away.

All right, Katie, calm down. It's just a weirdo artist's idea of a nice family photo album. But I couldn't talk my goosebumps down. I paced around the living room, rubbing my forearms and trying to think of something I could do to distract myself. There weren't a whole lot of choices, though, without any power: no TV, no radio, no reading—not comfortably, anyway.

I looked around, searching for ideas, and suddenly my eyes picked out the shape of the phone. Amanda had a regular "land line" phone, not a cordless, so there was a chance it was still working if, like the gas, the phone service hadn't been turned off yet. Maybe I could call Mom and see how she and Aunt Ida were doing in Florida. Or even Donald; he probably wasn't asleep yet. I could ask him what he'd thought of the interview. You never know; Donald might have taken up reading.

I picked up the receiver and placed it carefully to my ear, praying I'd hear the welcome drone of the dial tone. I was greeted instead by an eerie static. I spoke uncertainly, almost in a whisper: "Hello?"

The static rose and fell, like ocean waves. Then suddenly a hoarse, faraway whisper: "What do you think you're doing?"

"Shit!" I almost dropped the phone. It couldn't be Amanda! Yet the voice, disturbing as it was, did seem familiar.

"...you know?" The static rose, drowning out some of the words. "...coming back..."

Oh, Jesus!

"...expect me..."

The line went dead—appropriately enough. With shaky fingers I put the receiver down, then retreated to the sofa. What was that? As far as I knew, Amanda had been scattered in itty bitty pieces all over the Amazon four days ago. Was this really her ghost calling me from the beyond—or was I going crazy?

I ventured from the couch just long enough to grab a blanket and the bottle of Glenlivet I'd uncovered the night I'd arrived. Then I huddled there, applying liberal doses of single malt to try and calm myself. The dark apartment wasn't helping any. Wavering candlelight sent shadows dancing around the room and had me flinching every few minutes when one seemed to loom particularly close.

This had been a bad idea. Offering to clear out the apartment; staying here all this time. Oh, and the impersonating-the-dead thing. Especially that.

❧   ❧   ❧

Friday

A sudden noise roused me from my scotch-induced stupor.

What was that? It sounded like a door slamming! I dug my way out of the blanket I'd burrowed under and looked around. Still dark.

I stared groggily at the watch on my wrist, its hands barely visible in the light of the dying fire. Just past four—ugh! I was still wearing Amanda's watch! I snatched it off my wrist and threw it on the coffee table; it went skittering across and flew off the edge, landing on the hardwood floor with a *bang*.

An answering *bang* came from the kitchen.

I let out a yelp, jumping from the couch. *Oh, God, there's someone in the apartment!* A sudden shadow loomed in the kitchen doorway, and I'm sure what escaped my throat this time was a full-fledged scream. I turned to run in the other direction, and my left foot came down on the empty bottle that lay where I'd dropped it earlier. I had a brief glimpse of the room cartwheeling around me, then a blinding flash—from a gun?—behind my left ear.

Then nothing.

❧   ❧   ❧

"H-h-hey…" The wheezing, raspy voice from last night was back.

I answered with a groan.

"Are you OK?"

Cracking open one eye, I was greeted with too-bright sunlight.

And Amanda's silhouette.

I licked dry lips. "Am I dead?"

She laughed. "Not quite. Though you did bang your head pretty hard on your way down." She helped me sit up on the couch, propping me up with pillows she must have taken from the abundant pile on her bed.

My head felt like a tin can full of rocks. "Are *you* dead? I mean...*aren't* you?"

She seemed awfully cheerful for having just tried to kill me. She paused to clear her throat and take a drink of water; when she spoke again, her voice was clear and musical. "Well, I was hoping to stay dead just a little longer, but you kind of wrecked that plan. You know, I was pretty pissed off when I saw that interview yesterday, but then I got home and saw you lying here. You looked so pitiful, I just couldn't stay mad. Especially after you conked yourself on the head and passed out."

I scowled at her, which just made my head feel worse. Pitiful? Who did she think she was, calling me pitiful? "What's the big idea, pretending to be dead, anyway?"

Now she did look a little pissed off. "I certainly didn't expect someone to step into my apartment and start living my life. I was actually trying to set up a new show. The ultimate 'comeback tour.'" She sighed. "My pieces sell well enough, but I haven't had a good show in years. I thought I'd finally take advantage of all the rumors that seem to circulate around me and do a 'Back from the Dead' show. See?" She picked up the photo album from where I'd left it on the mantel and flipped it open. "I was going to put some cards together, make it like an invite to a funeral. Then I'd arrange all my new pieces around this big white casket, have lots of lilies all over the place..."

Amanda closed the book. "Still, I guess it's no big loss. It was a weird idea, anyway. And the interview...well, actually, it was pretty good." She grinned at me. "Quite a piece of performance art, I must admit."

Hmm. Maybe Amanda wasn't so bad after all. I liked the way emotions flitted across her face like weather.

"That whole 'cultural rhythms' shtick worked well. I haven't milked the Brazilian bit in a while."

"So, let me get this straight." My head was starting to clear, but I still felt like I was a few pages behind. "You're not actually dead. You never were. Were you even in Brazil?"

She shook her head, still smiling. "I was visiting my Mom in Hoboken."

"I thought your Mom was Brazilian!"

"Nah, she's from Jersey, born and raised. I did date a Brazilian guy once, though..." Her voice was getting hoarse again.

"Then how'd you get Dengue?"

She looked amused. "I didn't *have* Dengue." She spoke slowly, as if to a child. "That was part of the story."

Well, how was *I* supposed to know? "Then what was up with your voice on the phone? And why'd you try to scare me like that? I didn't expect anyone to be on the other end when I picked up."

"I had laryngitis; I figured that was as good an occasion as any to put my 'death' into action. And I wasn't trying to scare you; I'd been calling all day, once I figured out you must be staying at my place. I wanted to let you know I was coming back on the train from Jersey, and when to expect me."

Just then, I remembered turning off the ringer to spite Donald. I changed the subject. "So, how did you pull off the death thing? Or—almost, I mean."

"That was easy. I just printed up a couple of official-looking notices using my lawyer's letterhead. I sent one to my publicist—and one to Donald, asking him to 'temporarily oversee Ms. Brown's estate' while everything was put in order. That bastard." She looked around the room. "Not only did I not get any publicity, but in less than a week Donald's already trying to kick me out of my apartment."

"Yeah, well, if I hadn't been staying here, this place would probably be rented by now."

She regarded me with a raised eyebrow. "Yes, I see you've made yourself right at home."

At least I had the decency to blush.

Over a breakfast of bacon and buttered toast—I find grease does wonders for hangovers—Amanda regaled me with stories of Donald's general inadequacy, in bed and otherwise. I couldn't get over how different Amanda was from what I'd imagined. The persona she put forth as an artist—constructed solely for the purpose of making her art more desirable to shallow, easily influenced art collectors—was nothing like her true, quirky self. A self I was liking more and more.

"So, you really weren't in love with him?"

"With Donald? Are you kidding me? I mean, you know the guy. But would you give up a place like this? I had to keep it going till I had a lease in my hands. Besides, he started seeing that little flake Sandie a while back, and in return for my obliviousness he seemed to leave well enough alone."

Really, I couldn't help but respect her. "Yeah, apparently yesterday was their one-month anniversary."

Amanda raised her mug. "More power to them. They deserve one another."

Having met the airhead in question, I had to agree. We shared a laugh, then some more bacon.

❧   ❧   ❧

Saturday

So, my plan to spend the rest of my days as a New York artist hadn't really worked out. But in place of an avenging spirit, I seemed to have found a kindred one. Amanda and I spent the day Friday putting her apartment back in order. It was, after all, the least I could do. Really, she was very gracious about the whole thing. I think she figured the grief she would cause Donald by suddenly showing up alive and well—and in rightful possession of her property—was worth ditching her plans for a macabre art show.

She'd even offered me a place to stay in the city whenever I was in town; I think she'd been impressed by *my* chutzpah, too. But I thought it might seem a little presumptuous to move right in. So, today I was headed back to Buffalo. Maybe I'd see what sort of job opportunities might allow me to exploit my newly discovered dramatic talent.

As I walked slowly through a Penn Station crowded with travelers on this sunny October morning, I expected to feel more reluctant to be leaving New York. Somehow, Buffalo didn't seem as horrifying a prospect as it had when I'd left. I had come to New York not quite realizing that I'd been searching for something, and was leaving it today having found…I wasn't sure what.

I hitched my duffel bag up on my shoulder and headed for the gate, where the Empire Builder was starting to board. I smiled to myself: *appropriate name.* I found two empty seats and settled in for the long trip, putting my bag beside me to discourage talkative old ladies and lonely middle-aged men. As the train slowly inched out of the dark tunnel, I couldn't help but think to myself that a lesson had been learned here. Sometimes you just need to step back from your life to appreciate what it is you have. Buffalo wasn't a bad town; there was plenty of opportunity for a decent life there. Maybe the library would reconsider, and I could get my old job back. And so what if it didn't have the same night life as Brooklyn? It certainly was a lot quieter—peaceful, really. Now that

I'd stopped to think about it, I had a very good life waiting for me back home, a chance to—

A high-pitched trilling interrupted my reverie, an annoying waterfall of notes apparently emanating from the seat in front of me. I stood and peeked over the upholstered back: the seat was empty, except for a black leather jacket. From my vantage point I could see a tiny Nokia cell phone jutting out of the left pocket, a little red light flashing in time to the ring.

I glanced around. No one else seemed to be leaping for the phone, and the ticket stub tucked into the rail above the seat told me the previous passenger had been destined for New York. So, they'd gotten off the train, leaving the jacket behind.

People were beginning to shoot me irritated glances for not answering. I snagged the jacket, dropping it onto the seat next to me. Italian leather, very nice. I plucked the phone from the pocket and pressed TALK. "Hello?"

A gruff male voice assailed me over the bad connection. "Is this Rosie?"

Oh, what the hell. "Yeah…"

STILL LIFE

Carla Ng

"Shhh…Go back to sleep."

I keep my voice low—the words are meant only for myself. In her snowdrift of sheets, she sleeps on undisturbed.

The soles of my feet are numb against the cold floor. I stand, shivering in the cobalt light of predawn, and steal some moments to watch her breathe.

Her eyes are closed, the small line down the middle of her brow implying concentration, even now. Coarse blonde hair coils like rope about her face, and her mouth is slightly open, revealing a glimpse of teeth.

The light in the room is beginning to change quality, the blue leaching out as the sun comes closer to rising. I find my clothing and pad to the window to dress and watch the light intensify against my skin. It brings me more fully into my own shape even as it throws the buildings across the avenue into dark relief. I'd like to wake her, but I don't want to share the moment. Turning back, I trace her collarbone with a fingertip and, suddenly, find myself at the bottom of a flight of curved stone steps, facing the exit.

Outside, the light has yet to reach the streets. I navigate the narrow alley that opens out into the avenue. A few cars sweep by, headlights on, beams blending into the air like ghosts. Their drivers, dimly visible through glass, look serious.

Across the street, an old man patiently sweeps at a single spot of pavement. He moves delicately, like someone whose bones are fragile, or perhaps some-one who dances well. As if he senses me watching, he holds the broom still and looks up. We are the only two souls on this deserted street. I lift my hand to greet him, but he flinches from the gesture, ducking into the shadows, and hurries away.

I glance at my wrist, wanting to know the time, but my watch is gone. Funny that time should even matter now. Somehow it does, and I begin to plan my day. First, a shower, long and scalding, water so hot it feels cold. Then breakfast. Pancakes, I decide, with powdered sugar, lemon to make them melt in the mouth, and blueberries. My step falters, and the imagined taste of breakfast goes suddenly bitter. Richard will be there. It seems, lately, that he is always there. The thought of seeing him makes me both tired and nervous.

I navigate the near-empty streets on instinct, my mind occupied with Richard's hands. They're thin, long-fingered, and contain in them everything that made our marriage fail. Sometimes when we argue, his voice slowly fades away, and all I see are those hands, their delicate staccato fluttering—the wings of an injured bird.

The wail of a truck's horn breaks into my thoughts; I pull up short, holding myself from stepping off the curb. I look quickly left and right, but the street is deserted. Confused, I turn around. Here's my old building, standing at its usual intersection, but somehow I've arrived in less time than it's ever taken. I close my eyes, push fingertips against temples in an attempt to clear my head, and step inside. I climb the four flights in slow, deliberate steps.

I walk into my apartment quietly, leaving the lights off, and enjoy the familiar gloom. I do my best to ignore the kitchen as I pass by it. It is the one unpleasant room in this comfortable, familiar home, and I'll tackle it after I've had my shower.

An odd smell seems to follow me as I continue down the long hallway. Once I enter the tiled bathroom, I undress quickly, tossing my clothes on the floor. I turn the hot water full on, but the temperature will not rise past tepid. I stand frustrated, lathering up handfuls of liquid soap in a vain attempt to erase the smell of antiseptic from my nose. This isn't right. Everything is getting spoiled today.

"Richard!" I glare through the steam and turn off the water—suddenly scalding—with an angry twist...

"Richard, I will not stand for this, do you hear me? This is my place, and you've no right to come barging in here and ruining everything!" I throw my plastic juice glass into the kitchen sink and turn to see Richard perching, crowlike, on the counter. He does this every time, drags me somewhere I don't want to be, away from peace. My hands are smeared with scum from the dirty dishwater. I wipe them against an old dish towel, trying not to see Richard here in the kitchen, unable to stop myself.

…His suit is black, narrow with his presence. He looks like he is dressed for a funeral. I am struck with the irony of being haunted by a live man. The room is so white it hurts my eyes. I squint against the glare and cast about for the table. My hand catches the back of a chair and I grab hold before it—or I—can fall. I sit down and lean forward over my knees, breathing heavily. Richard is talking, but I have to concentrate, I have to shut him out and make the light go away, keep the apartment solid around me.

"Why won't you come back to me? There isn't anything wrong with you—not any more." His voice is thinner, sadder than I remember. "Wake up! I need you here."

It's hard to ignore him when he talks to me like this. I close my eyes and wave my arms in front of my face, as if he were smoke and, so, easily dispelled.

"If you would just move, just make some sign that you're here with me…" His voice breaks, and for a moment I almost don't hate him, almost feel him there beside me, holding my hand.

But then I realize what's happening, realize he's almost pulled me back into his world and I erupt out of my chair, the clatter as it falls against the linoleum growing louder as I struggle to make the room real again.

"You don't need me, Richard; you never have. You're perfectly capable of taking care of yourself. If there's anything you are, it's *capable*." I fling the last word at him like a person tossing a magic powder to ward off evil. The crow on the counter unfolds itself, its face no longer exactly Richard's, takes off in a confusion of blackness like spattered ink. The light in the room fades. Richard is gone.

In the silence that follows, the kitchen reassembles itself around me. In the softened light, familiar shapes solidify into stacks of dirty dishes, an almond-colored refrigerator, the old gas stove with its faulty pilot lights. I sink back into the wooden chair, now righted, and ease my breathing. It is getting harder and harder to fight Richard's pleas. They seem to come more often now; I think he must be desperate.

But that doesn't matter; I mustn't think of Richard. I have to concentrate on this home that I have made, a safe place for us, for Susan. If only this room were different. I look around, pitying the abandoned appliances of my mother's kitchen; their faded almond and avocado finishes look lonely.

The other rooms in the house are my own, mostly from my first real apartment after college. There's the bedroom, with the narrow twin bed and that crazy velvet quilt I found at a tag sale with a friend, the closet still stuffed with the clothes I wore then, my favorite red flannel robe slung over a chair. In the living room, my dad's old guitar leans against a couch that passed its prime decades ago. Oddly enough, the dining room is from the apartment I shared with Richard, but I have always loved that room with its white French doors opening onto a tiny wrought-iron balcony, full of sunlight. And in this version, all evidence of Richard is gone, the pictures and textiles transplanted from other places I've lived.

The kitchen, though, refuses to change.

A small scratching sound starts up behind me, and I know that I'm no longer alone. I turn in my chair to see a little girl seated at the table across from me, her head bent over a coloring book. Her frizzy blonde hair sticks out in all directions, and her four-year-old fist is clenched around a crayon.

Periwinkle blue.

The bottom drops out of my stomach, and I stand, edging my way around the table to sit beside the girl. Was I ever so small? She seems oblivious to me, all her concentration on the fire hydrant she is coloring blue. It's her favorite color, and the book is filled with it. The other crayons sit forgotten in their box beside her, their points still square and new. As she colors, she breathes shallowly, her breath rasping in cadence with the scratching of crayon on paper, and my own heartbeat rises to follow. She is waiting, waiting, keeping so carefully inside the lines so that her Mama will come.

A sound comes from beyond the kitchen, and I can *feel* the apartment shifting around me, an almost physical pain as that older, sadder place bleeds in. The little body beside me tenses, the crayon stilled. My mother emerges from the darkness of the hallway, walking slowly to stand in front of the sink. I close my eyes, struggling to will away the brick that has lodged itself in my throat.

Her back is to us, her dark hair a tangled mass of curls, and she has on her blue silk robe with the cherry blossoms near the hem. We call it her Before Papa Robe, from when she lived in the city, near Chinatown. She puts her hands on the counter, fingers splayed, and I can see they're shaking. I feel a little scared, but mostly I'm in love with those hands, hands I haven't seen in 22 years, their slim, tapered fingers and the pretty rings I used to play with.

The little girl beside me has gripped my hand; she knows what's coming now…

She's only four, waiting at the kitchen table for Mama to make them pancakes, sitting quietly with her coloring book and wishing Daddy were home. Because Mama isn't cooking, she's just standing there, staring into the sink, her hands shaking like they want to get away from her. And when Mama finally does move, the little girl thinks everything will be OK because Mama goes to the fridge and gets out the juice to fill up their glasses. But Mama's glass only gets filled halfway. And the little girl keeps on coloring, trying not to watch her, concentrating on the staggering blue line as her mother reaches under the sink and pulls out the bleach. Mama only cleans on Sundays, and it isn't Sunday. Slim hands no longer shaking, Mama tops off her glass.

…The crayon is stuck in my hands; my mouth is sewn shut; I can't say anything. I can only stare at my beautiful, beautiful mother as she sits down, smiling a little, that terrible smell drifting across the table to me.

❧   ❧   ❧

As the sun begins to set, I leave that house and set off to find Susan again. The day has left me drained in a way I didn't think was possible. Retracing my steps along the empty downtown streets, I chase the lengthening shadows toward that still blue room on the second floor. Before I can reach it, I spot the old man with the broom standing there in the shadows across the street, waiting for me. When he sees that I've noticed him, he goes back to sweeping, not even looking up as I approach. My feet make crunching noises as I walk, and I realize when I stop in front of him that we are standing in a pool of broken glass, rough pebbles like rock candy.

He stops sweeping and, leaning his weight against the broom, raises his head in that same graceful, painful, fragile way. Wisps of thin white hair that used to be blonde, like mine, drift slowly with the air currents.

"Daddy?"—my voice a whisper.

"Now look what you've gone and done, sweetheart." He gestures around him, and I see that the glass we're standing on is the remains of a windshield. There has been an accident; a dark blue car is tilting crazily against the curb, its hood buckled and twisted into a sneer.

"All this mess." He shakes his head, but his voice is kind, and I let myself fold into him, suddenly afraid. I am somehow smaller than this tiny man. He doesn't smell like anything: not like an old man, or a man at all, but as neutral as fog, or maybe glass. He leads me to the car, and we lean together against its scarred fender.

He doesn't say anything but waits patiently for me to speak, as if he knows that I need to. I feel an urge to explain myself; something I've done makes me ashamed to be here with him. Something about the car is familiar, in an uncomfortable way, but I can't quite remember what.

"I just thought it would be easier, Daddy, if I stayed here. I have my own place, and Richard is just fine by himself, you know he is, and it's nice here..." My voice trails off. It actually hasn't been all that nice here lately, with Richard becoming ever harder to ignore and then my mother appearing today. "If they would just leave me alone, it would be OK then, wouldn't it, Daddy? How can I make them go away?"

The shadow of a man beside me shifts, looking through the darkening air to the window across the way. "It isn't that easy, Suzie. You can't stay here; 'here' isn't much of anywhere. What you've got for yourself right now is a choice. Richard, when he's calling to you—that's not just Richard, baby; it's life. And it's got some unfinished business with you." He casts a deliberate glance at my stomach, and I wrap my arms defensively around it, as if I can already feel something there to protect. "Your Mama, on the other hand, well...I just never thought you were the kind to take *her* way out."

"Oh, Daddy, I would *never!* This is different." My voice is indignant, but I think I know now why I feel ashamed. I wonder if she ever felt ashamed, if she ever thought she was just making things easier. The child I was understood, to the core of her soul, the meaning of betrayal; she would be incapable of such an act. Yet Susan, sleeping up there by sheer force of will, is dreaming herself deeper into betrayal every moment. How could the woman ever have grown from the girl?

A shard of sunlight glances off the large window, painfully bright...

It's too bright, the headlights glancing off the rain that sheathes the car, blinding me. I can't see, and I just wish Richard would shut up. His reasonable, entreating voice makes me want to scream.

"Don't you see? This could change everything for us. We need this, Susan. We need to be a family."

How can he sound so glad, the son of a bitch? Was he gloating?

"It's too soon, Richard. I told you I didn't want to have kids for a while, and that hasn't changed. We're not ready. There's too much going on at work; we live in a tiny apart—"

"Susan, please, let's at least take some time and really consider this."

Time is what I don't have. I tighten my grip on the steering wheel as the panic wells up. I hadn't even meant to tell him, but I'd gotten angry, tried to use it against him, and now it sounds like this is what he's wanted all along. My eyes are watering, it must be from the glare, but I still see his hand reaching for me.

"Don't touch me!" Those hands, that needy body that did this to me, infected me, shackled me. Somehow, I know that if I have this child, I will lose myself. Just like my mother did.

I flinch away from his touch, taking the steering wheel with me, and the car swerves left. For a moment, as the small blue car travels across the lane into the stream of oncoming traffic, I feel the exhilaration of finally going outside the lines.

...I take a ragged breath, realize I've been crying against my father's shoulder. It feels like days have passed. The car we were sitting on is gone, though the sidewalk is still covered with glass. I feel calmer now, ready to go back to Susan. I know my father will remain, clearing away the mess as he has always done, has already done for me. I rub my face and turn to him, wanting to thank him, to say something, but he is already fading back into a stranger, a silent old man with a broom. As I start across the street, I can hear him sweeping, sweeping, raking up the windshield's shattered remains.

The door in the alley seems lighter now, the stairs not so winding, and as I enter the room it's just a little brighter, the details sharply outlined. I stand beside the bed and look down at Susan, this tall grown-up woman, blonde hair and fair skin, looking so much like my father but feeling, from the inside, more like my mother. I look down at this stranger, myself, and I let the world brighten around me.

❦   ❦   ❦

"Susan?"

At first I think I can still hear my father sweeping, but the sound resolves itself into the *beep-beep-beep* of monitoring equipment, and with it comes the hated smell of bleach. I can't really move, but Richard's pale and haggard face swims into view. He's gripping one of my hands, and as he sees my eyes focus on him, his knotted features dissolve into relief.

"Susan. Thank God."

His hand feels surprisingly good in mine, and though my mind is confused, I know I'm supposed to be here. With great effort, I raise my weakened, trembling arm, place his hand next to my face and try to smile against it.

His palm is cupped next to my ear, and in that space I can hear an ocean, the blood from two heartbeats coursing through me. Richard's fingertips tremble against my temple, and he begins to cry.

"Shhh..." I whisper, drifting back to sleep.

MY MOTHER NEVER UNDERSTOOD MY HAIR

Elizabeth Samet

My coif is enviable—strangers stop me on the street and ask about the long strawberry curls. But my mom? She can't see it. She's still focused on years of chasing me around the house with a fine-tooth comb, trying to excavate some non-existent 'do from my tiny little head. She thinks I'm beautiful, as a mother should, and smart and talented. But my hair? She has never forgiven it for being so curly.

The story of my childhood, however, is not one of unfulfilled expectations, nor is it the tale of a strained relationship. Indeed, my childhood has left me little to discuss with a therapist, unless I wished to pay someone $150 an hour to talk about my hair—about how a wealthy kid from the big city couldn't make peace with her own hair until she was well into her third decade of life. I suppose I could blame my mother for that and draw some connection to my lack of self-confidence. But I'd probably be making that up. So I have to accept that my childhood was relatively healthy, and only I am responsible for my issues.

It would be easier some other way, of course. I sometimes envy people who can blame their failures on their parents. Maybe I should talk to a therapist about that.

My perfectly normal childhood started in 1968, making me too young for the free-wheeling "me" generation of the '70s and too old for the free-wheeling "me" generation of the '90s. I got to spend my formative years in the Reagan Era, wearing cowl necks and leg warmers, my hair in a two-tone Flock of Seagulls style. Somewhere around 1985, I believe I had two different hairstyles on my head at once: a short wedge on the left and a long bob on the right.

When I look at those pictures, I think it should be more difficult to get a hairdresser's license.

At 12, I went on a comb and brush strike. Tired of my screaming, my mom reluctantly looked the other way. I undoubtedly looked terrible, but that was before boys and fashion and the like, so I felt no shame about the matted bird's nest atop my head. I was out to prove something—something about my independence or about my will or, perhaps, about being 12. But I had underestimated the cruelty of the girls at school. Three weeks in, I returned home in tears, explaining to my mother that "Scuz-head" was not, in fact, a term of endearment. She cursed them and held me close, then dragged me off to her beauty shop, where her stylist painstakingly brushed through the dreads, rewarding my aching scalp with luxurious hot oil.

In retrospect, it's probably a blessing that I spent my adolescense in the '80s, for I never had any problem achieving height in my hair. I could tease with the best of them. I will probably be spared the cancers likely to strike my generation of women; I never inhaled hairspray, for I never needed to use it. Once it was up, my hair stayed up—a mixed blessing, that. At one point, having reached maximum altitude on the top, I had a friend take buzz clippers to the sides. My father, who had previously stayed out of the Hair Wars, angrily remarked that I looked like a monkey. It nearly broke my heart; I think that was the only time in my life he has ever insulted me. I let the sides grow back.

By the end of the '80s, hair had reached its Rococo Period. Not since Marie let them eat cake had hair been any bigger—but when the bubble of the US economy burst, it deflated the hair of a nation as well. This left me, again, in an unwelcome situation. My mother was overjoyed when I told her that I was going to have my curls chemically straightened. She was further impressed when she learned that our black cleaning lady (who prided herself on her lack of nap) disclosed that chemicals were her secret. We made an appointment for the next day.

If the Devil is a woman, then she had a hand in the ensuing torture. I sat for an hour under an acid so pungent that it burned out not only curls but eyes and nostrils as well. Then, the rinse: cold water bringing relief (and a noticeably light feeling) to my head. My mother's face in the mirror remains vivid for me: the look of expectation; the hope that the one missing piece between me and perfection would be located; the grimace, masked by a nervous smile, when the blow-dry was done. And then I saw in her features something with which I was altogether unfamiliar. Disappointment.

My straightened locks hung limply from my head for over a year, until the regrowth was sufficient to allow a curl. It was the only time in my life that I ever went to the beauty shop religiously: every six weeks, to get the lifeless hair trimmed. It was also the longest time my mother has ever gone without commenting on how my head looks. She harbored a silent guilt over having encouraged the procedure; I spared her even one "this is your fault." I cried privately in my room but pretended that I didn't care. I experimented with barrettes and French braids and other things that had been inappropriate to my former hair. I mourned for my hair and promised myself that I would never forsake it again, and I haven't.

Four years ago, my mother got cancer. I had been out of the house for years, was married, and was living far away from my family. I began returning home often to see them and to give my father a break from taking care of her. By her third chemotherapy session, my mother had lost most of her hair. In anticipation of the event, she'd had a wig made—but she never wore it. She didn't seem embarrassed about her downy head. Sometimes she sported a floppy denim cap, but she did so to ease the discomfort of others, I think, more than her own.

After her treatments were finished and she was pronounced clean of the disease, her hair grew back rather quickly. She'd been warned of the side effects and thus was not surprised when what was formally pin-straight now grew in with sweet, soft curls. She called me for styling advice, and I taught her how to avoid frizz.

She hadn't colored her hair since her diagnosis; thus, her once golden locks were totally white. Her friends said it was beautiful; I said it made her look 20 years older. So she changed it back to the color she'd had as a girl—only better, really. Now, when people inquire as to where she got her curls, she always smiles when she gives her answer:

"From my daughter."

THE DETAILS

Elizabeth Samet

I arrived in New York on a dark and stormy day. All right, that's not true; I don't remember what the weather was like. God, I hate that about myself, my total lack of accurate recall. You know those people who remember the details of everything? Well, I am not one of them. Maybe my life would function more smoothly if I were.

Note to self: concentrate on the details.

So maybe it wasn't dark and stormy. It's just that "dark and stormy" sounds so dramatic. I have been accused of trying to inject drama where it isn't necessary, and now that I think about it, this is probably one of those times.

Anyway, I arrived in New York on a day that was maybe dark and/or stormy but probably was neither. I had two suitcases full of clothes that would turn out to be totally wrong for the occasion: half unsophisticated college wear, half unsophisticated post-college wear. At that point, I was still pretty unsophisticated. I was going to camp out temporarily in the apartment of my two best girlfriends. They lived in a tiny place on the Upper East Side that was not much different from the one we'd shared for two years during school in Boston: two bedrooms, a galley kitchen and a third room big enough for a couch and TV. The only differences were that a) this was a fifth-floor walk-up, b) they were paying $1,100 each, and c) the mice of New England had been replaced by the roaches of New York.

OK, so I arrived. My first task was to find my own apartment. I know you have heard that it's hard to do this in Manhattan, but let me define the word *hard* for you. Imagine trying to climb Mount Everest. Now imagine that your Sherpa thinks it would be funny to lead you in the wrong direction. Now imagine that his antics deplete your oxygen supply shortly before you reach the top and, struggling to maintain your consciousness, you must turn around short of your goal and race back to the bottom before you die of suffocation. Oh, and you are blind. And paraplegic. Now, if you throw in that your longtime love dumps you when you reach the bottom, and your car—specially outfitted with hand controls—just got towed from the outer Mongolia parking lot, even though you paid extra for the "handicapped" sticker…well, that's what it's like looking for an apartment in Manhattan.

Especially when you don't have a job.

So I arrived in Manhattan, stayed at my friends' and began my search for a place to live. *The Village Voice* comes out on Wednesdays but can be picked up outside the editorial building on Tuesday at midnight, so I headed down to the East Village at 11. Snaking around the corner from Lafayette to practically the subway station was a line of people not to be believed. If someone had put this particular assemblage into a movie scene, I would have groaned. "Oh, look," I would have said to whoever was seated next to me, "it's the Quirky Artist Line." There was the pink-haired pierced girl; behind her, someone of indeterminable gender; the club kid in 12-inch platforms; the heroin-addict rock-star wanna-be…all standing in line like a bunch of kindergarteners.

I took my place about 100 people back. If I'd had any money to spend on rent (or if I'd had a job), I'd have headed home and picked up the *Times* on Sunday, but since I didn't (and I didn't), I waited my turn—just as I would have to do at the apartments I would see the next day. Hundreds of bodies looking to claim each affordable yet horrid space.

Once, I saw this exhibit by an artist who had put an ad in the *Voice* for a studio apartment that was six feet by eight feet. I mean, she'd actually written that in the ad: "6 x 8." Apparently that is the size of a standard prison cell, although I don't think she was going for that particular irony. It was listed at something like $600 a month. There was a phone number, and when you called, the answering machine instructed you to leave a message about why you deserved the apartment. Then, at the gallery, the artist had built a six-by-eight "room" that really looked more like a broom closet. That's not such an astute observation on my part, by the way, because she'd placed brooms and mops inside it. And when you walked in, all the messages were playing. Everyone there was laughing, but I thought it was really sad. Anyway, the people who go to gallery openings probably got their places through the *Times*.

So the *Voice* came out on Tuesday night, and by 4 a.m. Wednesday there were people lined up at the Avenue B tenement that I chose to see first. It wasn't the cheapest apartment listed, but the ad had mentioned that the place had a closet, which I figured made it the most promising. I was about sixth in line, so I still had a shot.

At 7 the super arrived, looked over the line and rolled his eyes. Now, this offended me for several reasons. First, this guy was no *Times* reader himself. He looked as if he hadn't shaved in days, and he smelled like he'd smoked about a thousand already this morning. A cloud seemed to waft with him. I named him "Pigpen."

The motley line climbed the seven flights (no elevator, by the way—a building-code violation) and shuffled into the apartment in perfect order, which really didn't fit this group at all. Each filled out an application and, sight unseen, laid down a $50 returnable deposit. A stud-collared punk lent a pen to an anorexic actress. Come on! This etiquette confounded me. I really didn't get it. These people, who make it a way of life to be counter-cultural—why were they being so damned *polite?* I just wanted to go over to Pigpen and shake him. "I am not an artist. I am not a musician. I will have a job, eventually. Pick me. Pick me. PICK *ME!*"

I didn't get the place.

So now I was in a bit of a pickle. Ha, ha, ha. Oh, I should have mentioned before that the apartment was smack in the middle of the pickle district. It would have been funnier if you'd known that, as I did when I left the apartment. And don't act like you didn't realize there was a pickle district. You've seen *Crossing Delancey;* I know you have.

So, my strategy hadn't really paid off. I knew that I'd had the best chance with the first apartment I saw, since I was early in line; by the time I got to the next one, there would probably be a hundred applications already. Pigpen had mentioned that because the first two candidates had brought their 1040s and cash for a security deposit, one of them would definitely get the place. Excuse me: no one had told me to bring anything. I would really appreciate that, in the future, I be advised of these requirements. Thank you.

On to Plan B. That's me: "Plan B Girl." I don't think of it as an insult at all. The way I figure it, Plan B isn't that bad. I mean, it could be Plan C, or Plan F, even. So, I always come up with Plan B simultaneously with Plan A. And secretly, sometimes, I even make it better.

I've tried to play down the whole Plan B Girl thing in front of most people, ever since my ex-boyfriend told me he thought it was really negative. The ironic thing is that *he* was a Plan B.

In this case, though, Plan B was to check out the "Roommate Wanted" situations. My girlfriends had told me they knew lots of people who'd gotten super-great apartments that way. So I headed to Katz's Deli and started circling ads in the paper while eating a corned beef sandwich. It was really hard to concentrate, though, what with the rush of cholesterol into my bloodstream and all. I had been trying to watch my weight, and I do have a tendency to binge—but, man, I think I set a new record for fat consumption in a single sitting. Katz's is this large, cafeteria-style room, except there is no line, and you have to be really pushy and *scream* your order, hoping someone will hear you through the crowd, and since I felt really pissy about the Pigpen Incident, I was served pretty quickly.

I was totally enjoying my fat sandwich and checking out all the photos of Mr. Katz with celebrities when I noticed one of him with Meg Ryan and Billy Crystal. Yuck—I had completely forgotten that they filmed *When Harry Met Sally* here. I hate that scene where Meg Ryan does the whole fake-orgasm thing at the table. I know everyone thinks it was really funny and clever, but I find it so *obvious*. It probably appeals to the people who love Julia Roberts and Celine Dion and think that going to Disney World is a cultural experience. The whole thought of Meg and Julia and Celine and Mickey, it kind of ruined my appetite, so I decided to head back uptown and start making some calls.

I was trying to decipher the ads like someone would the Personals. I don't judge the Personals at all. I mean, if you are looking for love, I say good for you. I know two women who found their husbands that way, so I have proof that it works. I tried to convince my friend Jen to put one in. She's only 32 but is in heavy clock-ticking mode. She said, "Those ads are for losers," but I totally disagree; people don't just just pop into your life. I swear, she'd be married by now if she'd listened to me.

Anyway, I scanned for the ad that said "huge room with own bath in Upper West Side doorman bldg. to share with roommate who travels" and, if I was really lucky, "…a lot." But I'm not. So instead, I circled everything under $500 a month that seemed habitable, and I started making calls.

On the first two tries, I got answering machines. By the length of the beeps, I assumed they had already received lots of responses. That was probably because the first listed park views and the second, an elevator. On my third call, I finally reached a human being. I am not sure if this was better or worse. There is something pleasant about the anonymity of an answering machine: "Here's my information; take it or leave it." Then again, with a live person I could rely on my charm and really sell myself.

My game plan was to be funny. Everyone loves funny! The problem being that I am not very funny—at least, not on demand. Actually, I'm most funny when I am not trying to be, which of course makes me consciously *not* try to be funny, which has the same effect as trying to be funny, which is that I'm not. Are you with me? So right at that moment of "Hello?" I wished like hell that I were funnier, thus displacing my usual wish that I were thinner.

(I would restore the thin wish to its rightful first-string position when I visited roommate candidates number 4, both of whom worked for Revlon, and who weighed 110 pounds between them.)

But back to number 3. A real live man answered the phone, sounding as if I'd just woken him, even though it was 2 in the afternoon. He seemed confused when I explained that I was answering the ad in the *Voice*. I repeated that there was a "Roommate Wanted" ad in today's *Voice*. Either it clicked, or he just wanted to get me off the phone; at any rate, he said I needed to talk to Ian, whoever that was, and told me to come by after 8. I couldn't believe that I was the only one who'd called, and I wondered if there would be 700 people there "after 8." But I liked the name Ian, so I noted the time in my Palm Pilot.

Now before you go thinking I am all yuppie (or whatever they're calling it these days), I can explain. The Palm Pilot was a graduation gift from my brother, who *is* a yuppie. Palm Pilots are so totally not me, which proves it was from Jamie, because he's so self-absorbed and clueless that he always gets people gifts that he really wants himself.

I, on the other hand, pride myself on being a really good gift giver, always taking into account the recipient's tastes and needs. Last year, for my mother's birthday, I gave her a "bedazzled" baseball cap. Yes, it was very embarrassing buying the thing, but I sucked it up and explained to the saleslady and everyone in line that "My mother just loves sparkly things," and everyone nodded in understanding.

I finished making my calls and, after an hour, had about six appointments for the next day. I strategized about what I should wear and how to treat the unemployment situation, and I psyched myself into trying not to be funny.

Onto Thursday. The first apartment I saw was a "railroad" flat on the Upper East Side. If you have never seen one of these in person, then just imagine Jane and Bob's place in *Barefoot in The Park*. I entered through the front, directly into the kitchen. Luckily, because we no longer live in the 19th century, the bathtub wasn't just sitting there in the corner—instead, there was a shabby wall around it. The bathroom thus contained only the tub and toilet, the apartment's other water source being the kitchen sink. In this one about three days' worth of dirty dishes were piled up, along with eight toothbrushes and a razor. The woman showing me the place said that her roommate had given up on

New York and was moving back to Kansas City. I wondered why there were so many toothbrushes.

We proceeded back through the space. As you may have guessed, the odd thing about a "railroad" is that all the rooms are lined up in a row. So to get to the back bedroom, you have to walk through the front bedroom. This means that the front bedroom has absolutely no privacy, and of course *that* was the one that was available. I gave my life story to Kara, the remaining roommate, and tried desperately to not be funny, and unfortunately I succeeded.

I hated the location; seeing all those rich Upper East Siders sipping their $5 lattés always bums me out. I hated the apartment, a pitiful mess of a place making up in filth what it lacked in character. I hated Kara, an unemployed actress who clearly had competitive issues with her departing roommate and was both pleased that she had outlasted her and crushed that no one seemed to care. I hated everything about the place—but I was desperate. I felt as if my whole life would be in flux until I could find a home. I had convinced myself that doing so would be the hardest part of moving here (and it would be months before I realized how wrong I was). So I sucked up to Kara and made it seem as if I had something to offer her. I mentioned that my best friend was temping at the Equity office, and maybe I could ask if she knew someone who knew someone who could help Kara get her union card. I left feeling more down then ever.

I didn't have much time to brood, though, because my next three appointments were scheduled back to back. To spare you all the wretched details, here is a brief synopsis:

Buzzer rings.

Them: Who is it?

Me: It's Alyssa, about the apartment.

Them: Come on up. This is the kitchen. This is the bath. This is the available room.

Me: Uh-huh.

Them: So tell me/us about yourself.

Me: Blah blah blah.

Them: Well, I/we blah blah blah.

Me: Uh-huh, oh, how cool, yes, I totally agree.

Them: Well, we have a bunch of people coming, but we want to make a decision by Friday, so you'll hear from us.

Nothing special to note, except for (1) the aforementioned information about the skinny girls and (2) the observation that in Manhattan apartments, IKEA is ubiquitous.

Life sucks. I feel I need to add that right about here. Just remembering that whole day depresses me. I mean, I am a smart, sometimes funny, interesting girl. I have been reassured that I am a good roommate by everyone with whom I've lived. Well, with the exception of Jamie, but I don't care what he thinks since I hate him. And here I was, pandering to people who personify the word "yuck," practically begging them to take me into their miserable apartments and their miserable lives. Did I mention that life sucks?

So by now it was 7:30, and I figured I'd head out early to see Ian. Maybe if the comatose guy told everyone to be there at the same time, it would help for me to be there first. But when I got to the brownstone in Chelsea, no one answered the bell. I parked myself on the stoop and waited.

And waited. By 9 p.m., no one had actually entered the building—though I had sent away five other people who'd come to meet the mysterious Ian. "It's taken," I'd told them. Ha. Desperate times, desperate measures.

At half past nine, a crunchy-looking man in Birkenstocks appeared. He stared at me sitting there, and I tentatively asked, "Ian?" He affirmed that was he and seemed annoyed that his slacker roommate had told me to come by at 8—Ian worked at a film processing lab until 9 every night—and said that this was just another example of why he could no longer live with Paul, who never gave him his messages and was basically a pig who slept all day and worked as an orderly at Bellevue second shift (which didn't even pay that much) but who also was, in Ian's opinion, a very talented musician, and it was really a shame that he just couldn't apply himself. And I thought that I really didn't give a shit, and why was he telling all this to a total stranger?—but, then again, maybe this was a good sign. I decided I would play the confidante role, and perhaps he'd think that I would be good to have around.

We went up to the apartment, which was very clean and had beautiful details. Kitchen, bath, living room, bedroom…I was sure he was going to keep going when he pronounced, "So, that's it." I wondered out loud where the second bedroom was. He laughed and asked if I really thought an apartment that nice would go for $1000 if it were a 2-bedroom. He explained that the couch was a pull out, and that was where Paul slept. I took a look around and knew that he was lying: Paul didn't sleep on the couch. Well, maybe he did *now*, but that's clearly not where he used to sleep. For God's sake, I thought, we're in Chelsea. Didn't this guy get the telegram that it's OK to be gay?

My heart sank—I'd really been hoping for my own room—but I muttered that I guessed it would be all right. As I was walking out the door, Ian informed me that there was one other thing. He explained that he was a writer and was working on a novel. He insisted that he could only use a manual typewriter and often woke in the middle of the night with sudden inspiration. I looked over at his desk, which was stationed only feet from the couch. "But, really," he added, "It's not that disturbing; the noise is kind of…hypnotic."

Here is the pathetic part, in case you didn't think we'd gotten there already: I would have taken it. I would have lived on a couch in Chelsea with Ian, the closeted manual typist. I had not felt that desperate since I couldn't get a date for my Junior Prom and was reduced to asking freshmen.

In case you're wondering, I did eventually get a date, and not with a freshman but with a really cute guy from another school. But he spent the night trying to feel me up and then, when it was clear he wasn't getting any, got wasted and threw up on my best friend's shoes. It took her three weeks to forgive me.

So I headed back up to my girlfriends', where there were already two rejections on the machine: "You were great, blah blah, but we're going with someone else." I drowned myself in tears of frustration. Swimming in my head were images of all the fabulous people out there with fabulous apartments and fabulous jobs who'd had fabulous Junior Prom dates, while I would always have to settle for Plan B.

Oh, my God: this *was* Plan B.

The thought that my karmic standing might be slipping into the "C" range made me cry even harder. I got up to open the window and found myself screaming into the air shaft, "I hate my fucking life!"

And because this was New York, someone answered, "I hate it, too!"

My girlfriends returned from their sucky jobs and, as good friends should, proceeded to get me drunk on cheap Zinfandel. I regaled them with the story of my day, and they told me, "You're so funny!" See? My point exactly. I didn't *feel* very funny, and there it was.

I awoke the next morning and, can you believe, it was a clear and sunny day. Really. If I were the suspicious type, I'd have thought the weather was conspiring against me. Just when I wanted rain or hail or even a goddamn tornado so I could have an excuse to stay under the covers, the sun reared its ugly head.

I decided to nurse my hangover in Central Park, but the truth is that I was avoiding the phone; if I were going to be rejected, at least it wouldn't be in person. A little way into the park, I threw my towel into the middle of a big, grassy field, sat down and opened a can of soda. This place was startlingly quiet. I looked around me, surveying all of the buildings embracing the park for its entire 360 degrees.

Wow.

Once, in college, I dated this guy who had the most amazing dimples. He was by far the best-looking man I've ever been with. *Too* handsome, really. I used to look at his dimples and want to dive in—to live in them. That's what I felt like, sitting in Central Park that morning. Like I was living in this amazing dimple on a face so beautiful that I couldn't believe it would ever want me.

I sat there for a few hours, watching every sort of human go by. I defy you to say that Central Park is not the center of the universe. I'm not being hyperbolic here; I really, truly believe that it's the actual center of the universe. So I sat there, taking in that view, until I could no longer deny that I needed to pee really badly; six Diet Cokes will do that, you know.

I ran all the way back to the apartment. As I ran past the machine on the way in, I saw that it was flashing, and I knew (in the way that you just know) that those messages were for me. I took a deep breath as I walked out of the bathroom, recited my good luck mantra—"Please let it be good, please let it be good, please let it be good"—and pressed PLAY:

"Alyssa, hi, this is Kara. Listen, I thought you were great, but…"

Delete.

"This is a message for Alyssa"—it was Ian. "Paul and I have worked things out, and he is going to stay, but thanks for coming by…"

Oh, Ian. You were my last, best hope. I did understand, though: more was riding on a relationship in this city than anywhere else. After all, there was the real estate factor. I'd bet that Paul realized Ian was serious about kicking him out and knew how hard it would be to find another place to live. *Well, God bless them,* I thought, and wished them luck.

I imagined Ian typing away at his desk with Paul snuggled wamly in bed, and somehow, that image cheered me up. Maybe happiness was out there after all. Maybe we all could write novels on manual typewriters and wear "bedazzled" baseball caps and get our union cards. And if I didn't find a place to live that week, maybe the next week I would find two, or three even…

"Hi, Alyssa, you saw our apartment yesterday. We thought you were great, but…"

Delete—but gleefully. For the sun was shining, and I was here—mere blocks from the center of the universe—feeling shiny and full of hope.

I ended up getting the sixth place I saw, a totally nondescript post-war apartment. The owner is a paralegal who loves Celine Dion and owns DVDs of

The Little Mermaid and *Sleepless in Seattle,* and I adore her anyway. Months later, when I asked her why she picked me, she said that she thought I was really funny. Go figure.

OK, so I arrived.

PURE MAGIC

Emile Ferris

"Pure Magic." That's what's printed in black ink letters at the top of the square of cardboard the socks are wrapped against. The cellophane is flaky and yellowed. It's probably pretty old, like from the 1950s. It's hard to know what color the magic socks really are.

I got hold of the socks at the free thrift store run by the local church.

The basement where they have the clothes giveaway is lit up by only a couple of bulbs hanging from the ceiling.

Two Belizean ladies run it. These ladies are built like late-model Buicks. They have nice wide bodies and teeth as bright as new whitewall tires. They're generous women, and when I think of their hearts, I imagine those interiors to be real plush, like red Corinthian leather.

These ladies are always laughing. When I'm around, they like to tease me. They rib me about the hubcap hanging from a laundry cord tied around my neck.

They say, "Boy, you are some fine automobile, now why don't you make us all happy and get you-self off to a car wash?" Then they laugh. I don't pay no never mind. They don't understand why I became a car, and it would be too hard to explain. They're not bad; they just like to kid.

They joked about the socks, but I noticed they wouldn't touch the package with their bare hands. One of them wrapped a scarf over her fingers before she tossed the socks to the other one, who stepped aside to let the pack land on the floor. They were acting like it was all in fun, being afraid of the socks, but I could tell they didn't like the whole idea of magic socks.

Valencia, the one that wouldn't catch something with "magic" written on it, told me I could have the socks if I picked them up off the floor. The one named

Mathilde said, "What does a compact Ford four-door need wit' socks anyways?" And then they laughed like there was no tomorrow.

But when I reached down and grabbed up the socks, they stopped their cackling.

Valencia looked over at Mathilde. "If it says 'magic'…"

Then they both sucked in air, in a you're-going-to-get-it-now kind of way. To them, God walks the earth with a switch in hand, looking for people to lay a beating on.

While I was leaving, I heard them down there in the half-darkness, laughing. Probably about me and the socks.

I got outside and parked myself right here by the exit door so I could have my smoke. Opening the package of socks is like tearing away the years. Like opening a time capsule. I can finally see how pretty the socks are under the crumbling cellophane. They're blue-green with a lace pattern of tiny gazelles jumping all over them. They smell like ladies' face powder, and they remind me of my mother.

She worked the night shift at Blommer's chocolate factory. She was bald and red-faced, just like me, and just like me she was sensitive to vodka, Christmas, and the heat. She was as good and solid as one of them wood-paneled station wagons, the early-model kind with the plaid wool upholstery. Sometimes she knew about things before they happened. She always said I was like her that way.

I feel really different just holding these socks. I sense things I've never been real aware of before. And I have to say—and anyone at Mercy House where I live will tell you straight—that I'm not prone to exaggeration.

I'd better get back to my room and put on the socks and see what happens. But I'm sensing that something is happening already.

There's no denying it: the socks have power.

I'm swinging a left down Grant Street, and I start thinking about Paula, who lives on the ladies' floor of Mercy House.

She'll like the socks. She'll understand right away what a find they are.

A while ago, Maury Fentwick, who is a big dumb rusted-out beater, called Paula a moron. Even though a bunch of people told Maury to knock it off, no one but me denied what he'd said. No one said it was a lie.

But I don't think Paula is dumb. She's a quiet kind of smart, like an animal.

I'm hiding the socks under my coat as I make my way up the elevator and into my room. I parallel park alongside the narrow bed.

I'm sitting with my feet bare, and now the socks are going on. It's a somewhat tight fit.

I wait a few minutes for the magic to begin, and then there's a knock at the door.

I get up to answer it.

It's Paula.

This magic is exciting.

She says, "An earthworm has five hearts," and then she walks in and sits down on the bed. Her voice is always low and hoarse, probably from too many cigarettes. Most of her teeth are gone. The way she lisps from all the gaps in her grillwork, she sounds like a tough little boy.

Today she's wearing a stiff gray bowling shirt with the name *Ted* embroidered over the pocket. Her hair is brown and straggledy. Her eyebrows and eyelashes are missing. A long green knitted scarf is wrapped around and around her neck. Maybe she's not off the showroom floor, maybe she's even wrecked, but she's still beautiful. Whenever I see her, I think, *Lamborghini*.

"You're right as always, Paula-girl," I say in response to her earthworm comment.

Shutting the door, I realize I'm so souped up, I can barely breathe.

I sit down next to her and say, "Paula, I want you to be the only one I tell about the magic." Then I explain all about the amazing socks, and even though she doesn't blink much or move at all, really, I can tell she's pretty excited.

We sit there for a really long time. The light in the room gets sharp from the setting sun. I cough; she wipes her nose on a wad of tissues she's taken from her pocket.

Real soft, Paula says, "Some blackbirds learn to imitate the sound of car alarms."

I nod. "You're right, of course. But this time it's magic, Paula. I know it, I really do."

I'm revved about what's coming next. It could be anything.

We wait some more. Paula pinches the edge of her eyelid with her fingertips; she's found an eyelash that she missed pulling out. She goes at it until she gets it out. I turn my head, so that she can eat the eyelash. My mother was big on politeness.

The buzzer goes off for dinner.

"Magic, contrary to what a lot of people believe, takes time." I say this to be reassuring to Paula, so that she'll stay with me…but she stands up.

"A polar bear can eat 50 pounds of meat in one sitting," she says, and starts to go for the door.

I grab hold of her arm and say, "Paula, just look at me for a minute, this is big, this is important"—and that's when the magic happens.

She's hitting me, because I'd forgotten the rule that no one is supposed to touch Paula, but I don't even notice her punches when the convertible drives into the room.

This is nothing like the two angels I saw fighting in the laundromat or the dead cat that looked up from its place on the pavement and told me to quit smoking.

This is maybe the single most beautiful thing I ever saw in my life. It shines like a clean diamond, and its chrome is polished to blinding. It's blue, like heaven, which is the most beautiful color for anything.

A voice tells me to get in, and to make Paula get in with me. She fights me and fights me and opens her mouth like she's going to scream, and although I don't like putting my hands over anyone's mouth, much less Paula's, I do it because I have to.

The door swings open, and we get in. I pull Paula onto the seat beside me.

The interior of the convertible is plush. The seats are as soft and white as babies' clothes. Paula isn't excited any more. She's lying against me, and she's real still.

It's strange: everything outside the auto is different, even though nothing too much has changed. As always just before dinner, there's the smell of gravied meat.

The headlights go on.

The light they make isn't the regular kind. It's moving pictures; I can see them on the wall of my room. They're like home movies, with their tick-tick-tick sound and their shakiness. The ignition fires, and the engine rumbles. I check the rearview. It's reflecting the shape of someone, some man in the back seat—but when I look around, I can't see anyone there. I take the wheel, which moves in my hands. We're going somewhere…

I wish Paula would wake up for this. I wish she would sit up straight and tell me about how rabbits have twice as many tastebuds as people do, because then this pain in my head might go away. But she isn't moving.

Up on the wall, in the movie, there's this little girl running around in a weedy lot next to a brick building. She has really short hair. She's wearing a swimsuit and shoes with socks. She's talking, but there's no sound, so I don't know what she's saying. She picks up a broom that's leaning against the outside wall. The camera follows her. She swings the broom at the camera. Then suddenly there's…nothing. We're sitting in darkness; the thin bar of light under the door to my room is the only light.

The steering wheel turns hard in my hand. I can't stop it. I sense that the car is sad to show me what I'll see. The man in the back seat begins to tell me something awful. I can see his outline in the rearview. The engine roars, and I can barely hear him. I'm only catching stray words here and there. I start to turn around to ask him to stop all this, but then the picture comes back and it's the same little girl walking up these narrow, twisting stairs. She keeps turning around to look behind her at the camera. Her shoulders are shaking; at first I think she's laughing, but when she gets to the top and some light from a doorway hits her face, I see that she's crying. She looks so small up there at the top of the stairs. I want her to come down, or at least not stand so close to the edge. The man behind me whispers something, and now *I* begin to cry.

This magic is painful. The voice from the back seat has told me things I didn't want to know, and I wish Paula would wake up and tell me about how well manatees respond to words beginning with the 'ch' sound, or something like that, but she's still as a board.

The car stops. The engine is silent.

I pull Paula out of the convertible and lay her down on my bed. I sit down next to her and wipe the sweat off my forehead. I wipe my face on my sleeve and take the socks off my feet.

This magic is exhausting. It's emptied my tank.

Maybe when I get back from dinner, Paula will be awake.

I walk to the door, and I stall there. How can I leave her alone like this?

Just then, I hear Paula coughing, so I make a U-turn and sit back down on the bed. After Paula finishes her coughing jag, she looks at me for a long time. "You're alive," I say, glad as hell.

For a minute I think she's going to kill me—she's staring hatchet chops into me with her eyes—and then she rasps out, real angry: "Bluebirds cannot see the color blue."

"I'm sorry I had to…"

"A cow spends 18 hours a day chewing," she hisses.

"Don't be like that, Paula. Please. I had to do it; the man in the car told me to."

Paula rolls over and faces the wall.

I talk to her back. "I saw things, Paula, and I want to tell you about what I saw. I won't tell anyone but you. Please, Paula, I didn't expect to see you in the headlight movie. I didn't know the guy in the back seat would tell me how…how he hurt you."

Paula turns toward me.

"He hurt your neck, didn't he, Paula?"

She has her palm over her eyes. She's making a sad, shut-mouthed face, all squinched up, and she's curling into a ball like a sow bug. She shakes and shakes, and I want to touch her. I want to reach around the hubcap hanging from my neck and touch her back. I want to have hands like those big, soft felt strips that hang down in the car wash. I'd stroke her gentle and wipe the droplets off her windshield. But instead, I just keep watch.

Everything in my room is very still. Outside, in the hall, the last of the stragglers are heading for dinner.

Paula straightens out after a while, and when she pulls her hand away, I see that her eyes are wet. She sits up and unwinds the scarf from around her neck, letting it fall into her lap. She tilts back her head. The scar on her throat looks like a pale, pink string of melted wax. It goes from one side to the other, turning up at the ends like a matter-of-fact smile.

We sit there for a long time in the quiet left behind by everyone gone for dinner. The car isn't here any more. There's nothing but my bed, a big cardboard box of my clothes and two chairs in the middle of the room.

I'm looking into Paula's face. Her lips are parted, and I can see inside her toothless mouth. It makes me think about the dark basement of the church's free thrift shop, where all the treasures are.

"I'm sorry about the roughness of the magic."

She shudders like a motor that's been shut off too fast.

"The magic from socks," I tell her, "it isn't the conventional kind."

She turns her head and looks into my eyes. "One ostrich egg feeds as many people as 24 chicken eggs."

I nod slowly. That's my Paula, smart as a whip.

MY FAVORITE THING IS MONSTERS BY KAREN REYES

Emile Ferris

Some people say it is pretty weird to love monsters. They say that God could only love good people who do nice things. But I think that is wrong. Why do I think that? I will tell you.

In almost every case of when you have a monster it is not their fault. Monsters do not choose to be monsters. Like the Wolfman for instance. He was just a normal guy who was trying to save a woman from a wolf attack. Than he was bitten by a wolf who was really a werewolf who was really really a gypsy who was really really really Bela Lugosi. Than after the wolf bite Lon Chaney Jr. who plays the normal guy turns into a werewolf and everyone starts hating him. The worse part is that he started hating himself.

That was a bad mistake. Monsters always make that same mistake. It is sad. They can not live with the terrible things they do because they are monsters. They can not except that a monster is who they are.

Some people say I look like a werewolf. That does not make me angry because I like the way the Wolfman looks. We are a lot alike. I have shaggy brown hair and so does he. I have big eyebrows like him. I have a nose that is pushed in and small eyes that I can make look back and forth in a scary way just like he does. My bottom jaw sticks out and my teeth go at different directions too like his does. Also my teeth are sharper than average. I am growing my nails long and I sharpen them too.

You nuns do not understand this. Some kids don't understand about this too because they are too stupid or just plain dumb. Not a lot of kids and probably no nuns have seen the movies I have seen.

While my brother Deeze was gone I saw Creature Features at 10:00 every Saturday night. It is pretty late except that Mrs. Gronan who took care of me was at work all night until the A.M. Creature Features plays two movies. I drink tons of Coke so I can stay up for the second movie and not fall asleep before it is over.

Back in fourth grade my friend Sammy used to watch it too at her house. At school on Monday we would talk about the movies. But not any more. Now she likes boys instead of monsters. I think that is a bad mistake. Not because of God. But because liking boys has made her boring. Now she spends all of the time looking into the mirror. She used to give me her old monster magazines but now she gives me magazines about hairstyles. I use a ballpoint pen to change the ladies faces into monster faces and I hang them up anyway and they are just as scary. Sometimes more.

Clothes are important to Sammy too. Like last year she was begging me like crazy to look nice for her birthday party. OK I said.

So before he left for Nam my brother Deeze took me to the Salvation Army. He traded a pencil drawing of his for these black shoes and this blue party dress. I did not like the dress but Deeze liked the dress and the shoes.

He walked me all the way from Broadway to Sheridan Road like I was his date. I guess I know why Sammy likes the boy thing. I liked how big his muscles were and how good his tatoos were compared to other guys and he put his arm around me too.

Than he dropped me off to Sammy's. He stood by the doorman smoking a cigarette and smiling. We waved at each other until the elevator door shut.

Sammy lives pretty high up. When I looked out her windows I could see the whole north side of Chicago.

There were silver dishes full of food and a maid in a black and white dress to spoon it out for you. Sammy got a full set of drums and plenty of other stuff too.

Sammy and most of the other kids played pass the note and kissy games like that. A couple boys and me plugged in this machine that we found in her bedroom closet. It was shaped like a spooky castle. You could put strips of glow-in-the-dark plastic into the castle and it got hot (it stank) and than you cranked the handle shaped like a ghost and the plastic got molded inside. You could open the secret crypt and there was a monster inside that was made out of the plastic. There were a bunch of different monsters that you could make. They were standing on these pedestals that had their names written on them. Just like they were awards.

When it was my turn to make the Wolfman, Sammy's mother came into the room and said there was a man at the door claiming to be my brother. I did not exactly tell her right away that he really was my brother. I know what you would say. That to do what I did was a sin. But I wanted like crazy to make my very own Wolfman.

I could hear from where I was that the door bell was ringing over and over again and I started to sweat but not from the heat of the machine. The fact is that Deeze looks Mexican like our father and I look white like Mom did.

Sammy's mother kept Deeze at the front door with the door shut in his face and he started to bang on it and than the doorman came up. But finally I told her that he really was my brother and she packed a big bag of food for me to take with. I thought maybe this is the normal way rich people do things. But Deeze got red in the face and than we left. He took the bag and threw it in the plant besides the elevator. That was the only time in my life he ever hit me. On the way down in the elevator he slapped me and roared YOU WERE DILLY-DALLYING and NEVER DO THAT AGAIN!

For a minute I was going to cry and I don't care who knows it. But than I saw that Deeze was twitching and he put his hand over his eyes. It was not his fault. It was mine. I had not been greatful or anything. Than I felt sick in my stomach and weird about the Wolfman statue I was holding that was still warm. But I couldn't drop it. I loved it. Plus also I hated it at the exact same time. Feeling like that always makes me eat one box of vanilla wafers.

After Deeze shipped off to Nam I started to eat a lot. Mrs. Gronan said she was not being sent tons of extra money from Deeze to buy new school uniforms. They got small on me, which is OK. The sleeves of my white shirts have to be rolled up because the cuffs do not button. As for the skirts I hate them. I frankly do not think a werewolf would wear a plad pleated skirt, unless it was against his will. But the good part of it is that my clothes getting small makes me feel like I am the Wolfman in the part when he is changing and he is busting out. Which is about my favorite part.

Mrs. Gronan doesn't care about monster things like I do.

From the first day Deeze left I pretty much stuck with Mrs. Gronan wherever she went, except for her job of course. I especially liked it when she watched this baby next door. Mrs. Gronan always told me to put a dropperful of whiskey in the babies bottle to make him sleep. But I never did it because I liked the baby and wanted to play with him. Mrs. Gronan does not really like babies too much because they smell. She takes jobs like that to make money for beauty parlor trips.

Mrs. Gronan owns the building we live in. She grew up in the Depression and she said it was a bad time for everyone. From that time she learned to be careful and save things. Now she has a ball made of rubber bands in her kitchen that is the size of a globe.

She is careful with money too.

Deeze kept up the rent while he was gone and he made a deal with Mrs. Gronan to take care of me (he paid her good for it too), and he paid her in Viet Nam souvenirs for cleaning our place. While Deeze was gone I stayed upstairs with Mrs. Gronan. She had the space for me because her husband was in prison. Mostly I didn't go down to our apartment, except for on Sunday mornings, when I'd clump behind Mrs. Gronan down to our basement apartment carrying buckets and rubber gloves and pine cleaner.

Once Mrs. Gronan got angry and told me to walk like a lady and not to "tromp like an elephant."

After that I made up something that I call "stalk-walking."

It is where I walk real quiet up on the balls of my feet just like the Wolfman (who because of doing this leaves wolf tracks, not long one's like a man's) and Mrs. Gronan can not hear me or tell I am there. When she turns around I real quick act normal even though right before I am always about to grab her neck and suck out every drop of her blood.

One time she even forgot I was there. She thought I was not following her and when she turned around she screamed out "Oh my God!" I am not sure if she saw me looking like the Wolfman or not, but after that she locked her bedroom door every night. She also put away all the knives. But than she keeps a very neat and tidy house.

Cleaning is like a religion for Mrs. Gronan. She says it is that way because she has 75% German blood. She says that in Germany they wash the sidewalks every day. She told me that her mother had scrubbed the white enamel bathtub so hard that the whole thing just wore down to the black iron underneath.

Just like she is in church, Mrs. Gronan is quiet the whole time she cleans Deeze and my apartment, except for after she sprays Windex on the picture of Deeze in his purple high school cap and gown. Than she whispers "lady-killer" as she wipes the rag across his handsome face. Even though she is forty years old I should have known from that how crazy she was about him. But I did not realize it until the last few days.

But she is all right really.

She likes to say things like "Ah, what're you gonna do?" "Can't cry for laughing," and "Six of one, half dozen of another." She never calls me by my name, she only calls me "kiddo," and when we go out to shop she says, "Let's giddy up," like we were horses, or on them, or something.

Like a horse Mrs. Gronan has weird teeth. They aren't all missing or rotten. They are kind of sitting the way she does when she smokes her cigarettes, with her legs crossed. That's the best way I can describe it. They fold over each other. But she isn't bad looking at all. She is really sort of pretty if she doesn't smile.

Mrs. Gronan is a cocktail waitress in a big downtown hotel restaurant that has a lot of business from conventions. These guys show up all excited to be in Chicago. No wives, no kids, at least not with them. They for sure get drunk and flirt and if Mrs. Gronan flirts back she usually gets good tips.

She'd tell me in the morning, "I'm almost out of the barrel," which meant that she'd had good tips the night before, or she'd say "shrapnel only" if all she'd gotten was coins.

Mrs. Gronan would come home from work when I was getting ready for school. We had a kind of short hand between us because of how half-asleep I'd be and how half-awake she'd be. Mrs. Gronan told me from the beginning of my stay with her all about the different types of men that came from the small towns.

She'd say Nebraska Ranchers, and I'd know that meant she'd had a bunch of giant sun-burned men complaining that the steaks were no good and pinching her on the sly. About the pinches, she said there were always a few in every crowd, and I think she kind of liked it.

Oklahoma Preachers were the all-time worst and after I got out her cushion and put it on her chair we'd spend time eating our cereal and imagining out loud how mean their wives back home must be to cause them to act so bad when they'd gotten free.

About her bruised rear-end she'd raise her hands and say, "Ah, what're you gonna do?"

One night when Mrs. Gronan was gone at work, Deeze came home. I was in the middle of a dream. In the dream I had this gigantic goldfish in the pocket of the apron with big mod flowers on it that Mrs. Gronan made me wear when I ate ice cream in her living room. The fish in my pocket was gasping and I just needed to real quick find some water to let it plunk into so it could live. So I was going around Uptown asking people in stores and on the street for a glass of water, but it was like I was speaking another language. They all just backed away from me and the fish was flipping sharp as a knife in the apron pocket and opening its mouth really wide. I started running to the lake and than

Deeze woke me out of the dream and I asked him half asleep, "Is this you or a dream?"

Just like him, he pinched my cheek kind of hard and laughed and held onto me in the dark. He kept over and over smoothing down the hair on my head with his palm. His neck smelled like cigarette smoke and gasoline. Than he cried but I didn't make a big deal about it. Deeze is macho. I pretended to be more asleep than I was. He would not have wanted me to know that he could cry.

The next morning we went to a donut place, not too far from Wrigley field. A place where all the cab drivers and cops go to. Ben's Butter Up is a donut shop that got built on the triangle formed in the smack middle of where three roads meet.

Ben is a love-hate person, kind of like Dracula's hunchback. He loves donuts and hates vegetables and he loves the Cubs and hates the Yankees. Ben has really perfect white pretend teeth which if you tick him off by stealing the sugar packets he will spit out those teeth into your bag of donuts for a joke. But Ben is small and not too scary to anyone. His sign has a picture of a big baseball bat guy chasing a happy-looking donut man.

Deeze painted that sign for Ben back when Deeze had been at Lane Technical High School. My brother can paint anything you ask him to and whatever he paints looks just the way it is supposed to.

Before he'd gotten sent off, he'd landed a job at Bally, as a pinball artist. We both like the pinball machines front parts with the lighted up picture. Kind of like comic books.

Deeze had this big black leather folder called a portfolio. It had tons of pictures in it that Deeze had drawn and painted of lots of stuff like monsters and clowns and lady soldiers.

Ben had put sheets of cloudy plastic on all the windows, so that even when cabs and cops weren't parked all around, it would seem like there was something between you and the traffic coming on all sides.

The store always smells like old English colone and burned coffee and donuts, which is a mix that I would miss if I completely was a monster and couldn't go there any more. I would have to start loving raw organs and blood and stuff and I guess I would.

Deeze ordered donuts. He talked to Ben real fast. He seemed like he was in a hurry, like he was late for something that started since he was gone.

All of the guys, like Ben, who recognized Deeze were happy to see him. They smiled a lot until a hurt look came into their faces. Deeze does not smile back too much any more. There is a lot in between Deezy and the rest of the world. Like a tangled forest has grown up between him and everything and everyone else.

You can read about enchantments like that in fairy tales.

We got donuts and walked home. The sky was pink and blue like it was an old bruise and Deeze was eating donuts and sipping hot coffee from a styrofoam cup and telling me about the car he was going to buy.

When we got to our apartment he realized he had held the paper bag but did not offer me even one donut. But I told him that was OK. I didn't care. There was a lot left and I wasn't hungry right than I said. But I lied.

Deeze's nose turns red in the cold and it gets runny which would be gross on someone else but Deeze is so handsome you would not even care about his nose. Really I'm not kidding. Deeze is better to look at than donuts or wedding cake or eclairs or anything that I could dream of eating for the whole rest of my life.

Some of my friends brothers got sent back in 20 different pieces. One is even M.I.A.

But I am lucky. Which is not something I thought I would ever say again since Mom died. My brother is home.

For the first few weeks the bell rang and a lot of people came by unexpected. Sometimes if Deeze was in the right mood he was glad to see them. If his friends had brothers or sisters like around my same age than we goofed around out in the alley or at the Heart of the Immaculate parking lot.

If his friends are Army people than they usually don't have kids. Those times my brother sends me on a "mission impossible." As he calls it.

He pulls out a few balled up dollars from his pocket and sends me off to Brown's corner store for beer and chips.

By the time I get back, it is weird because the apartment is empty, except for Deeze who's dozing off at the kitchen table. Sometimes he burns incense and the house smells lonely.

Deeze put up posters and album covers on the walls. I am not going to write down about what they are pictures of. Because Sister Barbara, you would hate them.

Even I have started hating those guys who come over, because of the gross things they say about girls with me right there in the room.

At first it made Deeze mad when they talked dirty and I could hear Deeze yelling at them in the basement when I was out on the street. Than a day after that or so later those same guys came back and this time my brother was angry at me for hanging around. He pushed me out the door with no money to buy nothing and said to come back in an hour. I sat behind the Heart of the Immaculate bus and I cried hard and I don't care who knows it, because I wanted Deeze to see how swoll up my face was when I got back, but like always he was asleep when I got back, so oh well, what're you gonna do?

Deeze hasn't gotten a job yet, so a lot of times he goes upstairs to talk about the rent with Mrs. Gronan. He said that she was angry about it and for me not to come up. He'd be up there "getting things sorted out with her" for hours.

But I went up anyway, really quiet as a werewolf does it. Putting my wolf feet on every step very smooth.

I put my ear to the door and I heard Mrs. Gronan on the other side. It wasn't yelling, the sound she was making, and she didn't sound angry.

The next day at school, I told Sammy and she said they were you-know-whating. She said it just like that and I wanted to slap my hand over her mouth and yell, You shut up! but Samantha Kelly wears lipstick and eyeshadow (even though supposedly that's not allowed) and she just flipped her hair back and said, Don't get mad at me, cause I'm telling you about what is going on.

And I figure she's right, and if anyone knows about this stuff its Sammy. She has had more boys hands up her shirt than I've had Sara Lee pound cakes. That's the truth and at this point I do not care who knows about it.

So yesterday while I was thinking about my brother and Mrs. Gronan, together doing it, I finally threw up right onto the shiny gym floor and you put your arm around me and you washed my face. I told you that my brother was sinning with a woman and that the whole thing made me sick.

And sure enough you blinked over and over again (like you always do) and you took me to this dusty office and we got on our knees and we prayed together and than you called Deeze and said I'm sick and Lo and Behold, who shows up to take me home? Mrs. Gronan, and not just the regular Mrs. Gronan, NO, the new Mrs. Gronan. The very blond Mrs. Gronan, the one who stays on top of her dye job, so that you never see that skunk line of mousy brown and gray any more. The Mrs. Gronan who has started walking like her arms and legs are tied together by long strings only.

And than you looked at me and I nodded just like, Yes that's her.

Than you cleared your throat and made your eyes as narrow as pencil lines (which you do a lot). It is at this point that I knew why I always liked you. Because with your accent you remind me of Maleva the gypsy who takes care of the Wolfman. And plus you have always liked all the essays I have written to you.

Than after you did that thing with your eyes you looked Mrs. Gronan over from head to toe. Mrs. Gronan took a step backwards and than looked at me.

Outside on the walk home while I'm looking at the sidewalk, I said, I know everything about you and Deeze, right out loud.

Mrs. Gronan said nothing to me, but when we got to the building she took me to our apartment, Deeze's and mine and I started feeling afraid. But somehow Mrs. Gronan seemed more afraid than me, and I figured out all of a sudden why:

Mr. Gronan.

Even though he's in prison Mrs. Gronan is not going to want news going around about her and anyone else. Mr. Gronan is a gangster. One of those guys who sees life black and white and red all over.

Listen Missy, said Mrs. Gronan, you're only going to hurt yourself by snooping around and spreading tall tales. Do you know what your brother is?

And at that point she took me into our bathroom and reached up above the cabinet over the toilet and this is the part you do not know. She pulled down a little cardboard box. Inside of it was a bunch of burnt black spoons and a doctor type needle and a piece of plastic rope. That's when I looked up at her and I guess she saw how dirty it all was, the box, her showing me, just everything. And she started crying and saying, I'm sorry honey, I'm really, really sorry.

The funny thing is that all her pity for me and her guilt did not matter to me at that minute.

Yesterday I realized that Mrs. Gronan is so in love with my brother that it does not even matter how much trouble they will get in together.

Deeze has bad horrible dreams that make him scream. When he is dreaming he talks about there being children on fire. He says it over and over and over and than he hollers and his screaming wakes him up.

I think that those children are still on fire inside of him. I think they are thirsty and drinking up all of him and he is drinking up all of everybody and there isn't enough water to put out the fire. Not even enough water in me.

So yesterday I left that bathroom bent over like I just had got a punch in the stomach from Sammy or someone. I did not even want eclairs. Not even if you offered them to me and said they will never never make you fat, eat all you like. I would have said no.

Food was not going to do it this time.

Deeze used to be the person I could turn to when I was in trouble. He always had a sort of magic icing on him that made things work out for me. Like when he came to school and charmed everyone and got me out of hot water after my hitting fight with Sammy. (Even you liked him a lot, you said you did.)

But now Deeze is the trouble.

You had prayed with me. But I could not see how God cared that much about Deeze. What with the Heroin and all.

But than I started to think of the baby that Mrs. Gronan and I used to take care of on Saturdays. Thinking of that made me calm down a lot.

One time in the summer I was holding the baby and Mrs. Gronan was watching TV and the baby looked at me for a real long time. Usually babies look at you and than they look away from you. But this time the baby was touching my face and his eyes were big and wide open and his mouth was open too like he was astonish at me. And than he laughed like I made him happy and kicked his legs and went back to touching me. After that minute I had the idea of how God is. Just like that baby. Always in love with everyone.

Yesterday I laid down on my bed underneath a pile of three weeks of dirty laundry and I prayed up to baby Jesus to take all my big problems into his little hands.

When I got up this morning I got up like I did when I was little with Christmas presents to unwrap.

Deeze was already up. He had spread out his portfolio on the kitchen table.

Before he left for Nam he had spent a lot of time covering each picture with special artist plastic. He had made me promise not to take it down and show anyone and not to leave it on the floor in case our apartment had one of its' regular floods.

This morning he was looking at all of the pictures and eating a dry piece of toast.

He was wearing his sweatshirt. The one with a hood that zips up the front of it. The one that is missing the cord for the hood. It is very dirty, even to me who doesn't care about stuff like that. It has dark pit stains and everything. His legs have gotten thin and kind of gray, but he is still the handsomest guy in the neighborhood. And I do not care who knows that too.

First thing out I think God has heard my prayers because Deeze smiles at me just like he used to do.

He walked to the stove. It's pouring out, he said and he lit a cigarette off the stove. He sat down at the table again and I poured a bowl of cereal and than filled it with tap water and ate it standing up so I would not get near his art with food.

Yeah, I said I heard the sky cracking open in the night.

I looked over his shoulder at this one painting while I spooned cereal into my mouth. It showed this weeping knight. He was wearing a gold helmet. In front of his feet was a dead dragon. All cut open and bleeding. The blood was splattered up the legs of the knight and it was even in his hair. His sword stuck out of the dragon's belly. It was really cool that picture. It had surprises. If you looked close you could see there was a woman inside the dragon. The back of her hand rested against her forehead. The sword had gone into her too. Deeze had won an award for that one. He had been so proud of it that even though it cost a lot more he got that one framed in a gold foil mat.

Deeze went upstairs to Mrs. Gronan's. He came back down a minute later with a white garbage bag. He cut two holes on the sides and one hole at the sealed bottom and than he turned it over and slipped it over my head. Than he put my head and my arms through the holes.

A raincoat, he said with a big smile.

And than he put his hands with all the handsome veins all over them on my plastic cover shoulders.

He said Karen, it's been tough for you, I know that, but things are going to get better.

Yeah? I said to the walls. I could not even look at him. And than suddenly I felt how rotten things were. And than suddenly I started crying like I was a baby.

Yeah? I said again, but my voice was high and squeeky.

He said, You let me worry about it, just like his old tough self and than he made like his thumbs were wind-shield washers on my face. Than he made sound effects, swish, swish and than he used his thumbs that are always all black from ink to back and forth wipe away my tears.

I laughed and said something, but I don't remember what, all I remember is that it came out all spitty and sputtery. I felt like a big fat dope.

But still Deeze leaned in and kissed my forehead, really gentle. I knew I was going to take it for my raincoat. But I can tell you I didn't care cause Deeze had made it for me.

So when I got to school this morning I hung up my raincoat as proud as I could be even with the noise from kids like red face Jerome McMichael.

On most rainy days I smell the most. But today I was lucky it was the glue that smelled the most. You had it out for the afternoon art project. The one that you assined us about cutting out the egg-shaped parts of styrofoam egg cartons to make flower booquays, (in the case of the girls) or rockets (in the case of the boys.)

Pretty much everyone did what they were supposed to do.

That is, except for me and LeRoi Vallenceau.

LeRoi is one of those people you are talking about when you tell us not to stare at people. Of course that's hard when like LeRoi you are a giant in sixth grade.

Sure I am sometimes dirty. (You are good at reminding me about that Sister Barbara.) My shoes are too small. I look like Lon Chaney Jr. in The Wolfman at about one half the way through the change from fat upset man into fat upset werewolf. But there is always someone who is worse off than you are and I admit I sometimes tried to stay away like the other kids. But also like you say we should be merciful. So I have sometimes tried to say hello to LeRoi. But Sister, LeRoi is not a friendly kid.

I thought maybe everyone from Loiusianna was like him. I thought maybe all the black people from Loiusianna are the color of iron and quiet as death like LeRoi. But the kids who are black in class say no to that. They say he is just plain dark and they call him Africa. I do not say that. They say he is ugly because of his dark skin and how his upper lip is scarred and crooked. They say mean things and you should know about it so you can put a stop to it.

Do you know that Jerome McMichael calls LeRoi "Blackenstein"?

Today LeRoi made a booquay like he was not supposed to do. Only girls were supposed to be doing that. I am not telling on him but that is what happened.

Me and about six other kids were busy taking our turn with the glue. I was gluing together my hat made of felt with styrofoam hills all over it (the one you said was creative) when Sammy, who was next to me, looks out the window and says, "Isn't that your brother?"

I have taped so much around the frames of my glasses to keep them together that it is hard now for me to see out of them. So I squinted through the glasses and the Scotch tape and the foggy window and the rain and across the schoolyard. Yes that was Deeze in the sweatshirt and jeans. He was leaning on the black rot iron gate that goes around the whole school. He was talking to this guy.

He pulled something flat out of a white garbage bag and handed it to the guy. It shined even from far away like gold.

I have to go to the bathroom! I yelled. Than I bolted out of the door before you could catch me. Sister Barbara I know you were angry because you did not even have the chance to assine me a bathroom buddy.

When I got outside Deeze was the only one there and he was turning to walk away. He had sold his picture to the guy. I know he saw me, but he walked away. He said nothing to me, even though I was standing in the pouring rain shouting out Deeze! at the top of my lungs. He just disappears into the rain, just like that.

When I turned around to go back I looked up to see the whole class standing at the windows. The floresent lights were glowing up there and the kids were all shoving each other to get a better look at me. Than you snagged me by the ear and than I could hear the whole class wooping it up in your absense.

The other nuns wanted to cane me but you said I would not feel it as good, being fat and all. That was OK by me because caning is embareassing. Than you sentenced me to 6 on each hand with a wooden ruler. Than you explained to the class how nice and neat the arithmetic worked out:

It's 3 for lying and 3 for trickery and 3 for breaking the rules, and than you looked around because you had only gotten to 9. Than I argued that lying and trickery are really the same thing, and than you sentenced me to 3 for correcting my elders.

You said that 12 was a special number to our Lord because of the apostles. Than you said, "hands."

So than I held my palms out. Just like you might instead of hitting me be going to rest a cake right between them.

I wouldn't have cried but than I'm at number 12 and I saw my raincoat. Whoever was in charge of collecting the garbage stapled shut the holes and filled it with trash. So I went over and kneeled in front of it and I said, my raincoat, and I thought to myself where is baby Jesus? The coat that Deeze made me was ruined, but for no good reason I still wanted it. I just did.

You said that is a trash bag and not your raincoat but than Sammy says real loud yes it really was my raincoat and than the whole class laughs like hienas.

You said stop your laughing, someone elses misfortune is no cause for humor. Karen, I'm going to the janitor to get another coat for you.

When you left is when the chant started. It was white-trash bag, white-trash bag, white-trash bag, over and over again.

Jerome McMichael was leading the chant. What made me stand up and look was hearing the voices of the girls who were my friends two years ago. They were chanting along.

The chant started to get quieter and slower when Jerome McMichael got near to me.

He turned to face the class and his back shook from laughing than he turned to face me again. His eyes were all sharp and glittery and mean. He held out his hand to grab the gluey bag.

Let me put it on you he said and he grabbed it.

Suddenly the class was quiet as a pin drop. LeRoi Vallenceau was standing right behind Jerome.

When Jerome turned and looked up and saw the hate in LeRoi's face Jerome dropped my raincoat and walked back to his seat and sat down. No one called Jerome a chicken or even said a word. No one would fight LeRoi. He is the scariest.

You came in than and you put a trash bag, a new one, on my desk. Than Jerome said LeRoi had attacked him. But that was a big fat lie and you should know about it.

Than you said tonights homework is to write about your favorite thing and we will sort this fight mess out in the morning.

And than the bell rung.

Everyone was leaving. Even Sammy.

LeRoi stayed behind after even you had gone. He put on his raincoat.

I never saw this one thing about him before: Leroi moves very slow, very graceful like a swan.

He put my hat made of egg carton bumps on my head and tied the strings under my chin. Than he held open one side of his yellow slicker for me.

I was still holding the rain coat that Deeze made from a plastic bag. I moved close to LeRoi. It is weird and I don't care who knows it but LeRoi smells like Tabu perfume which is a better smell than some nuns I know.

That's how we walked side by side in the rain.

When the rain stopped I went to get out of his coat but LeRoi just held onto me. We didn't hold hands or anything weird like that. We only stopped for one minute to look at a bunch of tulips. The tulips were growing on the other side of a chain link fence. They were mostly green stalks with just a few red petals holding on for dear life.

MOMS DON'T EAT THEIR BABIES

Drew Downing

Eight or nine years ago, when I was in kindergarten, we lived at the end of a cul-de-sac surrounded by the thick, green lawns and giant elm trees of a typical suburban midwestern neighborhood. The cul-de-sac was paved with a fresh coat of thick asphalt that glistened under the summer sun. On especially humid days, the asphalt would shift under your feet and leave gooey black stains on the soles of your shoes. The kid that lived next door, Pete Wallach, told me one afternoon that if you stood on it for too long without moving, you'd start to sink, and the asphalt would suck you up like quicksand. I remember riding my bike up and down the street, pedaling my ass off just to be safe.

There were four houses on the cul-de-sac: the house where Ma, Dad and I lived; the house to the right, where the old Wyler couple lived; the house to the left, where Pete's family lived; and the Woods' house. The Wood family had three sons: Mark, Ethan and Brett. Mark and Ethan were both in high school and never around much. Brett was younger than his brothers—about ten back then. But that wasn't the only way that Brett was different.

Pete said Brett was a retard. At day camp, he would tell me stories of how Brett liked to bite other kids and pull their hair if they entered the Woods' yard. He said that one time, Brett had attacked the mailman and bitten him in the nuts. Pete said that he was pretty sure Brett was part werewolf, and probably part vampire, too.

"Make sure you don't go outside at night," he told me at lunch one day, between bites of peanut butter and jelly, "because that's when the Woods let Brett loose to roam the neighborhood."

From that day on, I would get off the bus from day camp and sprint down the cul-de-sac, even though the sun still hung high in the sky.

My afternoons were spent at the big bay window in the living room, playing with my GI Joes and Transformers and watching for Brett. A little bit before 3:00, a short yellow bus would pull into the Woods' driveway. Mrs. Wood always walked out from the garage to make sure Brett got off OK, then would take him by the hand and walk him inside. A few minutes later she would let Brett out the front door into the yard, where he would spend the next couple of hours until dinner time.

The first thing I noticed about Brett was that he was slow. Really slow. I mean the way he walked with sort of a limp and held both arms out in front of him, like Frankenstein. He had a mouth that looked crooked to me because it was always open, with the bottom jaw cocked to one side. Pete said that Brett could talk but that he drooled and spat a lot, and the words were hard to understand.

"Sometimes he just makes grunting and whining sounds."

"How do you know?" I asked.

"Because I used to play with him until one day he attacked me."

"What did he do?"

"Same as he does to everyone that goes into his yard. He pulled my hair and tried to bite me. That's why you gotta stay out of there."

The main thing I noticed while watching Brett was that he loved to touch things. Out in the yard he would stumble around, stopping to bend down and run his hand through the grass or rub the bark of the sagging oak tree at the side of the Woods' house. He especially liked to stand at the mailbox and flip the red flag up and down over and over again. Mrs. Wood always opened the front door and yelled at him to stay away from the street. Most times, though, Brett would sit in the middle of the yard, not quite Indian style because his legs didn't work like most people's. He'd have something like a sponge or an empty milk jug, and he would spend all afternoon touching and rubbing and squeezing it until dinner time.

"Ma, what's wrong with Brett?"

We were eating lasagna at the dinner table one night as the warm summer air blew in through the kitchen window over the sink.

Ma took a bite of garlic bread and chewed it slowly. "Well, hon', Brett's brain doesn't work as well as yours."

"Pete says he's a stupid retard," I said, stabbing my lasagna with my fork.

"Andy, that's not a nice thing to say."

"Pete said it. Not me."

Ma scooped up a big piece of lasagna. "Well, I'm sure Pete's mother would love to know Pete's opinion of Brett."

I stabbed my lasagna again and started to twist it around in circles on the plate.

"Stop playing with your food," Ma said, letting out a big yawn.

"I'm not." I cut the lasagna in half and separated the pieces. "Ma?"

"Yes, Andy?"

"How come Brett likes to play with garbage all the time instead of GI Joes or Transformers?"

"Honey, he does not play with garbage."

"Yeah, he does. I saw him playing with a toilet paper roll today."

Ma put her fork down and took a real long sip of her coffee. Then she looked at me for a minute and took another sip of coffee. "Honey, Brett's mind is simple. He likes simple things."

"Why's Brett's mind simple?"

Ma looked down at my stabbed lasagna. "Will you finish your dinner if I tell you?"

I nodded.

"Well, when Brett was a baby in his mom's stomach, he had problems and didn't develop quite right."

"Did Mrs. Wood eat Brett?"

Ma's eyebrows wrinkled up and lowered over her eyes. "No, Andy, of course not." Then she smiled. "Moms don't eat their babies. The baby develops in the mother's stomach until it's time to be born."

"Why didn't Mrs. Wood develop Brett right?"

Ma reached for her coffee again. "Andy, it wasn't Mrs. Wood's fault. Sometimes babies aren't born in perfect health."

"Why not?"

"It just…happens. Now, eat your lasagna."

I stared at one of the chopped pieces of lasagna on my plate, then touched it to see if it was still hot. "Ma?"

She let out a deep breath. "What?"

"Does that mean I'm perfect?"

"Go play with your Transformers."

Once day camp was finished for the summer, I spent my days in the living room, making forts—and watching "Reading Rainbow" because Ma made me watch it. After all the stuff Pete had told me, there was no way I was about to go outside and risk getting attacked by Brett.

One day while Ma was cleaning, she came through the kitchen toward the living room, dragging the old vacuum cleaner across the tile behind her. "Andy, turn off that TV and get your butt outside so I can vacuum the carpet."

I cried and begged for her to let me stay in the house.

"Andy, what is wrong with you? Why in God's name would want to spend your summer vacation inside?"

"Because Brett's out there and he's part werewolf and maybe part vampire and I don't want him to bite me and pull my hair!"

"What? Where on earth did you get that idea?"

"I'm not telling you!" I yelled.

"I know who told you. For godsakes, Andy, Brett is not a werewolf. He's a human being, just like you and me. Do not listen to Pete Wallach. That boy has an overactive imagination." She kneeled down so her face was right in front of mine. "Honey, look at me."

I didn't want to, but I looked.

"Brett is not going to hurt you. He's just a boy. OK? Now go out and ride your bike and get some fresh air."

"But what if he chases me?"

"He won't chase you. Mrs. Wood doesn't allow him to leave the yard."

"How do you know?"

"Because she told me so. Now, go. You'll be fine, I promise."

I took my time walking out to the garage. As I wheeled my bike onto the driveway, Ma opened the garage door.

"Stay on the cul-de-sac, Andy, and watch out for cars." She smiled at me, then shut the door.

It was hot outside. Maybe the hottest day of the summer. Pushing my bike down to the end of the driveway, I inspected the Woods' front yard: no sign of Brett. I swung my leg over the seat and pedaled down the street, slowly, cautiously—until I glanced down and noticed the glistening, gooey asphalt. I pumped my legs faster and rolled down to the end of the cul-de-sac. As I pedaled, I peered at the Woods' house, looking for any sign of Brett, half expecting him to bound out the front door or limp around the side of the house and hobble after me.

After a few passes up and down the street, I forgot about Brett and started to get bored. I decided to ride over to Pete's and see if he wanted to ride bikes with me. But after I turned around at the end of the street, the handlebars of my bike started to wobble. As I passed alongside the Woods' front yard, the wob-bling got worse real fast. The next thing I knew, I was holding the handlebars in front of me, but they weren't connected to my bike! I lost my balance, and the bike veered off the road and into the big ditch at the very front of the Woods' yard. I tried to jump off but the bike fell under me, and I landed right on top of it. The pedal must have jabbed me in the stomach because I couldn't breathe. I rolled off the bike and tried and tried, but still I couldn't breathe. Just as I started to worry that I might never breathe again, I tried once more and felt the air shoot into my lungs. I exhaled it with a grunt and felt a pebble in my mouth. I spit it out, and a bloody tooth bounced off the front fender of my bike with a *PING*. I felt tears filling up my eyes, and I started to bawl.

After crying at the top of my lungs for what seemed like forever, I heard a voice talking, but it sounded like baby talk. I looked up and there was Brett, at the top of the ditch, staring down at me. He was saying something, repeating it over and over with his crooked, drooling mouth.

This scared the living crap out of me, so I screamed even louder. Where the hell was Ma? How long did I have to cry?

Brett kept mumbling and making noises, but he didn't attack me like he was supposed to. Instead he limped down into the ditch and slowly bent over and picked up the handlebar from my bike. He held it in the middle and stared at the green rubber grips at both ends. He put his other hand on one of the grips, just his fingers at first, slowly, awkwardly sliding them along the bumps and ridges, a soft humming sound coming from his throat.

I sniffled a little bit, my cries having turned to whimpers. There was a big scrape on my knee with black smudges from my bike chain mixed in with the blood, and seeing it made me cry again. I looked back up through teary eyes at Brett. He still clutched the handlebar but was now looking down at me with wide, curious eyes. He stared at me for a few seconds, head cocked to one side. Then he slowly held the handlebar out to me. I didn't want it, didn't want any-thing except to sit there in the ditch and cry until Ma came and carried me home.

Brett made a thick noise in his throat that rose at the end like he was asking a question. He inched toward me and carefully placed the handlebar in my lap. Then he bent down and tried to pick up my bike. His hands were curled and his fingers were kind of twisted and bent, so he had a hard time. He grunted and struggled and was able to stand my bike up on its tires. He turned and looked at me briefly, then started pushing the bike up out of the ditch.

I sat there bleeding and whimpering, watching Brett as he huffed and growled and wagged his head from side to side, straining to make his legs push the bike and the rest of his body up the side of the ditch and onto the street. I could've pushed the bike up and rolled it back down at least five times while I sat there watching him. One of his feet was bent inward and it kept sliding back down the grass. I wondered why he couldn't make his legs work like mine.

Finally, he reached the top and carefully held my bike upright while turning around to look at me, breathing heavily, sighing victoriously with each exhalation.

I realized that he was waiting for me. I grabbed the handlebar off my lap and stood up slowly, wincing as the scraped skin stretched over my knee. I saw the bloody tooth next to my shoe; I bent down, plucked it out of the grass and stuck it in the pocket of my t-shirt. Then I climbed out of the ditch and stood by Brett.

He was only a little taller than me. He stood there staring at me, his mouth all covered in spit bubbles, and I noticed that his lips were curled up at one end. He giggled and hunched over and started rolling my bike along the soft black asphalt, limping toward my driveway.

I wiped the tears off my cheeks and the blood off my mouth and limped after him.

NEW KID

Drew Downing

The locker room smells kinda funny, and I think the fat kid on the bench next to me might have something to do with it. He's bent over, trying to stick his pale, doughy legs through a pair of old ratty-looking gym shorts. His big ass is covered by a pair of tighty-whiteys (more like tightey-*off*-whiteys) and it's, like, two inches from my face.

The smell is more like a combination of smells. There's a dirty-sock smell, like socks you play hoops in, then chuck in your closet and forget about. There's also B.O. (body odor, which is OK 'cause, c'mon, it's a locker room) and A.O. (ass odor, which is *never* OK, especially when it's two inches from your frickin' face!). I feel like I'm gonna barf, so I slide down the bench away from that big ass before I actually do. I grab my new Nike Airs out of the rusty locker and slam it shut. Speaking of barf, all the lockers are painted this dull puke-orange color. I've seen this color at every school I've ever been in. It's one of those ugly-ass colors that was popular in the '70s. They probably used that color so it would blend in with the rust.

I slide my Nike Airs on, get up and walk over to the bathroom to get away from the stink and take a leak. The only people left in here besides me and the fat kid are the two kids at the lockers across from us. One's black, one's white, and they're both loud as hell. I've been pretending like I don't notice them, but they're bouncing around with their shirts off, whipping towels at each other and shouting the words to "Mama Said Knock You Out."

Someone must've just taken a thermonuclear dump because it smells even worse in the bathroom. I finish and flush and go over to the sink. While rinsing my hands I stare at myself in the mirror, wondering if I look like the average seventh grader. Skinny, average height, grayish-brown eyes, brown hair. I'd probably blend in pretty well if I wasn't new.

I walk over and sit back down by the fat kid, and I take my time tying my Nike Airs so I won't have to go out in the gym and stand around like a frickin' loaner, waiting for gym class to start. There's a fourth smell, one I can't figure out. The fat kid is trying to put on a pair of beat-up Adidas Sambas; he loses his balance and almost falls over. He straightens up, turns around and lets out a loud burp, and I realize that the other smell is peanut butter.

The black kid and the white kid are still whipping the towels at each other and yelling "I'm gonna knock you out! Mama said knock you out!" over and over. The white kid's got one of those creaky puberty voices that a lot of kids get, and it's echoing off the tile walls and killing my ears. They're both pretty muscular, and both have armpit hair. The white kid even has face hair. He snaps his towel, and it smacks the black kid's shin.

The black kid lets out a half-scream, half-laugh. "Daaamn, man! Time out!"

The fat kid laughs at this.

The white kid looks over at us. "You want some-a-this, Fat Stu?"

I look at the fat kid. His eyes widen, and the smile on his pudgy face shrinks. He holds his hands up in front of him while shaking his head and says, "No-o-o way, Tony."

Tony twirls his towel and looks at me. "What about your little butt-buddy there?" He has the most perfectly spiked hair I've ever seen, like a bed of nails. He flips the towel out at me, and it cracks like Indiana Jones' whip. "You want a piece, new kid?"

"No thanks," I say. My throat's dry, so I barely get it out.

Tony gives me a grin. "I love new kids. Don't you, Reggie?"

"Aww, yeah," the black kid says. "Especially in gym class." His voice is really deep, but you can tell he's faking it. He has a flattop with one of those little fake parts on one side, like all the rappers have.

"You remember the new kid last year?" Tony asks.

"Yeah," Reggie says. "Short, skinny-ass kid, baby face. Kinda looked like *him*," he says, pointing at me.

"Yup. A real mama's boy," Tony replies.

"He got messed up pretty bad in gym, huh?"

"Mm-hm. Got hurt pretty bad." Tony looks at Reggie, and they're both trying not to smile.

"Yeah, they had to call the ambulance and shit."

"Never saw him again after that."

"But now we got a *new* new kid." Reggie smirks.

"A new mama's boy," Tony says, staring me down.

They laugh and high-five. Reggie glances back at me. "Mama said knock you out, new kid."

Tony stares at me with bulging eyes and an evil smile. His voice drops to a whisper: "Newwww Kiiiiiiiiid…"

I look down at my shoes but can still feel his big eyes on me.

"You the man, Tony," Fat Stu says. He's all excited, bouncing around on his feet and wiggling his fingers.

"You the Fat, Stu," Tony replies.

Reggie laughs at his joke, but Tony just keeps looking at me. Fat Stu laughs and walks down the hall to the gym. I finish a double knot with shaky hands and quickly follow him around the corner. He's skipping now, *skipping* down the hallway, talking to himself as he passes an office with a sign by the door that says MR. POLLACK. An old guy sticks his head out the door. "Stuart!"

Fat Stu stops skipping and turns around. "Oh, hey, Mr. P.," he mumbles.

The old guy is pretty old, and he has a whistle hanging around his wrinkly neck. "You're going to take a shower after class today, right, son?"

Fat Stu raises his eyebrows real high. "Oh, yeah! Of course, Mr. P."

"Make sure you do. Remember: if you don't care for your body, no one will care for you."

Fat Stu gives him a goofy wave and continues on his way.

Mr. Pollack turns and looks at me. "How ya doin', son?" He's wearing glasses, but his eyes are all squinty, like he still can't see. "You must be the new student."

I nod.

"What's your name?"

"Craig Mitchell."

"Ray?"

"Craig."

"Well, Ray, ready to have some fun today?"

❧   ❧   ❧

It's so bright in the gym that I'm practically blinded, and I have to squint for a minute till my eyes get used to it. It's a big-ass gym, twice as big as the one at my old school. I count ten basketball hoops: six with glass backboards, four with metal. On the left side of the gym, a bunch of girls with jump ropes are giggling and screeching and babbling like girls do. A few are doing that Double Dutch stuff, y'know, where two girls hold the rope and sing a gay little song while another one jumps to the beat. On the right side of the gym, all the guys in my class are pretty much standing around, joking and screwin' off. I don't know what to do, so I bend down and pretend to adjust my shoelaces until Mr. Pollack walks out. He has a clipboard in one hand, a big mesh bag full of red rubber balls in the other and a white bowling pin stuffed under each arm. He sets down the pins and the ball bag and blows his whistle.

"All right, fellas!" he shouts. "Line up on the baseline."

Out here in the bright lights of the gym, I can see him better, and *man!* He's like 70 years old with thin white hair and wrinkly skin, but he's got huge muscles. He's wearing a tight Ford Junior High Braves T-shirt, so tight that the Indian-head mascot is stretched out across his chest and his giant arms are bursting out of his sleeves. His shorts are so tight that you can see his package, and his calves look like softballs. I've never seen an old guy with such big muscles. He could whip my grandpa's ass. Maybe even my dad's.

"Let's go, fellas," Mr. P. says, looking at his watch. "Time's a-wastin'."

We're lined up now, so he looks down at his clipboard. "Allison."

"Here."

"Brosky."

"Here."

"Bruenner."

"Here."

I look down the line, checking everyone out, counting, and I'm almost to the end when Tony leans out and turns his spiky head toward me. An insane smile spreads across his stubbly face as he mouths the words "Newww kii-iid"—real slow, so I'll understand.

"Erickson."

"Here."

"Farelli."

"Queer, Mr. Small-Dick!" Tony yells.

I turn to watch Mr. P.'s reaction, but he just continues with attendance like he didn't notice. "Gullickson."

The skinny kid next to me is laughing so hard at Tony's joke that he can barely spit out his "Here." He has braces, and his top two front teeth stick out really far, which I guess is why he has braces.

Mr. P. goes past the Ms and all the way to Wilkinson without calling my name. I'm kinda glad he missed me, but then he says, "Before we start today, I want to introduce you all to a new student in the class." He looks over at me and points.

All the guys lean their heads out past the guy in front of them to look at me.

Mr. P. squints up his eyes at me. "Ah, what did you say your name was, son?"

"Craig. Mitchell."

He stops squinting and says, "Oh, yeah. Everyone say 'hi' to Ray Mitchell."

No one says anything, except for Tony and Reggie, who cup their hands over their mouths and start chanting "Neww Kid! Neww Kid!"

"Actually, my name is Craig." I say it loud so Mr. P. can hear, but he ignores me.

"Dude, he's deaf in his right ear," Gullickson, the-kid-with-braces, says.

"Really? What from?" I ask.

"I don't know. Some war or somethin'."

Mr. P. picks up the bowling pins. "All right, fellas, I think you know what we're playing today."

"Aw, yeah!" Reggie says. He gives Tony a high-five.

Mr. P. starts blabbin' away about game strategy and tactics.

"Are we bowling?" I ask Gullickson.

"No way, man! The name of the game is 'bombardment.'"

"How do you play?"

"OK, there's two teams. Each team has a pin, and you try to knock the other team's pin over by chuckin' balls at it."

"That's it?"

"Yeah. No, wait! If you hit one of the other team's players, then they're out. But if they catch your ball, *you're* out."

"...and remember, fellas: pay attention." There's a vein on the side of Mr. P.'s neck that moves when he talks, and it's the size of a frickin' python. "I know it's tough with the ladies prancing around over there, but you have to be 'heads up' at all times."

"Yessir, Mr. Ball-Lick," Tony shouts.

Everyone cracks up, and I hear Fat Stu say, "You the man, Tony."

"Now," Mr. P. says, "Tony and Reggie fought to a standstill and were the only survivors last week, so they'll be the captains. Go ahead and pick your teams, fellas." Mr. P. hands the pins to Tony and Reggie and walks over by the bleachers. Then he gets down on the floor and starts doing push-ups.

I lean over to Gullickson. "What does he mean by 'survivors'?"

Without looking at me, Gullickson says, "You'll see."

Reggie picks first, then Tony, and I start hoping to God I'm not the last one picked. Finally, it comes down to me, Gullickson and Fat Stu. It's Reggie's pick, and he looks at both of them for a minute, then at me. He says, "Damn!" and points at Gullickson.

"Yess!" Gullickson says, and jogs out to join the other guys on Reggie's team. Then he glances back at me and shrugs his shoulders, like he's sorry.

Tony rolls his eyes and drops his head to the side. He exhales all loud, like this is the biggest pain in the ass ever in his entire life.

Fat Stu rocks back and forth from foot to foot. His stubby fingers wiggle like earthworms.

I look over at the jump-roping girls, some of whom are looking over this way, and I pull my lower leg up behind me, like I'm stretching. Like this is *not* totally humiliating.

Tony turns to Mr. P. and says, "Hey, Mr. P, do I *have* to pick one of these two?"

Mr. P. is now over at a chin-up bar on the wall, massive arms pumping up and down. He doesn't stop.

"Hmm," Tony says. "Skinny turd or chubby choad. Tough choice."

"Hey, T-Man, just pick one," Reggie says. "They're both gonna be out first anyway."

Tony exhales again, totally exaggerating. "Well, the new kid's unproven. I'll take Fat Stu; at least I *know* he sucks."

Fat Stu claps his hands together, does a little jump and struts on by me. "He *knows* I suck."

I walk over to Reggie's team. Gullickson gives me five, and we follow Reggie and the rest over to our side of the court. A lot of the girls are now moving closer to our half of the gym.

"Hey, new kid!"

I turn around, and there's Tony, slapping one of the rubber balls around in his hands. "Nuts, stomach or face?"

"Huh?" I say.

He's smiling like the devil now. "Nuts it is. Same for you, Gully." Tony turns and jogs back to his team, yelling, "I'm gonna knock you out! Mama said knock you out!"

"What's he talkin' about?" I ask Gullickson.

"He's callin' his shots. You know, like Babe Ruth."

Waiting for the game to start, I watch Tony, who's yelling orders at his team. I wonder what he puts in his hair to make those spikes so perfectly straight. I bet if he got hit in the head with a ball, the spikes would pop it.

Gullickson is stretching his legs and making grunting noises. His face is strained and looks weird from the side because his bottom lip is tucked behind his big buck teeth. He looks like a rat with braces. If Gully got hit in the mouth with a ball, I wonder if his braces would pop it. "Gotta look good in front of the babes," he grunts. He nods over at the girls, who are gathering at our side of the gym. "You don't think they pay attention, but they do."

My stomach starts to feel like it's floating. "It's just gym class."

Gullickson looks at me like I'm in Special Ed. "Dude, who you crappin'? This is way more than gym class. This is make-or-break time."

"Whaddaya mean?"

"Look, I don't know how things were at your old school, but here, how good you are in gym determines how popular are. Especially with the chicks."

Mr. P. rolls five of the rubber balls over to us. Reggie snags one; a kid with curly hair and glasses gets another. None of them come my way.

Gullickson leans over to me. "Speaking as a former new kid: watch your ass. They'll be gunnin' for ya."

Mr. P. rolls four balls over to the other team. Tony gets a second one; a kid with a bowl-cut grabs one. One ball rolls right past Fat Stu.

"All right, fellas," Mr. P. says, "remember what I told you: pay attention."

Gullickson jogs up behind him. "Hey, Mr. P., can I go to the bathr—?"

Mr. P. blows his whistle to start the game. Before the whistle-blow even ends, a ball whizzes through the air and drills Gullickson dead-on in the crotch; he squeals when it hits, and you can hear all the breath blow out of him. The girls shriek as his hands shoot down to his blasted nuts. He twists around so he's facing our team: he looks like he just saw Bigfoot. After a few seconds his eyes squint up, and he tips over like a sawed-down tree.

Mr. P. is doing push-ups on the sideline.

I look over to see who threw the ball that pelted Gully, and there's Tony with his hands behind his head, pumping his crotch at the girls. Out of the corner of my eye I see a ball flying at me; I duck and hear a loud slap and a grunt. I look up, and the kid standing behind me has his hand over his mouth. "H-hanks, ahhole!"

I stand straight and move a little to the left. Reggie winds up and whips a rocket across the court at a kid wearing a Hard Rock Cafe T-shirt; the kid sees the ball coming and tries to jump out of the way, but the ball catches his feet in mid-air, knocking them out from under him. He lands on his back with a *thud*.

"Yeah, bitch!" Reggie yells in his fake low voice as the kid gasps for air.

After this, things start happening too fast for me to notice them all. Balls speed through the air. A few are caught, but most hit their targets, who aren't paying enough attention. With every throw, Tony lets out this crazy scream-laugh that sounds like a rabid hyena. The girls are cheering him on. Every time he hits someone, he wags his tongue or pumps his crotch.

Reggie has a frickin' cannon for an arm. No one could catch his throws, even if they wanted to. Two kids on the other team actually try, and they both end up walking to the sideline clutching their beet-red arms to their aching chests.

Fat Stu runs away from every ball. I don't think he knows how to catch.

Mr. P. is now doing sit-ups.

I'm under constant fire, ducking and hopping and sliding away from balls that are either too high or too low to catch.

"What's the matter, new kid?" Tony yells. "Afraid of the ball?" I don't have time to even look at him. Gullickson was right: they are gunning for me.

I actually manage to get a ball—once—but as soon as I grab it, Reggie claps his hands and yells, "Right here, new kid!" so I toss it to him. A bunch of girls scream, "Go, Reggie!" That's all they say: "Go, Reggie!" or "C'mon, Tony!" every time either one of those two gets a ball.

There's a kid on the other team whose shoe just fell off; he darts over to grab it. He's a couple of feet away when Reggie launches the ball I gave him, and it beans the kid on the side of his head. His neck jerks back, along with the rest of his body.

The girls all go, "Ohhhhhhhh!"

His shoe stays where it is.

Tony is laughing his ass off, even though this kid is on his team. The kid sits on the ground for a few seconds, touching his head. Then, as balls continue to fly over him, he starts to cry.

Mr. P. finishes a set of sit-ups, hops up to his feet and blows his whistle. "Hold on, fellas!" He jogs out, helps the kid up and grabs the shoe as they walk off the court. Right before he takes the kid into the locker room, he blows the whistle again, and the game's back on.

More balls fly. Some are caught; some are dropped. More kids get drilled. All of a sudden, there's only six people left standing, and somehow, I'm one of them. On our side are me, Reggie and the kid with curly hair and glasses. On the other side are Tony, Fat Stu (a miracle) and a kid with a bowl cut.

We all just stand there, holding our balls. The rubber ones, I mean. Everyone's quiet, even the girls. The only sounds in the gym are the low groans of

Gully and some of the other guys laying along the sideline. With his free hand, Fat Stu picks his ass.

Tony stands totally still. "What's it gonna be, Reg'?" He glances at me, then back at Reggie. "Looks like you're pretty much screwed."

"I wouldn't be talkin'," Reggie says. "*You're* the one with Fat Stu."

The kid with curly hair and glasses laughs.

Fat Stu sticks his chin out, trying to look mean.

Tony turns and whispers something to the kid with the bowl cut.

I hold my ball tight, rubbing my palms around on its surface to get the sweat off.

Staring straight ahead, Reggie says, "Nobody throw till I say so."

Curly-haired kid nods.

I nod, too, and wonder how this whole thing is going to end. And when.

It's a stand-off. No one makes a move for, like, a couple of minutes. Tony keeps whispering to Bowl Cut. Fat Stu has his arm cocked back, ready to throw. Each side waits for the other to move.

"Hell with this," Reggie grumbles. He leans over to Curly. "All right, man, we're goin' for Fat Stu on the count of three." He looks at me and says, "New kid, whatever you do, *don't* throw your ball." He stares down Tony, who stares right back.

"One..." Reggie says.

Tony starts slapping his ball back and forth in his hands. I hear one of the girls whisper, "What are they waiting for?"

"Two..."

A drop of sweat rolls down the back of my leg. I want to wipe it, but...

"Three!"

Curly plants his foot and hurls his ball at Fat Stu, who yells, "Oh crap!" and holds his ball up to cover his face; as soon as Curly lets loose, Tony and Bowl Cut fling their balls at him. Reggie fakes his throw at Fat Stu, pivots, fires at Bowl Cut. Curly's ball slams into Fat Stu's unprotected gut. Curly catches Bowl Cut's ball with his arms—and Tony's ball with his *face*, which snaps his glasses in two.

"New kid!" Reggie shouts. "Ball!"

I flip my ball to him, just as the one he threw hits Bowl Cut on the tip of his chin. Quick as lightning, Reggie *whips* my ball at Tony, who is giggling at Curly like a lunatic.

It's the hardest ball Reggie's thrown all game, and I know what's going to happen. I can see the ball sail through the air and pop Tony right in the nose. I can hear him shriek with pain. I can see the blood gush out of his nostrils. I can hear him whimper. I can see him dropping to his knees. I can hear him crying out one word: "Mommy!"

...but no. It *is* the hardest ball Reggie's thrown all game—but that bastard Tony notices at the last second and gets his arms up to wrap around the ball as it smacks his chest, and Reggie is gone.

All the girls cheer and clap and yell, "Good one, Tony!"

Reggie rolls his head back to one side and says "Damn!" under his breath as he walks to the sideline.

"Nice try Reg," Tony says, shaking his head. He cups his hands over his mouth and yells, "I'm gonna knock you out! Huh! Mama said knock you out! *Get* down!" Then he starts to Moonwalk.

I'm lost for a minute, trying to go over everything that's just happened. I feel like I've been watching a movie on fast-forward—except I'm *in* the frickin' movie! Looking around, I see Curly crawling around on the floor, looking for the pieces of his glasses; Bowl Cut curled up in a little ball, his hands cradling his face; and Fat Stu laying on his side, holding his stomach, looking sick.

And then it hits me that I survived...

"Newwww kiiiiiiiiiiiiid."

...and that this is a bad thing.

Tony looks like the Joker now, smile spread clear across his face, wild eyes glaring. His porcupine hair is still perfect, not one spike out of place. He spins Reggie's ball on the tip of his finger. "Just so you know, you only survived 'cause I let you." His smile grows even wider.

One of the girls yells, "C'mon, Tony!"

He looks over at her, licks his lips and growls like a tiger. Then, slowly, he turns back to me.

I hear a sound like someone spilled a cup of water, and I follow it to the sideline, where Fat Stu is barfing on the floor.

All of the girls go, "Eeeeeewwwwwww!"

Reggie shakes his head. "*Nasty!*"

All I can think of is peanut butter as Fat Stu upchucks a couple more times, then flops over onto his side.

"Jesus," Tony says. He turns to me once again and stares me down for what seems like 10 minutes. "Say your prayers, new kid." He says it real slowly and grins all proud, like he invented that dumb line.

He takes a few steps back, eyes on me the whole time.

I really have no idea what to do.

Another girl: "Go, Tony! *Whooooo!*"

"New kid! C'mon!" Reggie growls from the sideline—"dead," but team captain still. "Pick up a ball."

I hadn't even thought about that! I flick my eyes down at the floor a couple of times. I don't want to take my eyes off Tony for too long. I glance around again and see a ball off to the right, just a few feet away.

Tony sees me looking at it, and he nods. "Go ahead."

I side-step over to it, keeping my eyes on him.

"Don't worry, new kid, I'm not gonna throw at you."

I know he's full of crap, so I watch him while I bend down and feel around for the ball. As soon as I get my hands on it, Tony jumps out and winds up to throw. I try to pick the ball up and shuffle backward at the same time, but I trip over my own feet and fall back on my ass.

He was only faking it.

All the girls point at me and giggle, their hands over their mouths. Some of the guys laugh, too—even some of the injured ones. I scramble to my feet like a spaz—nearly bumping into our team's bowling pin in the process—then try to look as cool as a dude can after falling on his ass (which isn't very).

"Way to go, nut-sack," Tony says.

The girls stop laughing, and the gym is silent again.

Tony bounces his ball a couple of times. "I dare ya to throw it."

I think about it for a minute. No way. He caught Reggie's ball, and there's no way I could throw anywhere near that hard. So I just stand there and wait.

"All right. Enough jerkin' off." Tony licks his hands and rubs the soles of his Nikes.

I hear Reggie laughing under his breath. "Mama said knock you out, new kid." My captain.

Tony palms his ball with his right hand, searching for the perfect grip. He looks over at the girls and waves his arm at them to start cheering. They all start clapping and screaming.

On the sideline, I hear a weak, raspy voice crying my name. I glance over and see Gully, on his knees, hands still cupping his blasted 'nads. "Make...or...break...time." He nods toward the girls—then sinks to the floor.

Tony's face is all twisted up, and his lips are pulled back so you can see all of his big white teeth.

The girls are screaming, and I want to tell them to shut the hell up, but then Tony lunges back and bursts forward, howling his head off.

Would anyone notice if I crapped my pants? I bend my knees and grip the slippery ball with sweaty hands.

Tony plants his foot and yanks his arm forward and the ball *explodes* from his hand.

The ball's getting bigger—fast. At the last moment, I drop my own ball, hold my hands out and close my eyes. A cannonball hits my chest, and the force knocks me back so hard and so fast that my feet are no longer under me, and I sail through the air and land on my spinal cord, and my head bounces off the gym floor.

The first thing I notice is that I can't breathe. I see lights, bright lights, just like—oh, shit—like when someone dies in the movies but no, no, it's just those bright-ass gym lights. I find my breath, take it, raise my aching head off the floor. Everything is blurry. I look down past my stinging, swollen chest, my swirling stomach, my shrunken sack, and I see a red blob rolling out between my feet. It rolls along, slowly, slowly—then it bumps into a short, white blob. Knocking it over.

The girls start screaming again.

And then I hear Tony: "I'm gonna knock you out! Mamma said knock you *ouuuuuuuuuuut!*"

And that's when I remember that this is only second period.

THE SYCAMORE TREE

Lisa Beth Janis

It's odd. I love sycamore trees. I should hate them, really.
I'll tell you why.

❧   ❧   ❧

When I was boy in Wheeling, West Virginia, I had a friend named Joseph. Joseph Seidler. He came to Wheeling when he was seven to live with an aunt, and we met in Miss Thurston's second-grade class. Joseph told me his mother was in a sanatorium for "two-boy-sclerosis." I didn't know what he meant; I figured she was crazy. That's what I thought sanatoriums were for.

Joseph would come to my house after school to play spy-man. We'd pretend to be secret agents tracking evil villains. Usually the villain was my older brother, Harold. Sometimes—particularly when I'd misbehaved and been made to regret it—it was my mother. Joseph and I hid under furniture and in the backs of closets, taking notes. We listened to my mother on the phone and learned about neighborhood ladies with boozy breath and roving husbands. When Harold went to study with his friends, we followed, carefully noting how his "studying" involved smoking and flirting with girls in the parking lot of Chubby's Diner.

Joseph would do just about anything. One afternoon when my mother and father were arguing in their upstairs bedroom, Joseph climbed onto the roof to spy. I stood on the lawn as his look-out man. The roof had a steep slope, and I was secretly glad he'd ordered me to stay on the ground. When my parents' argument lost his interest, Joseph moved over to the chimney and shouted down to me: "I bet you five dollars I can jump clear down it, right into the living room fireplace."

"You better not," I shouted back. "What if you get stuck in there?"

"Come on," Joseph argued in his gravelly voice. "I'm not gonna get stuck." He clutched the chimney rim and peered inside, his black hair hanging over his eyes. "It's huge. There's tons of room!"

I held my finger up to my mouth. "Shhh! Don't talk so loud."

"You're a chicken."

"You're an idiot."

We argued back and forth until the sun set. Then a light came on in the kitchen; my mother stood in front of the sink, looking tired. She snapped on her yellow kitchen gloves and opened the window. "Lenny, it's time for Joseph to go home for dinner. Where is he?"

"Um, I don't know."

"You don't know?" She didn't believe me.

"We're playing hide and seek."

"Well, seek him out and tell him it's time to go home."

I could barely see Joseph any more. I knew he'd heard my mother, though, because he scampered around, trying to keep his balance, searching for a way back down. Every few steps, his shadowy figure would wobble and swing its arms, like a little ghost dancing on the rooftop. Joseph finally made his way to the lowest spot and leapt off; he landed with a heavy *thud* and a groan but quickly stood, all recovered, and ran to my post on the lawn. "I'm gonna do it next time," he laughed, and pushed down on my head with the palms of his hands—his usual way of showing victory.

"Oh yeah?" I didn't know what else to say; I believed him.

Joseph pulled away, turned in the direction of his house and took off with a bouncing trot. "Yeah!" he shouted as he ran. From down the street I heard him call, "Just wait!" His body had disappeared into the dark.

By the next time I saw him, he'd forgotten all about chimney jumping. There were new plans in the works.

Joseph's mother came home from the sanatorium when he was eight. Mrs. Seidler was thin and pale with big, brown eyes. She had a heavy accent, and sometimes I didn't know what she was saying. It didn't matter much; her eyes explained a lot. They told when she was angry and when she was sad. She used to pat me on the head and say things I couldn't understand, but I knew she liked me.

Whenever I went over to Joseph's house, his mother was sitting on the porch in a rocking chair. Even in the winter she sat there with a blanket on her lap. She wanted to be outside.

"I wish I could play like you boys," she once told us, rocking gently in her chair. She couldn't, though. She was still weak and fragile; she moved slowly and slept a lot.

She was also timid with strangers. Not long after Joseph's mother had returned from the sanatorium, my mother walked over to the Seidler house to fetch me for dinner. Mrs. Seidler stood up from her rocking chair and said quietly, "How do you do?" She ran her hands over her tattered cotton dress and smiled softly. "Your Leonard is a very good boy."

"Thank you, and we always like having Joseph at our house," my mother replied, politely making her eyes avoid the shabby dress.

I once asked my mother why Mrs. Seidler was crazy, because she didn't seem like it to me.

"She's not crazy," my mother said. "Whatever gave you that idea?"

"She was in a sanatorium."

"She was in a sanatorium for tuberculosis—not because she's crazy."

I still didn't get it, but I let it go.

My mother unfolded her ironing board, keeping her gaze fixed on me as she pulled out the stiff metal legs. "Mrs. Seidler is not well, and I hope you don't go over there and make trouble for her."

"I don't make trouble; Joseph does." That was partly true: he usually started the trouble, and then I'd go along. "And I don't think his mother is that bad off. She seems OK to me. Yesterday she was outside banging nails into the porch with a hammer."

My mother look puzzled. "Banging nails? What for?"

I explained in detail what I'd seen—how Mrs. Seidler had been sitting in her usual spot on the porch when she noticed that a board in the steps had come loose. She was worried someone would trip, so she went inside and came back with a fistful of nails and a hammer. Then she hiked up her dress and got down on her knees on the lower steps. She hit the first nail all the way in—till the head was flush with the wood—using just a few strokes, then started to do the same with the other nails. We wanted to watch, but she kept waving us away, like we were ruining her concentration. Joseph's Aunt Sarah came outside to see what the noise was and nearly had a fit when she saw Mrs. Seidler lying over the lower stairs with her hammer, just banging away.

"What did Joseph's aunt say?" my mother asked, turning her iron on.

I put my hands up to my cheeks, like Aunt Sarah had, and did my best to imitate her anxious, high-pitched voice: "'Oh, Eva, what are you doing? You mustn't! Let Morris do that when he gets home from work.'"

I could see my mother fighting back a little smile, so I kept going.

"Mrs. Seidler just stared at Aunt Sarah like she was stupid and kept banging the nails in. She was muttering something, but I couldn't understand it. See, Mom? Mrs. Seidler's not as bad off as she looks. She seems OK to me."

"Well"—she licked her fingertip and tested the iron to make sure it was hot—"you're no doctor."

"I know," I said, a little mad that my story hadn't convinced her. I played with a plastic place mat on the table, tracing its brown circles with my finger.

"Lenny." My mother looked up from her ironing with a stern expression. "Mrs. Seidler has had a very difficult life." She stood the iron up on its base. Her voice softened a bit. "Did you know that her husband and their two older daughters were killed in the war? She was rescued—she and Joseph. But the rest of the family didn't make it."

I hadn't known this—not all of it, anyway. I didn't know what to say. "I knew his father was dead, but I didn't know the rest. I wonder…why didn't he didn't tell me?"

"He probably doesn't remember them. He was just a baby."

"How do you know all of this?" She barely ever saw Mrs. Seidler, not nearly as much as I did.

"Lots of people know." She picked up the iron to resume her chore. "People talk about these things."

❧   ❧   ❧

After that, I knew why Joseph's aunt and uncle seemed so worried about Mrs. Seidler. I understood why she always wanted us to play in the front yard where she could see us from the porch. We used to try to sneak away, but after the talk with my mother I felt bad. I'd try to convince Joseph to stay in his mother's sight.

It was hard to be good with Joseph; he was full of energy and didn't mind his mother. She never scolded him, though, even when he was bad. Once, Joseph decided we should steal Uncle Morris' car keys and take his new Thunderbird out for a ride. Joseph wasn't tall enough to see over the dashboard, so we filched some of Aunt Sarah's cushions, too. We'd made it a few yards from the driveway when Uncle Morris came running out of the house, screaming

things that would've made my mother faint. Mrs. Seidler wasn't around to wit-
ness the crime, but when she returned, Uncle Morris made us confess. Her
head shook in disapproval, but she didn't yell or seem angry. She stared at
Joseph for a while—her big eyes moving up and down, sizing up her fearless
son.

Joseph looked back at her. I could tell he was trying to look innocent, but
then he smiled, and his long black eyebrows arched mischievously—like they
always did.

Mrs. Seidler shook her head some more. Then, with a faint smile, she said,
"You boys go play."

❦   ❦   ❦

Some nights after dinner, Joseph and I would visit my neighbor, old Mrs.
Calhoon. She lived in a yellow bungalow across the street with her daughter-
in-law, Gloria. It was just the two of them; both of the Mr. Calhoons were
dead. Gloria was pretty: she had blonde hair and wore shiny red lipstick. My
father made fun of Gloria behind her back; he called her "Hot Pants." Joseph
had a crush on Gloria and looked embarrassed whenever he was around her. I
liked her, too—not so much for the reasons Joseph did, but because she made
me laugh and let me call her by her first name.

Old Mrs. Calhoon was my favorite neighbor, though. She made jerky in her
backyard and smoked a pipe on her porch in the evenings. She was part Cher-
okee Indian; she once showed us a picture of her mother—a real squaw, just
like in the history books, with long black hair and big, tall cheekbones. We
asked Mrs. Calhoon if she used to look like that too.

"Oh, sure I did." She smiled at the picture with her crooked yellow teeth.
"Long time ago."

Old Mrs. Calhoon always wore a white smock with lots of pockets over her
dress. That's where she kept her tobacco and her jerky. My father liked to make
jokes about her too, saying she kept food in there she'd stashed away during the
Civil War. When my mother served something for dinner that he didn't like,
he'd say, "You pull this out of Old Lady Calhoon's pocket?"

My mother would say, "Oh stop it, Howard," but you could tell she thought
it was funny.

Gloria and old Mrs. Calhoon were always bickering about something; I
could never tell if they liked each other or not. Joseph and I loved it when they
got into fights, though. Boy, could they be mean! One time, Gloria lent their

car to her new boyfriend, a man named Jack Stanley. Jack was supposed to bring the car back in an hour, but it'd been four days, and no one had heard from him. Gloria and old Mrs. Calhoon sat out on the porch day and night, hoping he'd show up. Joseph and I came by one evening while they waited, and old Mrs. Calhoon decided to tell us what had happened.

"See that floozy?" She put her needlepoint down on her lap and pointed to Gloria. "She gave away my car."

Gloria was sitting on the opposite side of the porch from us in a plastic beach chair, smoking a cigarette; she scowled at old Mrs. Calhoon. "Honestly, old lady, you can't even get your facts straight any more. I oughta put you in a home." She paused to take a drag from her cigarette. "And it ain't your car."

"It sure ain't," old Mrs. Calhoon muttered, "belongs to Jack Stanley now." She winked at us and looked over at Gloria. "Now, when do I get to go to this new home? 'Cause I tell ya, I'm countin' the minutes."

"If I had the money, you'd be there yesterday, old woman." Gloria chewed on her thumb nail and watched a car go by. It was maroon, the same color as theirs, but it kept on driving and didn't stop.

"I see." Old Mrs. Calhoon pretended to be very interested in her needle-point, holding it up to admire it. "That Jack Stanley got all yer money then, too, did he?"

Gloria crushed her cigarette in a little gold ashtray. "All my money's gone to doctors to keep a certain rickety heap o' bones I know from fallin' to pieces."

"Hah!" Old Mrs. Calhoon pretended to pick some lint off her needlepoint. "If you were half as sturdy as myself, you'd be thankin' the Lord for your good fortune."

Gloria looked at me and Joseph. "I just think 120 years is too long to stay around, don't you?"

Joseph giggled.

I said nothing, afraid to interrupt for fear they'd stop and end the show.

Gloria sighed. "Gotta make room for others. Out with the old, in with the new."

"Out with the old, huh?" Old Mrs. Calhoon glanced at Gloria with a fake look of surprise. "Well then, I guess *your* time'll be up soon, too." She cackled, and her teeth made clicking noises.

"Oh, I doubt that, Granny." Gloria turned her gaze back to the road. "Not before you—that's for sure."

"That right? Well, you'd better be careful, then." Old Mrs. Calhoon set the needlepoint down on her lap and leaned back in her chair. "'Cause one o' these days some man's gonna leave the car and the money, and he's gonna take yer soul instead."

Gloria stared at the old woman. "Oh, come on," was all she had to say. No one spoke after that; we all just sat in the dark and listened to the crickets chirp.

After a while Gloria went inside, and old Mrs. Calhoon filled us in on the neighborhood gossip, like always. I think she liked to spy on folks just as much as we did.

※   ※   ※

Besides Gloria and old Mrs. Calhoon, I didn't really know the other gentile neighbors—just Dr. Palmer and his wife. Dr. Palmer had an office right in his house where he took care of adults in the neighborhood. When my mother went in for her appointment, I would wait in a little room with white wicker furniture and a table with magazines and a Bible. There was a rocking chair that I liked to rock back and forth on, but Mrs. Palmer—the doctor's wife—always interrupted my rocking. I didn't like her much; she was tall with black and white hair that stopped at her chin. She didn't use lipstick, and she always wore denim shirts and men's trousers. She would eyeball me above her little half-glasses and call me "young man."

"Hello, young man," she'd say. "Have you seen our flowers this year?"

I knew she was going to make me look at them no matter what, but to be polite I'd say, "Yes, ma'am, they're very pretty."

"Well now, do you know the difference between dogwood and azaleas?"

"No, ma'am, not really."

"Well then, I'd like you to come out here on the porch, young man, and I'll show you." Then she'd grab me by the arm and "escort" me around the garden, which was really more like dragging. She had big hands and a harsh grip, like a prison guard. "Now, these are rhododendrons," she'd say, "and that's our state flower. Did you know that, young man?"

I knew because she told me every time, but she wasn't the kind of lady you'd want to embarrass, so I'd say, "Is that right, ma'am? I didn't know that."

"Well, you ought to. This is your state, and you should show some pride in it."

"Yes, ma'am, you're right."

Dr. Palmer wasn't much like his wife. He was tall like her, but bonier, like a skeleton. He had the deepest voice I'd ever heard, and when he talked, his

Adam's apple moved, and the hollow dents under his cheekbones deepened like craters. His manner was slow and sure, not pushy like Mrs. Palmer's. Dr. Palmer didn't smile or laugh much, but he looked me right in the eye when he spoke to me, and he always remembered my name. He kept candy in his office—peppermint-flavored hard candies, wrapped in cellophane. When it was time to go, he'd give me a handful and say, "Mrs. Palmer sees that, she'll snatch it back quicker than a hungry snake in a mouse hole, so keep it in your pocket till you get home."

🍁   🍁   🍁

Joseph and I had a friend named Frankie Fox, but we called him "Frankafox." Frankafox had curly red hair and big buck teeth, and he could do all the math problems in his head without even picking up a pencil. He was the smartest kid in our class, but you'd never know it by looking at him. His buck teeth made him look like a half-wit—like the kids from the mountains.

One summer day, Joseph and I were stretched out lazily on the grass, wondering what to do, when Frankafox came running into my yard carrying a long, heavy rope. "Look what I found!" Frankafox swung the rope tip over his head like a cowboy.

"So what?" said Joseph. "It's just a rope."

"Yeah," Frankafox panted, "but guess what…we're gonna do with it."

Joseph and I stared, waiting for an answer.

Frankafox looked mildly annoyed. "Don't you remember?" He continued swinging the rope, waiting for a response.

"Remember what?" I asked, hoping he'd whack himself with the loose end.

Frankafox pointed to a far corner of the yard. "Remember when we talked about putting a rope swing on that big tree?"

Now we knew what he was getting at.

"Hey," Joseph smiled, "good work, Frankafox."

Secretly I agreed, but I refused to give Frankafox the satisfaction. I just kept quiet and looked over at the tree. My dad called it a "mutant tree" because it was so huge—bigger than most sycamores, anyway. It stood maybe a hundred feet high, and the base was almost as wide as a small car. About four feet from the ground, it split like a 'Y' into two smaller trunks. It was like having two trees in one—both of them perfect for climbing. Thick branches grew from both trunks, strong enough to hold the weight of a few boys; even some of the thinner boughs had withstood years of abuse from Harold and me and our friends.

"So?" Frankafox tapped my shoulder. "You wanna do it?"

"Come on, let's go!" Joseph was already making his way toward the tree. I followed, like always, and Frankafox too—both of us yelling for Joseph to wait up.

We got to work, picking the perfect branch and deciding who was most qualified to climb up and tie the rope for the swing. Joseph got the job and started up the tree with the rope looped around his shoulder. About mid-way up, Frankafox and I began to holler directions to him from our safe posts on the ground: "Not that branch! That's too weak!" "Move to your right!"

Joseph had been on the job for about three minutes when Frankafox got impatient.

"Hurry up, will ya?"

"Hey, shut up!" Joseph shouted back, "I'm trying to concentrate!" Normally we'd have ignored the request, but the tree was so colossal, and his bravery so impressive, that we did as asked. We stood on the lawn with our necks craned and watched Joseph climb higher and higher until he'd disappeared into the leaves. Here and there, the silence was interrupted by soft rustling and the crack of dry branches.

"I found a good one!" Joseph was no longer visible, and his voice seemed to call from the sky, but we could see the thin branches surrounding him shake as he tied on the rope. Soon his gleeful face popped out from the leaves high above. He called down to us, boasting of his work: "I tied it on good! It's ready!"

"OK, now move down to the jump-off branch," Frankafox instructed, "and bring the rope with you."

Joseph came down the tree like a mountain climber who'd lost his footing, swinging from the rope and searching clumsily for branches with his feet. He finally landed on the jump-off branch, and we could hear him cursing.

"What's wrong?" I shouted.

"Damn! I got rope burn!" There was no soreness in his voice, though, or self-pity; he was too much of a show-off for that. He showed his palms to us like a soldier displaying his war wounds.

"We can't see your hands from down here," I yelled.

"Well, get up here, then!" I could see Joseph smiling, eager to get started. "It's time to start jumping!"

Frankafox and I scrambled up the tree; its ash-colored surface crumbled a bit under our tennis shoes, exposing the white bark underneath. Frankafox's climbing always surprised me—he was pretty good. He'd grab branches and pull his whole body up over them, like a gymnast. When we got to the jump-off branch, Joseph was busy tying knots in the rope.

"This one's to sit on," he explained, holding up the bigger knot, "and this little one's for your hands. Got it?"

"I got it," said Frankafox, looking at Joseph and then at me. "So, who gets to go first?"

"*I'm* goin' first." Joseph poked his chest with his thumb, "I'm the one who did all the work."

"Fine, fine," Frankafox whined, "just go already!"

I said nothing, happy to let someone else go first, in case the whole branch ended up snapping from the weight of the swing.

"OK. Watch me, and tell me how far out I swing." Joseph took hold of the bigger knot and stuck it between his legs. "Ready?" Joseph smiled. He wasn't stalling; he was playing with us.

"Go on." Frankafox's eyes were wide and his mouth slightly open. His teeth shot out from his face, like they too wanted to gawk at the daring feat about to be performed. "I mean, if you're ready."

Joseph hesitated, just for a second—then jumped from the branch, swinging out into the air. "Wh*ooaaa!*" he screamed, his face lit up with delight. I could see him clutching the rope tightly as he swung back and forth, but he didn't seem scared.

Frankafox cupped his hands around his mouth: "Now, swing back to the branch!"

"I am!" Joseph yelled back. He managed to swing back to the jump-off branch and get one leg over it, but the rest of his body was hanging off the side of the tree, suspended from the rope. "Pull me back on!" Joseph was struggling a bit, but still smiling.

Frankafox grabbed Joseph's shirt and dragged him closer so we could pull him up. When he was safe on the branch, Frankafox started giving instructions. "OK, when you swing, you can only swing out once, otherwise you won't have enough momentum to get back here."

"All right," I said, impressed enough by his use of the word *momentum* to take whatever advice he gave.

"Right," said Joseph, as if he'd already thought of it but just hadn't said so. His striped T-shirt had a big pouch in it behind the left shoulder, where

Frankafox had stretched it out; Joseph must've felt it, because he reached back over his shoulder and tried to push the little hump down.

"And," continued Frankafox, "whoever's closest has to catch the jumper." He looked at me. "Just grab 'em by the shirt," he said, as though he'd been working on this strategy all day.

"Got it," I said.

"Let's go again!" Joseph grabbed the rope.

"Hey, you just went!" Frankafox pushed Joseph's hand away. "It's our turn." He looked at me. "I'll go next. You can go after. Oh, and watch Joseph's catching technique while you're waiting, so you'll know how to haul someone in by the shirt. Just watch how Joe does it." With the rope in hand, Frankafox moved to the edge of the branch so his toes were just hanging over. He peeked down at the ground below and hesistated for a moment. With his free hand, he lifted the bottom of his red shirt to his face—exposing a glimpse of his freckled white belly—and blew his nose in it.

"Come on!" said Joseph. "You're taking all day! If you're scared, let Lenny go!"

Frankafox turned and glared at Joseph. "I'm not scared!" he declared, then continued in a shrill, teacherly voice, "I'm just *preparing* myself to jump. OK?"

"Fine." Joseph smiled at me.

I rolled my eyes.

"OK, I'm gonna count to three," Frankafox announced, turning his head briefly toward us to make sure we approved of the plan.

"Do whatever you need to do," Joseph counseled.

"Take your time," I added. "There's no hurry."

Frankafox turned again to see our expressions. "Never mind," he said, irritated. "OK, I'm just gonna jump." He gazed again at the ground, then at us.

"Try just jumping without thinking about it," Joseph advised. "That's what I did."

"Yeah, OK." Frankafox looked nervous, but he took a deep breath and hopped off the branch. With his mouth hanging open and his teeth chopping the air, he screamed, "Yeee*aaaaa*!" On his way back to the jump-off branch, the rope twisted and began to spin Frankafox around wildly. "Whooo*aaa*!" he yelled, whirling toward us. "Catch me!"

Joseph's eyebrows drew together. "Hey, what if I grab where he wiped his nose?"

Still spinning, Frankafox started to swing away. "Guys? Hey!"

I thought about it for a moment. "Just try to grab the *back* of his shirt." As I explained the plan, Frankafox came hurtling back toward us. Joseph reached way out, taking hold of a smaller branch to stabilize himself, and seized the snot-free side of the shirt. I grabbed Frankafox's foot. We pulled him in, grunting and panting.

When he was finally sitting safely on the branch, Frankafox took a deep breath and let it out. "Phew! That was close! Whoa! That was fun! I mean, it was like flying!" He stared at Joseph and me with wide eyes, to make sure we got his point. A bead of sweat dripped from his temple onto his flushed face. "You gotta try it, Lenny!"

I did, and though I was just as frightened as Frankafox, as soon as I left the branch, fear turned to excitement, then bliss: I was flying, flying, soaring through the treetops. I jumped again and again; we all did. My stomach dropped each time my feet left the tree, but then the cool air whizzed by, and the thrill of flight rushed through me. My heart raced and my head tingled, and I couldn't get enough.

My mother called out to us at one point. She stood near the basement steps in a light blue dress with a white apron, holding a basket of laundry. "What's all that yelling?"

I could see her, but I'm not sure she could see us. The yard was big—maybe an acre or so—and we were in a far corner, hidden by the dense leaves and broad branches of the old sycamore.

"Lenny!" she shouted. "What are you boys doing?"

"We're just playing in the tree, Mom."

"Be careful!" she warned.

"We are!" I lied.

We got bored after a while just jumping from the branch and decided to try some new stunts. Frankafox thought it would be fun to make a real swing—one you sit in. He took over, making a loop at the bottom of the rope and tying a special knot. "This'll never slip," he said, weaving the end of the rope in and out. "I learned it from my big brother. It's from the Boy Scouts."

"Are you sure about that?" I asked. I imagined the knot coming undone just as I jumped from the tree.

"This is a bowline knot," Franfafox said indignantly. He slowly repeated his previous line, emphasizing each word: "It's from the Boy Scouts."

"OK, fine," I said, still a little uneasy.

"You're a worrywart," said Frankafox. "You're like my grandma."

"Yeah," Joseph chipped in while examining the rope. "Don't worry so much, Lenny." The knot passed his inspection, and he volunteered to try it out first.

"OK," Frankafox approved, "you go first and then tell me if the loop is too big or too small."

We helped Joseph into the loop-seat, holding the rope while he slipped his legs through. "Ready, men?" he asked, daring us to be frightened.

"Yeah, I'm ready," Frankafox said, "but I'm not the one who's jumping, so who cares?"

Joseph ignored Frankafox and looked at me. "Ready, Lenny?"

"I guess." I was worried—and I was pretty sure I was right to be. I looked at Frankafox leaning on a branch, all antsy and impatient, and then at Joseph, who stared into the abyss before him with smug self-assurance. I was pretty sure both of my friends were idiots. For a second, I wondered what I was even doing there.

"If you're scared, I can go first," Frankafox suggested haughtily—trying to regain a bit of his previously lost dignity.

Joseph just snorted and jumped from the branch. He flew into the air, legs stretched out in front of him, with perfect grace, then swung back to us and flung his legs over the branch. He sat casually in the loop with his legs anchored to the tree, like someone laying out by the pool after a hard day's work, and joined his hands behind his head, elbows out. "Nothin' to it."

Then we all had to try. We took turns sitting in the loop, then standing. "I told you my knot would hold, Lenny," Frankafox said—about ten times.

On the eleventh boast about his famous bowline knot, I finally told him to shut up.

"Hey, don't tell me to shut up, Lenny," Frankafox whined.

"Ahh, he didn't mean it," Joseph said.

"Yes, I did! Do you have to tell me about your knot a million times, Frankafox? I got your point the first time!"

"Yeah, but you didn't believe me." Frankafox remained convinced that I didn't fully appreciate his knot tying skills. "You thought I didn't know what I was doing."

"But now I believe you," I said, trying to be calm. "What do you want, a knot-tying award or something?"

Frankafox stared at me with an earnest expression. "Well, maybe."

"Hey, look at me," Joseph said, fiddling with the loop at the end of the rope. "I'm gonna be a bird." He put the loop around his chest, under his armpits, and turned it so that the knot came up just behind his head. "I'm gonna fly," he said, smiling.

"You mean, like this?" Frankafox leaned over and stuck his arms out straight at both sides.

"Yeah," said Joseph.

"OK, try it," Frankafox approved.

I wasn't paying much attention. I was too busy trying to figure out how Frankafox could be so smart at school and so dumb everywhere else. I never stopped to look at the position of the rope and give my seal of approval.

"Watch this, Lenny!" Joseph called, his raspy voice ringing with excitement.

I was preoccupied, deciding how to word my next attack on Frankafox.

"Hey, Lenny, watch this!"

I turned and saw Joseph's eager face; he was waiting for me to look before he took off. And then he jumped from the branch with the rope tight around his striped t-shirt. And very quickly, something went wrong. Too quickly, before I could fix it. I didn't know, you see; I was ten—I was only ten years old. I didn't know that would happen. He'd jumped, and the weight of his body was too great; his chest slipped, and the rope caught under his arms, but the weight was too great, and the rope pulled his arms up and caught under his chin, and there was a loud cracking noise, and I thought a branch had broken, but no branch fell. His limp body didn't fall, either; it hung from the end of the rope, from the noose, twirling around and around, and every few seconds I would see his face, frozen in joy and anticipation…and then he would turn away.

Frankafox and I ran to the house, screaming for my mother. She opened the screen door from the kitchen and rushed out onto the grass; she must have known from the tone of our cries that something bad had happened. She ran to us so quickly that she tripped: her tall, elegant body lurched and almost fell flat on the ground, but she thrust an arm out and saved herself, and continued stumbling toward us. "Good God, what's wrong?" she cried. Her voice had a deep, hideous pitch that made the back of my head tingle with horror.

I couldn't speak.

"Joseph got hurt on the tree!" Frankafox yelled.

Then my mother kicked off her shoes and ran. I'd never seen her run before, but she ran to the sycamore tree so fast, we couldn't keep up. I heard her scream—a real scream, like in the movies—and the feeling of horror swelled; I suddenly realized we couldn't just call a do-over. Still, I thought *something* could be done, that we could fix it, that everything would be OK. She screamed out again, in that dreadful deep voice, this time for my brother: "*Harold!*"

Frankafox and I had caught up, and we stood with my mother under the tree, under Joseph, but we could not reach him. She grabbed our hands and squeezed so tight, I thought she'd break my fingers. She said nothing to us; she seemed to be holding her breath. Frankafox's nose dripped onto his upper lip, but he didn't wipe it. A car drove up the street behind us: the whir of its motor broke the silence, then dully faded away. I heard the screen door open and slam shut and felt Harold's hard footsteps running in the grass.

"We're over here!" my mother called, her voice now shrill.

"Ma? What's wrong?" Harold asked, trotting over. He was only 16, but he was as tall as my father, and I thought he was a man. His left hand was up at his brow, blocking the sun, but under the huge branches of the tree it grew shady, and he brought his hand down. "Oh, shit."

Normally, my mother would have had a fit if she'd heard Harold curse, but she didn't seem to hear him this time. She put a hand on her chest below her neck and took a deep breath. "Please get the ladder from the basement, Harold."

"What happened?" Harold asked, looking at me.

My mother's face contorted, and suddenly it was like a dam broke, and everything came rushing out at once: "*The ladder, Harold, there's no time for questions now! This boy is hanging from the tree!*" She was roaring at Harold, shrieking, but he was long gone; he'd sprinted off to the basement the instant her voice rose.

Frankafox began to wail. My mother let go of our hands and turned to Frankafox, bending down so her eyes were level with his. She placed her hands on his shoulders and tried to sound calm and stern, but her voice still shook: "Franklin, please stop crying. I need you to do something for me. I need you to run down the street to Dr. Palmer's house and get him."

Dr. Palmer! The name gave me hope.

"Can you do that for me, Franklin?"

Frankafox was still crying, but he nodded his head.

"Do you know where Dr. Palmer lives?"

He answered in a thin voice, "Yes, ma'am."

"Thank you for helping me, Franklin." She squeezed Frankafox's shoulders. "Lenny's father is away for the day, so I need you boys to help me. I need you to be strong." She looked at me, too. "Can you do that for me?"

I nodded.

Frankafox's eyes were red and swollen, but he looked determined; his chest puffed up a bit. "Yes, Mrs. Simon, I can do that. I can run to Dr. Palmer's house. Do you want me to go right now?"

"Would you, Franklin?" My mother looked pleased.

Frankafox's chest puffed up a bit more. "Sure," he said, in an unsure voice. He wiped his nose on his forearm and started to run, but he kept looking back at us.

"Franklin!" my mother yelled after him. "Tell Dr. Palmer that it's an emergency, that he must come now! Tell him…"

Frankafox stopped running and looked back, waiting.

"Tell him that Joseph Seidler has broken his neck."

      ❧   ❧   ❧

Harold brought the ladder; it was wooden with metal braces that clicked flatly into place when you pulled the sides out. I watched as he positioned it under the tree. My mother watched, too. She was not holding my hand any more. Her own hands rested flat at the top of her chest, one palm over the other, as though she were gently choking.

Harold began to climb up, then hesitated for a moment and looked at my mother. "Should I…?"

She nodded her head.

Harold looked up and wrinkled his nose; he looked confused. I thought he was going to say something or come down off the ladder, but he didn't. He looked down at the ground, staring at the grass, just standing there on the two lowest rungs of the ladder, and shook his head back and forth like he was arguing with someone, though no one was talking. Then his left hand let go of the ladder and covered his mouth, just for a second. When he pulled his hand down, it gripped his face and pulled his lips into a strange, stretched-out frown; when he started to climb, the frown stuck. If I'd seen him looking like that any other day, I would've thought he was being funny. I would've laughed and told him he looked like a ghoul.

Harold stopped climbing, but from where he stood, he could only get to Joseph's legs; the rest of his body was out of reach. He grabbed Joseph's legs but then realized he couldn't get him down that way. He let go. "Can you come hold the ladder?" Harold said quietly, looking at my mother. "I have to climb higher."

My mother walked over silently and gripped the sides of the ladder.

Harold moved up to the next rung, from which he could reach Joseph's waist. He grabbed Joseph's body and tried to push it up, to free it from the rope, but the rope was caught under Joseph's chin and wouldn't come free. Harold tried to wiggle Joseph's body a bit, but that didn't work, so he jerked him—pretty hard.

My mother didn't like that. "Come down from there," she said curtly. "I'll do it myself."

"Sorry, Ma." Harold looked down at her with surprise. "I didn't mean to…I mean, I'm just trying to get him down…"

"I understand that," she said in a clipped voice. "I'm not angry; I would just like to do it myself. Please get down."

She sounded angry to me, but I didn't say anything.

Neither did Harold. He crawled down the rungs and stood on the grass.

My mother was still wearing her blue dress and white apron. She untied the strings of her apron; it fell on the grass, and the starched cotton gathered in stiff peaks. Her dress buttoned down the front, all the way to the bottom. She leaned over, pulling the bottom of the dress up, and began to unbutton it. She stopped when she got to the middle of her thighs. Grabbing the two ends of the dress, she pulled them above her knees and tied them in a knot. A white slip showed beneath the tied dress. With a hand on the ladder, she balanced herself and pulled the slip down around her ankles, then off, leaving it in a pile on the grass. When she turned her back, I took the apron and threw it over the slip, to hide it.

She grasped the sides of the ladder and pulled herself up. The knot on the dress bumped against the rungs, but she didn't seem to notice. She climbed right up, without stopping to think or frown. Harold and I stood beneath and held the ladder. When I looked up to see what she was doing, all I could see was the back of her knees. I looked at the grass instead. It was thick and green, growing high around the base of the tree, and I thought, *If only he had fallen, the grass would have cushioned his fall.* I heard my mother's breath, deep and uneven, and held the ladder as tightly as I could so it wouldn't tip. When my mother moved her weight, the wooden sides creaked, and the feet sunk deeper into the earth. Suddenly, the ladder jerked; she slipped a bit but didn't fall.

"I got him," she said. "It's OK."

❦   ❦   ❦

Harold held Joseph: one arm under his shoulders, the other in the crook behind his knees. He was whispering to my mother. I watched her place her fingertips on the sides of Joseph's neck. She whispered again to Harold and shook her head. Then I thought I heard her say we shouldn't lay Joseph on the grass. I said I'd get something, and both of them turned to me, looking guilty.

I ran to clothesline, grabbed a white table cloth and hurried back. I gave my mother the table cloth, and she shook it out in front of her; it billowed in the air and smelled clean. She laid it on the grass: it was dry but hadn't been ironed, and my mother seemed bothered by this.

She looked at Harold. "Just a minute." Kneeling on the grass, she smoothed her palm along the wrinkles, trying to flatten them out. When Harold put Joseph down, I watched my mother move his head this way and that way, trying to make him look less twisted.

Frankafox finally appeared with Dr. Palmer and his wife. All three ran from the street into our yard.

"My heavens." Mrs. Palmer's gruff voice was almost breathless.

She and Dr. Palmer went to the edge of the table cloth and squatted down. Dr. Palmer felt the sides of Joseph's neck like my mother did. Mrs. Palmer put a hand on Joseph's cheek and gently turned his face toward her; she looked at Dr. Palmer. "He's broken his neck, all right."

"I never felt a pulse," my mother said quietly.

"Oh, it must have happened in an instant," Mrs. Palmer said. She stood, slowly, and stuck her hands in the pockets of her denim trousers.

Dr. Palmer didn't move; he was kneeling on the white table cloth, and he touched Joseph's cheek softly. I thought he was going to do something to help, since he was a doctor. But he just closed Joseph's eyes.

"Dr. Palmer ought to be the one to tell the mother," Mrs. Palmer announced. Her hands were out of her pockets now; she stood on the grass like a general, hands on her hips.

No one disagreed—or, if they did, they didn't say so.

"She's a frail woman," continued Mrs. Palmer. "Her health might not tolerate another tragedy."

My mother nodded in agreement.

Dr. Palmer was still on his knees. He took a handkerchief out of his pocket and wiped his brow. "I reckon Mrs. Palmer's right." His voice was slow and steady, like always.

My mother's hands were at the top of her chest again; she looked at Dr. Palmer.

"How will she survive the death of her son?"

❧   ❧   ❧

It was then that the whole world seemed to shrink into my head. The voices outside were muffled, the way they sound under water.

I just thought he'd broken his neck. I didn't know Joseph was dead.

I heard Frankafox crying, but the sounds were far away. Maybe he hadn't known, either. He asked Dr. Palmer to check again, to make sure he was right. That's what I thought, too—that maybe they were wrong. Couldn't they try something else? Why weren't they trying harder? Someone responded, but all I heard were dim noises. Only Dr. Palmer's words cut through the haze. His deep voice vibrated in the air and rumbled through my body.

"I'm sorry," I heard him say, "but the boy is surely dead."

❧   ❧   ❧

Dr. Palmer told my mother I'd be all right; he said I probably just needed a drink of water and a little time to breathe. He asked if I felt like I might be sick.

I shook my head.

Mrs. Palmer asked Frankafox if he'd like her to call his mother.

He nodded, biting his lower lip.

Mrs. Palmer said, "Let's go call her now." She took his hand and began walking toward the house; Frankafox followed, walking quickly to keep pace with her long legs.

My mother sat on the edge of the table cloth. She told Dr. Palmer that she would wait with Joseph while he went for Mrs. Seidler. She asked Harold to please take me inside to the bathroom and to make sure I drank some water.

I made Harold wait outside while I went into the bathroom. I locked the door behind me and sat on the floor, in front of the toilet, waiting…but nothing happened. I got up to splash water on my face, and I looked in the mirror.

I watched myself blink.

I looked at my eyes; they looked back at me.

I pressed my lips together and watched the face in the mirror do the same.

I couldn't look away.

Harold banged on the door and asked if I was OK.

I didn't say anything.

My lips felt dry and tight, but I stretched them anyway. I made an *O* with my mouth. The face in the mirror did the same.

I moved my face right up to the mirror and touched my nose to his nose.

Harold banged louder and told me to open the door.

I didn't want to.

Harold yelled and kicked the door; his voice was frantic. I didn't want Harold to be scared, so I opened the door and said, "Sorry." He was nice—he put his arm around me. He filled a glass of water for me and said we should go back outside. When we walked down the hallway I felt every footstep, like the floor was metal and my feet were magnets. I looked out of my head through my eyes at the photos hanging in the hall: Grandpa and Grandma; Harold with his catcher's mitt; me when I was little, sitting on a rock near the seashore, holding a stuffed bear.

❧   ❧   ❧

Mrs. Seidler hadn't come yet, but some of the neighbors were in the yard, gathered around the edge of the table cloth. They must have seen Dr. Palmer on his way to the Seidler house and asked him what was going on.

Mrs. Fessinger from down the street was there. She wore a brown dress with yellow and orange flowers and held a pair of black sunglasses in her hand. She was talking to Mrs. Miller, her next-door neighbor, in a low voice. All I could see of Mrs. Miller was the top of her gray-haired head; she was bent over, hunting for something in her purse. While she searched, I heard her say, "I can't believe it, I really just can't."

Mrs. Fessinger gave her a half-hug from the side, and her gold bracelets made a clinking noise; she looked at my mother, still sitting next to Joseph. "Where is Howard?"

"I'm afraid he's gone to Charleston for a car show." My mother looked worried.

"Oh, my." Mrs. Miller found the tissue she'd been looking for and dabbed the corners of her eyes. "Oh, that's too bad."

"It'll be OK, dear." Mrs. Fessinger patted my mother's shoulder. She pulled a cigarette from a small silver case, lit it and took a heavy drag. "Oh, here come the neighbors. Anne, would you like me to go talk to them?"

"Please." My mother managed a very slight smile.

Mrs. Fessinger went over to meet Gloria and Old Mrs. Calhoon as they walked from the street into the yard. The three of them stopped on the sidewalk and spoke in hushed tones. I couldn't hear what they were saying, but I saw Gloria put a hand over her mouth and look over at Joseph. Gloria stayed on the curb, whispering with Mrs. Fessinger, but old Mrs. Calhoon marched over to where we were sitting. "Damnation!" she yelled.

My mother looked a little stunned, but said nothing.

Old Mrs. Calhoon was the only person so far who seemed angry. I wondered if she was angry with me—for letting it happen.

She wore boots under her dress and stomped her feet a bit in the grass. "Damnation," she said again, but this time she said it more like a question than an exclamation, less angry than sad. She walked to where Joseph's body lay, then squatted at the edge of the table cloth and ruffled his hair with her hand. "It just ain't right."

My mother gazed at Joseph and shook her head.

Mrs. Miller looked at the old lady, "No, it doesn't seem fair."

"I suppose God has His plans," Old Mrs. Calhoon said quietly. "But I can't say I like 'em. Long as I live, I'll never understand 'em, either."

My mother and Mrs. Miller both nodded, murmuring quietly in agreement.

A brown Oldsmobile pulled up at the curb. Mrs. Fox jumped out of the car and ran onto the lawn. She was short, with brown hair and wide hips, and she was always talking. She yelled as she ran: "Franky! Franklin…oh, where is he?"

Frankafox had been inside with Mrs. Palmer, but he must have heard his mother's voice, because he came running outside to meet her. She hugged him violently and kissed his face. Her eye make-up had bled, and black tears fell down her cheeks.

Mr. Fox had gotten out of the car; he stood on the lawn, reflecting. He had red hair and a gap between his front teeth; he was quiet, unlike his wife. Mr. Fox walked to the table cloth where I was still sitting with my mother and the other women. He put his hand on my mother's shoulder, then bent down and said something to her in a low voice. Her face looked pained; she grabbed his hand and held it.

Mrs. Fox had taken a handkerchief from her purse and was helping Frankafox blow his nose.

"I told you, Franklin, I told you never to play with rope swings because something like this could happen!" Her voice was loud and harsh. Mrs. Fox started crying again; under the black tears, her face was red and blotchy. She moved closer to my mother and, in an accusing tone, said, "How could you let them jump from the tree like that, Anne? Weren't you watching?"

Everyone stared at her in disbelief, even Mr. Fox. I could see Mrs. Fessinger with her mouth wide open, coming over from the curb; Gloria followed behind.

Mr. Fox looked embarrassed. In a stern voice, he said to his wife, "Stop it, Sheila."

Mrs. Fox looked offended.

"I will not stop it!" she whined. "This is a terrible tragedy, and it didn't have to happen."

My mother pursed her lips. Her hands flitted up to her collarbone.

A little bird sitting somewhere in the sycamore tree made a squawking noise.

Mrs. Fessinger walked up to Frankafox's mother and, looking straight at her, remarked dryly, "I hardly think now is the time to discuss this, dear."

Staring at Mrs. Fox, my mother added flatly, through white lips, "I think you're upset, Sheila. Perhaps we should talk about this later."

Old Mrs. Calhoon stood up from her spot on the table cloth; she stuck her hands in the pockets of her smock and walked over to Mrs. Fox. Calmly, she said, "It was an accident, and an accident ain't nobody's fault." She looked over at my mother, then at Mrs. Fessinger. "What good's a tragedy if it only breeds ill will? Hmm?"

I didn't know what she meant by that. Maybe my mother did, though. She stared at her lap like a little girl who'd been scolded.

I'm pretty sure that Mrs. Fox didn't know Old Mrs. Calhoon; she gaped at the old lady in the stained smock, looking horrified.

Old Mrs. Calhoon moved closer to Mrs. Fox and poked her on the shoulder. "Maybe you oughta think about that."

Mrs. Fox recoiled, like she'd been touched be a leper. She stepped back, pulling Frankafox close to her chest.

Just as she opened her mouth to say something, Mr. Fox spoke: "I think I see the doctor coming with Mrs. Seidler." He looked at his wife. "Please, Sheila."

Mrs. Fox closed her mouth.

Everyone was silent.

❦   ❦   ❦

I heard them before I saw them—heard the crying. First came Uncle Morris, his hands on Aunt Sarah's shoulders. She was stooped over, sobbing while she walked. Dr. Palmer followed, his arm linked with Mrs. Seidler's. She looked straight ahead, and her eyes were dry.

The rest of us moved off the table cloth, making room for Mrs. Seidler. Dr. Palmer and Mr. Fox helped her sit; both carefully held her arms while she bent her thin legs and lowered herself down. Harold lifted Joseph's body up to make room; Mrs. Seidler gestured for him to lay her child down. Together, the two of them positioned Joseph as Mrs. Seidler wished, with his head and twisted neck resting in her lap. Joseph looked just like he was sleeping, though his face was a funny color and his neck badly bruised. Mrs. Seidler stroked his hair and whispered quiet words to him that I couldn't understand.

We all stood close, watching but not talking. Only old Mrs. Calhoon was standing by herself, preoccupied with the high branches of the sycamore tree. Her head was tilted back, and she squinted up toward the sky. She shook her head, muttering "Mercy," then started to walk away. I watched her. Some of the others turned their heads to see where the old lady was going. She crossed the street and headed to her bungalow.

It seemed like no one knew what to say to Mrs. Seidler. Finally, like she'd been holding her breath and just had to let it out, Mrs. Fox gasped, "Oh, Eva!" Her lips trembled, and a lone, thick tear streamed down her cheek. "I'm so sorry. How could this happen?"

Then the others began to chime in, offering their condolences:

"We're so sorry for you…"

"Anything we can do…"

"He was so young; it's so unfair…"

Mrs. Seidler said nothing; she didn't even look up. She stroked her son's hair and held one of his small hands in hers. Somebody said, "It's such a horrible tragedy."

Mrs. Seidler lifted her head and stared at the crowd, like she couldn't believe what she was hearing. I'd seen that look on her face before, the day Aunt Sarah told her to stop banging nails. Mrs. Seidler's eyes were defiant; not angry, but steadfast—fiercely so.

"There is no tragedy," she said. "I was lucky to have him."

A minute passed; we all stayed quiet, not knowing what to say. Then I saw old Mrs. Calhoon heading back toward us from her bungalow, carrying a small pillow. She walked across the grass and straight through our little crowd to Mrs. Seidler. "There you are; that's for the boy." She handed Mrs. Seidler the pillow: a needlepoint with a picture of a stubby house and blue corduroy backing. The needlepoint looked unfinished, like someone had given up on it about three-fourths of the way through.

"Thank you," Mrs. Seidler said. "Is this yours?"

"Oh, yes, ma'am," Old Mrs. Calhoon replied, "but I'd like you to keep the pillow as a gift from me."

"Thank you, dear." Mrs. Seidler's eyes smiled. She squeezed the old lady's hand, then gently placed the pillow under Joseph's head.

"Well." Old Mrs. Calhoon turned to the group. "Let's give the lady some privacy." She pronounced *privacy* funny, so that the *i* rhymed with *pig*. It wasn't clear if she was talking to Gloria or the whole group, but no one seemed to listen to her.

Gloria looked embarrassed.

Old Mrs. Calhoon motioned to her, pointing to their house. "Come on, then, let's get going."

Gloria looked confused for a moment, but she finally walked over to join her mother-in-law, and the two of them headed back to their bungalow.

As the two women walked away, Mrs. Seidler quietly told the doctor she would like to sit in the shade. The men moved in quickly to help: Harold lifted Joseph's limp body. Dr. Palmer and Mr. Fox helped Mrs. Seidler up, walked her over to the sycamore and slowly lowered her back down. Harold placed Joseph just as he had before, with his head in his mother's lap.

Everyone was quiet. No one consoled Mrs. Seidler, I guess because no one could. But she leaned into the wide base of the great sycamore tree, and let it support her, and took in its shade. And she stayed there for a long time.

After it had been dark for a while, my mother asked Harold to take me upstairs to bed. Once he'd turned out the lights, I waited a minute, then got up out of bed, went to the window and looked out.

Most of the neighbors remained. They sat with my mother on an old quilt on the grass, not far from Mrs. Seidler, and drank iced tea that Harold had made. They said they would leave when my father got home, but I knew they would stay as long as Mrs. Seidler stayed. I could still see the outline of her body under the sycamore, sitting with Joseph in the dark.

And I prayed she'd never leave.

About the Authors

Laura Allen-Simpson has written (as Laura Allen) two nonfiction books for children: *Clever Letters: Fun Ways to Wiggle Your Words* (Pleasant Company, 1997) and *The Quiz Book: Clues to You & Your Friends, Too!* (Pleasant Company, 1999). She grew up in a house like that of her protagonist, Paula, in Wilmette, Illinois, but now lives in "a treehouse-like condo" in Evanston. From there she walks to her job as an editor at McDougal Littell Publishing Company and delights in life with her husband, Sid.

Sarah Morrill Condry was raised in North Carolina and now resides in Wilmette, Illinois. A former elementary school teacher, she is currently at home as a wife and as mother to her two greatest accomplishments, Grant and Lindsay. Sarah thanks her Dad for the storytelling and her Mom "for the push."

Betsy Doherty grew up in Madison, Wisconsin, and is frequently asked why she left. She studied biology at Northwestern University and now lives in Chicago's Lincoln Square. With remarkable models in her parents, she has been writing for a couple of decades and hopes to keep learning how it's done.

Drew Downing was raised in Michigan and attended Michigan State University. He now resides in Chicago, where he is studying to be a teacher. "Self-discipline permitting," Drew says, he hopes to "one day be a serious writer."

Emile Ferris is a writer and visual artist who grew up in Santa Fe, New Mexico, and in Chicago; she now resides in Evanston. Her second story in this book is excerpted from a novella-in-progress, *Charon's Planet*. Emile is pleased and honored to be a part of this anthology.

Lisa Beth Janis grew up in Marin County, California. She has a master's degree in philosophy from Oxford and is earning her PhD in psychology at Northwestern University. A self-described "starter, not a finisher" of many projects, Lisa notes, "My contribution to this anthology, being finished, marks a hopeful turning point in this trend." She lives in Chicago.

Paul McComas grew up in Milwaukee and lives in Evanston. He is the author of the short story collection *Twenty Questions* (Fithian Press, 1998), now in its third printing, and two novels: *Unplugged* (John Daniel & Co., 2002) and the "nearly-completed" *Planet of the Dates,* from which his second piece in this book has been adapted. Paul teaches fiction writing both in Northwestern University's Minicourse Program and in his own Advanced Fiction Workshop, whose students are the other contributors to this collection. For more information, go to **www.paulmccomas.com**.

Carla Ng was born in São Paulo and raised in Brooklyn. She is currently pursuing a PhD in Chemical/Environmental Engineering at Northwestern University. In her spare time, Carla enjoys long walks on the beach and sunsets. She lives in Chicago with her two cats, Maggie and Watson, who are similarly inclined.

Elizabeth C. Rossman was raised on the Outer Banks of North Carolina. She lives in Chicago, where she is pursuing a Master of Arts in Literary Writing at DePaul University. Her second story in this collection is excerpted from an as-yet-untitled novel-in-progress.

Elizabeth Samet was born in Pittsburgh but has made limited-engagement appearances in Providence, London, Rome and Venice. She spent the last 10 years working as a creative director for a multinational ad agency in Manhattan, where many of her single-girl-in-the-city stories take place. These are quickly but not quietly being replaced by tales of the married Mom in the suburbs, as she is expecting her second son this winter.

0-595-30195-9